April's Fool

I0536707

A Novel

by

Harry J. Truman

Racketty-Packetty Press   Kendallville Indiana 46755

Harry J. Truman is the publisher and principal writer at Racketty-Packetty Press.

Non-fiction written by Harry J. Truman:

Ten Habits of the Spiritually Tough

Co-written with Steven J. Herendeen:

My Grandfather's Grave

Racketty-Packetty Press   Kendallville, IN 46755

© 2017 by Harry J. Truman

All rights reserved. Published 2017

Printed by CreateSpace and its affiliates

ISBN-13: 978-0-997012545
ISBN -10: 0997012544

This paper meets the requirements of ANSI/NISO Z39.48.1992 (Permanence of Paper)

Cover photograph provided courtesy of NASA and the Beaver Island Chamber of Commerce
All rights reserved © 2017

For my children… that they may each find their passion in life and a love for another person which gives that passion its real meaning.

~ 1 ~

If there was a speck of dust in William Riley's apartment, it was hiding for its life. There were just four in all — rooms, that is — five, if you included his bathroom. His was one of eight flats in a two-story wood frame building. The style was of a type lost to architectural memory (if it even had a name to begin with), and the units were accurate reflections of the exterior's squat, cramped expression. Still, it was one half of William's world and he made the most of it.

His bedroom was to the right of a central hallway leading from the apartment door to a large space serving as both William's living room and dining room. An oak four-poster bed fashioned from mahogany dominated this space and made his bedroom appear even smaller than it already was. Neither the ten-foot ceiling or the one window helped to alter this impression.

Two dressers, one low and long with a beveled oval mirror framed on its long axis and a highboy were the only other pieces of furniture in the room. Whereas the bed was precisely dressed, the top of the low dresser was naked save for a linen runner embroidered in the hardanger style and, on that, a framed photograph of William's parents.

Across the hallway was a second bedroom William used for storage (in the five years since moving in, he had yet to entertain a single overnight guest). Even in this room, order and cleanliness ruled. A stranger peeking into it might conclude Mr. Riley was about to move on to greener pastures. His family and friends knew otherwise.

As for what William called his front room, he had placed an Antebellum swivel card-table with its top unfolded in front of the picture window overlooking the street below. Set in opposition were two of four matching chairs. In the center of this table lay an artificial arrangement of flowers in an opaque white vase atop a small linen doily.

The third chair of the set occupied the space in front of a nineteenth-century roll-top desk which William used as his at-home work area. The fourth chair was in the storage room.

William's front room was large enough also to include a sofa, a 1940s era radio console, end tables clad in tiger maple and embossed leather ascents, and a matching coffee table. Two lamps fashioned from white marble were set on the end tables and an oriental rug completed the cozy yet antique feel of the room. William had never owned a television. Even if he had, it would have looked out of place here.

The kitchen was located to the left of the front room — if one was looking out the picture window. Accessed as it was by way of an open threshold, it matched the front room's length but had only a third of its breadth. A visitor might have been surprised to discover modern appliances in it.

The fridge, range, and microwave were all newer models. The sink, countertops, and cupboards were not. These were original to the apartment when it had been built in the 1920s and bore their age well. The sink was white porcelain with a contemporary faucet which did a good job of not looking like a replacement.

The cupboards began about twenty-six inches above the countertops and climbed all the way to the ceiling. Double doors with cut glass inserts allowed William visual access to all but the topmost shelves. A small curtained window was located above the sink, and the sink itself faced the street-side of the building.

While every room in William's apartment was tidy, the bathroom was the best reflection of his personality: compact, efficient, and (above all other traits), cloistered. It held no extraneous objects — just the toilet, sink (with mirror), and bathtub (without shower) all in that same white porcelain. For storage, there was a narrow linen closet out in the central hallway next to the bathroom door.

Forget finding a crumpled sock jammed in a corner; the only signs of use were the smudges left behind by evaporated drops of water. Even those things one might expect to find in a bathroom (towels, for example) were stowed as if the room was onboard a submarine. William would have cringed at such an analogy; he had no particular love for either water or boats.

Still, the submersible imagery was fitting — if not to efficiency, then at least to remoteness. While William Riley lived almost dead center in the village of St. James, the community itself might as well have existed in the middle of an ocean. In point of fact, it was in the middle of that great inland sea called Lake Michigan. Except during the summer, Beaver Island doesn't get many visitors.

William Riley lived and worked in a place which was remote by North American standards. Putting aside places like the High Sierras, the Oxbow Quadrangle, or the Yukon — places with natural incentives to keep out all but the most fearless of people — Beaver Island is near the top of any list of the least-known yet inhabited places within the continental United States.

Located almost thirty miles due west of Cross Village, Michigan, Beaver Island is the kind of place where Father Time wound his watch but then forgot to start it. And that's just the way the locals like William preferred it. Of course, this meant William kept time the way he knew best: By the whine of charter flights taking off; brass tones from the Catholic church; ferry whistles, and especially through the detailed rhythm of his workday.

William (Bill to his friends) held the dual positions of director of Beaver Island's Chamber of Commerce and curator of the island's museum. Only he knew where one job ended and the other began. To the tourists who visited the island, William was, 'that nice young man who worked in the basement of the King Strang Hotel.'

For seven years (since the age of twenty) he had been keeping this daily pace by himself. This bothered no one — least of all William. He had watched and worked along side his father practically since the day he could walk. The islanders took comfort in knowing another generation of O'Riley's was following the family tradition.

Someone from William's family had served as caretaker of the island's historic treasures since the very beginning... the beginning, that is, which came after the Mormons were violently evicted from Beaver Island. If there was one subject William Riley knew and appreciated, it was his island's history...

~   ~   ~   ~   ~

The Mormons were responsible for bringing European civilization to Beaver Island in the 1840s. Up until then, the locale had been a long-established sacred domain and trading post for numerous Indian tribes and clans.

At first, Mormon occupation of Beaver Island was welcomed. Just about everyone in that neck of the woods saw it as a success; that is, until their leader, James Jesse Strang, declared himself king in 1850.

Brigham Young had removed Strang and his followers from the main body of Mormonism after a power struggle in 1844. While Young and his people went west, the Strang cohort went north into Wisconsin and denounced polygamy. In 1847, he moved his group to Beaver Island because he was attracted by its remoteness,

As if declaring himself king wasn't enough of an issue, Strang soon revived the practice of polygamy. When word of these things reached Washington City, President Millard Fillmore was at first inclined to send a gunboat to the island to set matters straight. He thought it such a good idea that it was exactly what he did. Strang and his followers were arrested on minor federal charges, but eventually found not guilty. This only emboldened King Strang, and he soon became a power-broker in the Michigan State legislature.

By 1853, Franklin Pierce had inherited the presidency and the "King Strang problem" (as he called it). But America's current chief executive was distracted by the recent death of his son. The idea of having these Mormons nicely packed away on some remote island in the middle of Lake Michigan was appealing to him and many other politicians (all outside of Michigan, of course).

Pierce and Congress were also in the midst of the conflict over States' Rights and the border war between Kansas and Missouri. The last thing any of them needed was another crisis. Therefore, a plan was hatched to quietly grant James Jesse Strang his kingdom in the middle of nowhere. They had, in essence, passed along this 'problem' for someone else to clean up.

And clean it up someone did, but much sooner than anyone in Washington expected. By the time President Pierce's executive order reached Beaver Island in August of 1856, Strang was dead and his Mormon followers rounded up and sent packing by Irish fishermen from Mackinac Island.

George Whitney was one of the men responsible for getting rid of Strang and his followers, and good old George always knew an opportunity when it stared him in the face... as it did when he held onto President Pierce's decree.

Who in Washington City would possibly care that he, Whitney, was an Irish fisherman instead of a Mormon? The order stated that the king (but failed to mention Strang by name) and his descendants after him could keep the title and their kingdom as long as the decree was publicly read every year on the first day of April. As soon as this stipulation was broken, the sovereignty of the island and all its inhabitants would revert to the state of Michigan.

After its first reading in 1857, the decree was transcribed onto a cross-stitched tapestry twelve by twenty inches in size. The entire piece was rendered in silk thread with the lettering itself done in metallic gold thread. After the Strang Tapestry was created (George Whitney himself named it as a joke), William's great-great-great-grandfather Peter O'Riley took it upon himself to keep it safe. After all, his newlywed wife had done most of the work on it herself.

Thus began the tradition of William's family being charged with the care of Beaver Island's most prized artifact. It was a tradition each generation of O'Riley men proudly maintained... except for Peter who burned up the original decree when he drunkenly used it to start a fire in his pot-bellied stove in the winter of 1859.

~ ~ ~ ~ ~

Maintaining the integrity and security of the Strang Tapestry was William Riley's most important function. As his father had done before him, William always removed the tapestry from its protective case and inspected it on the first working day of the month.

William faithfully comported himself to the rhythm of this particular day, Monday, October 2, 2000. It was going to be another sun-soaked day on Beaver Island, though there was a noticeable chill in the air. The trees — and the island had plenty — were just coming into their peak coloration. Most things came late to the island; autumn being Mother Nature's odd contribution to this trend.

William took the final sip from his teacup and finished washing his breakfast dishes. He carefully dried each item before returning them to their proper places. The radio was tuned to a classical station out of Harbor Springs. As he did every workday, William listened as National Public Radio brought that particular hour's broadcast to a close. As the show's theme music began, he cut power to the vacuum tubes within.

Stepping into his bathroom, William secured the top button on his shirt and made a final adjustment to his solid green tie. After one last look around, he drew forth his overcoat from the bedroom closet and put it on along with his black earmuffs. Then he turned off the lights to his apartment and made his way to that other hemisphere of his life.

His office in the basement of the King Strang Hotel was less than two blocks away. If he had bothered to check his watch, William would have seen that it was two minutes before eight o'clock.

By 8:00 a.m., William was unlocking the door to the museum (the Chamber of Commerce materials occupied three square feet of counter-space on the front desk). The museum's hours of operation were from 9:00 a.m. until 4:00 p.m. Monday through Friday and from 9:00 a.m. to noon on Saturday. William always enjoyed that first hour of uninterrupted quiet; and especially savored such moments during the summer when the museum was often packed with tourists. Visitors to the museum in October would be a trickle in comparison.

By 8:01 a.m., William had placed his earmuffs and overcoat on the hat stand in his small office and was set to take his usual walk-through to see that all the display artifacts were in their proper cases. Having satisfied himself in this regard, he strolled over to the Whitney Family Collection in an adjacent room.

From his pants pocket, William drew forth a set of old keys. Having found the correct one, he carefully inserted it into the lock securing the top drawer of the desk; the location which had been the resting place for the Strang Tapestry for the last eighty years. Pulling on the twin brass handles, William found the tapestry — missing!

~ ~ ~ ~ ~

April was looking forward to her upcoming assignment in New York City. Next week would mark the first time she had been back there since taking her current position.

The plan was for her to visit a number of wealthy art collectors in their homes in Manhattan to make a survey of some sixteenth through eighteenth century Oriental and European rugs. Some of these artifacts were quite rare and most of the rarest had not been examined by a professional like April in more than three generations.

For a year and a half now — ever since her graduation from the Institute of Fine Arts at NYU (with honors), April had been employed by the DIA. She enjoyed using just the letters when telling strangers where she worked. Their eyes might go wide with wonderment or they might tilt their heads and shift their body-weight to show how impressed they were that a woman so young worked for the Defense Intelligence Agency. Then April would smile and explain that *her* DIA was the Detroit Institute of Arts. Unless the person was from Michigan, this harmless ploy usually worked.

There was one aspect of meeting new people April despised: They would almost always use the word *young* to describe her, but April knew too many of them were really thinking the word *black*. Their eyes usually gave it away. Her father had told her years ago, "When in doubt, sugar, look to the eyes." April had learned over time to trust this advice.

April Anne Smith was a twenty-five year old black woman — and a professional one at that. Her pedigree, sadly, was almost as rare as the artifacts she was privileged to authenticate. The irony of this was not lost to her, but April had chosen to interpret this as a compliment paid to her by the institute. They were, after all, in the business of acquiring the best: be it the finest artworks or the most competent personnel.

And this was precisely what this trip to New York City signified. Her department head at the DIA, John Risner, was counting on this expertise to help him determine which of these rugs the institute would attempt to acquire.

It was a responsibility April relished, and one she was more than ready to take on. Her parents had raised April and her siblings to always meet challenges without fear of failure. It was how they also had been raised…

April was the youngest of the four children of Richard and Margaret Smith. Richard had been an engineer for General Motors for over forty years and had recently retired as a vice-president in their New Materials Division. As a young man, he had been a top student at Pontiac High School, and won a full scholarship to General Motors Institute, Flint. He had been among the first black men to graduate from there after World War II and did so with high marks.

Even with his impressive intellect, Richard found the company reluctant to hire him. On his first day of work, he was astonished to discover he had been placed under a two year probationary status. No one openly raised the issue of his skin color, but as the only black man to graduate in his class, no one had to.

Like he had always done, Richard made the best of whatever situation confronted him. To counter the few friendships and constant scrutiny, he poured himself into his job. It was here Richard found his reward: the cutting-edge work in automotive manufacturing and, of course, the pay. For a young, single man of any color in the 1950s, Richard's paycheck was enormous.

Richard was also astute enough to live well below his means. He saved and scrimped for seven years until he met Margaret at a church function. They were married a year later by which time Richard had saved enough money to build a house without having to go to a bank for a mortgage. The look on the contractor's face when Richard and Margaret handed him the certified check for $22,385.70 was one the couple would never forget.

April's mother was cut from the same cloth as her engineer husband: hard-working, fiercely determined to rise above her lower class roots, and filled with faith in God. She had already come too far herself to permit any of her children the luxury of taking it easy.

As a housewife and mother, Margaret saw that everyone did his or her fair share around the house. And after the evening meal, both she and Richard oversaw the completion of all assigned homework. The one area where she and her husband differed was in their use of coarse language. Margaret was generally soft-spoken and did not permit profanity in her home. It was the one rule her foul-mouthed husband habitually broke — to her repeated displeasure.

The Smith's first child, a son named Allen, was born in 1962. A daughter they called Susan (after Margaret's mother) came along in 1964. A second son, named after his father, joined them in 1969. April was what used to be called a *change of life* baby even though Margaret was in her early forties. She got her name for the simple reason of being born in that particular month in 1975.

~ ~ ~ ~ ~

Tom Zurakowski ducked his head into April's office. It never failed to amaze him that someone so talented could also be such a clutter-bug. The place was a total disaster... papers, books, and boxes in stacks all over the floor...

"Hey, April, how about some lunch? We could go down to the cafeteria or maybe pop on over to Greek Town. Waddya think?"

It wasn't that April disliked Tom, it was more the case she liked him better in group settings. The way she saw it, Tom wore his intentions like the less-than-subtle billboards along I-75. Her sarcasm aside, April had to admit Tom wasn't the only man trying to put the make on her. There were two others at the DIA alone who cast their gaze her way.

"No, Tom," said April as she looked up from a report she was preparing, "not today. I have to finish cataloging the items donated by the Mansfield Estate, and some of this stuff is difficult to describe. I think Charles Addams was their interior decorator," she concluded with a smile.

"Fine, April, but you know what people say about all work and no play…"

With that, Tom gave April a half-wave and spun around on his heels. She heard his footsteps echo off the polished marble hallway and then mercifully fade away.

April paused from her work and wondered if she had some sort of disability when it came to relationships. Like her brothers and sister before her, she was considered a gifted student. Additionally, April had been a standout in girls' track at the Chandler School; the Birmingham area academy from where they all had graduated. Unfortunately, learning how to date was not a course the school offered its students.

April enjoyed challenges be they physical or intellectual, but apprehension always rose in her when the challenge in question concerned dating. It didn't help matters her parents had found 'the perfect match for you, dear' as her mother phrased it. April thought it made her sound like someone's misplaced shoe. In this case, that *someone* was a young, black attorney by the name of Jeremiah Wheeler — Jerry, as he insisted she call him.

Jeremiah Wheeler had everything going for him and he knew it, too. At thirty years of age, he was tall with the chiseled facial features of an athlete and was already someone to be reckoned with in GM's legal department.

Richard Smith had met Jeremiah a few years before he retired, and the two of them formed a mentoring relationship. Jeremiah had the virtue of reminding Richard of himself at that age. And with his engineer's mind, he postulated there was no one better for his youngest child to marry than the kind of man he knew best.

What Richard Smith's youngest child knew was she could no longer continue to be indecisive when it came to her parents' pick. She had put off Jeremiah's advances so many times he had begun to refer to April as his *maybe baby*. While she could hardly blame him for that label, she also wondered what he saw in her. Aside from the color of their skin, the two of them had almost nothing else in common.

Jeremiah was mostly bored around art. He tried to hide it, but April saw the truth etched on his face every time he visited her at the institute. She, meanwhile, had little interest in contract law. Jeremiah ate, drank and breathed it like an addict. The first time she met him — a month ago at a dinner party at her parents' Florida home — the two of them could barely find anything to talk about. This experience only served to reinforce April's resolve to forget about relationships for the time being.

April pulled her thoughts back to the gothic confusion which best described the Mansfield Estate's manifest. Though it was time-consuming work, she drew comfort from the knowledge it would keep her occupied until her trip to New York City. She smiled as this thought passed through her mind: "For the moment, at least, all my relationship problems are beyond my ability to control."

~ 2 ~

The garage door lifted quietly at Phil Kerschner's house. It was a screw-type mechanism instead of the more common chain-driven model, and represented Phil's fifth (and hopefully final) attempt at placating his exacting spouse. At 3:30 on a sultry Tuesday morning, it was possible for his wife to sleep through his return; possible, but unlikely.

"No point in tempting fate by coming in through the front door," Phil said under his breath.

Marla Kerschner always had difficulty sleeping when her husband was flying. Phil's best hope was that she would sense the vibration generated from the garage door going up and then drift back into slumber.

Phil's flight from Chicago to Dallas had been over six hours late in departing. He didn't know if he should be angry with the airline or his travel agent.

"To hell with them all!" he hissed. Yet even Phil admitted to assuming some of the pain: "If I hadn't sold my Cessna, none of this mess would have happened."

Whoever was to blame, these once-a-year weeklong fishing trips with his old navy buddies were getting harder to endure. Last year, it was a relatively easy drive to the Ozarks. This year — if Phil had still owned his airplane — he could have picked up and dropped off Larry in Indianapolis going to and coming back from northern Michigan.

"That would have been real clean. But not this: sixteen hours from Charlevoix to Dallas, for Christ's sake," he mumbled as he eased his car into its place in the garage.

That calculation, he knew, didn't include the two and a half hour ferry ride from the island or the sixty-minute drive from Dallas-Fort Worth International Airport to his home in Richardson.

Phil turned off the engine and emerged from his car — the silent garage door already on its merry way back to concrete. He threw the satchel containing his dirty clothes next to the washer. His fishing equipment was treated with considerably more care in spite of the fact he wanted to break something. With a sigh born from experience, Phil began to stow his gear. Last but certainly not least, he reached for his tackle box (it was always a mess after a flight), found a place to sit, and opened it. He stared at the thing which was scrunched up on top.

"What is that…a scarf?" With thumbs and forefingers, he carefully lifted it as if it were some kind of dead critter. He hadn't remembered ever owning something like this. "What the hell is it doing in my tackle box?" He felt as if he really should know. And then the truth started to come back to him: "Damn!" he chuckled to himself. "Marla is always saying I never bring her anything from these trips. Well, this will shut her mouth… she loves fancy crap like this. I just won't tell her I won it in a poker game."

Then he recalled the hand…"Got it with queens over sevens from the guy who took us around the waters of upper Lake Michigan. What was his name? Terry? Barry? Oh, who the hell cares you old fart! Go to bed and finish it in the morning."

With that, Phil Kerschner — master fisherman and former Marine Corps aviator — opened the door leading into the mud room, turned off the garage lights, stepped into his home, and placed his most recent catch on the kitchen counter where Marla was sure to find it.

~   ~   ~   ~   ~

Her office phone was ringing as she hurried to unlock the door. April's overcoat was still on from her Tuesday lunch-hour trip to a small deli a city block from the institute. Without removing it, she reached for the handset.

"Hello?"

There was a pause as she listened to the voice on the other end.

"Yes, Mr. Risner, I can come right now."

Another pause…

"No, I'll probably not finish that until Thursday or Friday."

Once more…

"Yes, sir… right away. Good-bye…"

"That was odd," April thought as she returned the handset to its base unit. "He just gave me the Mansfield project, and now he wants me to put that aside for 'something more important'? What could be more important than all of this?"

April looked at the papers and photographs strewn across her workspace. It had taken six months of delicate negotiations just to secure the opportunity to inspect this manifest. "Good Lord! The Chicago Institute of Art almost got it instead of us," she vented.

After hanging up her overcoat, she left her office for John Risner's located one floor above with the other department heads. April hadn't walked ten feet toward the stairway before literally bumping into Tom Zurakowski.

"Hey, baby," Tom said with a very poor imitation of Cary Grant's voice. "Why are you so good to me?"

"Um… I'm not." April replied absent-mindedly as she maneuvered around him.

Tom watched as April quickly ascended the stairs. "Wow! She sure is fine," he said under his breath. "If I could only figure out what makes her tick."

~ ~ ~ ~ ~

John Risner heard a light rapping on his partially opened door, looked up, and saw April peeking around it. "Thanks for coming so quickly," he spoke as he waved her into his office, "Anthony will pick up the Mansfield material from you at four-thirty. Can you have it gathered up for him by then?"

"Uh, yes, that won't be a problem, Mr. Risner, but…"

April's voice trailed off and she knew that in spite of all her best efforts, she was looking stunned. Risner saw the expression on her face and pointed his assistant to a cushioned leather chair in front of his desk. "April… relax! You're not being demoted."

April smiled as she dropped her gaze to the floor for a brief moment. When she looked up again, she said, "I'm sorry, sir. I wasn't worried about that. It's just, well… this all seems so 'cloak and dagger'… you know… mysterious."

"That's precisely what it is, April," John said evenly and without embellishment.

The changed look on April's face told John that April understood the seriousness of the moment. April's attention was now fully engaged; waiting for her boss's next words.

"I received a call this morning from a client," he began. "About three years ago, the institute — that is to say, I — did an appraisal for him on a unique needlepoint artifact. This relatively small piece of linen chronicles one of the most unusual — and least known — chapters in nineteenth-century American History. It is irreplaceable. I knew that with your knowledge of woven artifacts and having an academic minor in criminology, you were the best person in my department to assist him."

"But, why do you need... Oh, I understand, sir. The artifact has been stolen. That's it, isn't it, sir."

"Yes, April..."

Before John could explain further, April interjected with a question: "Aren't the police better equipped to handle something like this, Mr. Risner?"

John paused to consider his next words carefully. He rose from his seat and stood behind it as he cleared his throat. "Well, there is a small question of legal jurisdiction. But, beyond that, the client wishes to keep news of this theft as quiet as possible. His thinking is that the thief may try to sell the artifact on the black market. Bringing the police in at this point may only serve to alert the thief instead of lulling him into a false sense of opportunity."

April leaned back into the rich comfort of the chair and considered the implications of what her boss had just told her. The DIA didn't make a habit of this kind of assistance, she knew, so this was a rare chance for someone in her position. April did like a good mystery and knew this particular quality of hers had made John Risner's decision to hire her in the first place an easy one. April pursed her lips and gave her head a small, quick nod.

"Very well, sir. Tell me what you need me to do."

"Great! Well, April, as for right now, just to take the next two days to transfer out your current assignments to…"

"There was only the Mansfield project… and my preparations for that trip to New York City, sir."

"Oh, thanks for reminding me about New York, April." John said as he retook his seat. "We'll put that project on a back burner for now, ok? I'll make the necessary calls and explain the situation to our Manhattan clients as best I can. In the mean time, here is the client's file," he said as he picked up a large manila folder and handed it to his now clearly disappointed assistant.

"Read it over and let me know if you have any questions. You'll probably have one or two…"

With that, April understood the meeting to be over. She stood up from her stunned comfort and looked at the name on the file: Riley, William. As April left her superior's office, she knew only one thing for certain, and she voiced it: "Whoever you are, Mr. Riley, I already hate you!"

~   ~   ~   ~   ~

Marla Kerschner knew the value of a bit of well-placed positive reinforcement... and now so too did her husband.

In the thirty-seven years since his wedding night, Phil couldn't remember ever being awakened the way Marla had done so this morning. His journey getting home had worn him down and he had looked forward to some horizontal inactivity. But now...

"My God, I'm exhausted all over again," he thought to himself. Phil eyed his bedside clock and was shocked to see it read 1:25 p.m. "That can't be right!" But it was, and the truth of it made him smile. "Not bad for an old fart, even if I do say so myself," he said in a whisper. "There's certainly no need to go to the gym today to work out the kinks from hours of sitting around in airports."

The sound of the shower stopped and Phil heard the swoosh of the curtain as Marla stepped out onto the bathroom rug. A moment later, she came into the bedroom wrapped in her powder-blue bathrobe.

Marla could see her well-loved husband still had one of those 'cat-that-ate-the-canary' grins on his face. The *cat* spoke first: "Am I to assume, my dear wife, you found something in the kitchen which tickled your fancy?"

Marla sat on the bed next to Phil and continued to dry her hair. She looked at him with a grave expression such that her spouse was suddenly unsure of himself.

"What's the matter, Marla?"

Those few seconds before she answered became an eternity to Phil. Finally, she replied, "You know I love you, Phil, even though you can be a jerk sometimes. I'm reluctant to say this because I know it will just go to your head... Phil, that needlepoint piece is simply the most beautiful gift you have ever brought me from one of your fishing trips. Now, go get cleaned up while I make lunch." With those words, Marla Kerschner first kissed and then smacked her husband's balding head.

~ ~ ~ ~ ~

Thick, calloused hands pressed onto Perry Whitney's hair-challenged head. No matter how hard he applied pressure to his scalp, he couldn't make the throbbing go away. It was late Tuesday afternoon and he still hadn't recovered from the weekend.

He looked at his fishing cruiser *Morning Glory* docked in its usual slip at the marina in Paradise Bay. It was a good thing he had cleaned it up Sunday afternoon. He didn't think he would have had the strength to do it today. It was a thought confirmed by a lack of any meaningful activity since leaving home at 7:00 this morning. Even that effort was an improvement: Perry never made it out of his house yesterday.

Last week had been very good for business; in Perry's case, the fishing excursion business. The four men who chartered his boat paid him a lot of money. That fact alone made his current state of wellness tolerable; with Perry's residual queasiness holding up two object-lessons he thought he'd already learned: do not drink more than you can handle and do not play poker. "Here's a third lesson," he added under his breath, "never do both those things at the same time!"

Perry took a pack of unfiltered cigarettes from the breast pocket of his red-plaid shirt. At the same time, the sun dove under a thick cloud-bank so Perry snatched an opportunity to open wide his eyes behind the increased comfort of his shades.

As he did all this, he shook loose a smoke and nipped the end with his lips. He'd gone as far as drawing a flame from his lighter before the pain in his skull convinced him smoking — at this particular moment at any rate — was not a good idea. He snapped shut the lighter and returned the cig to the pack and the pack to the pocket.

Perry removed his sunglasses and gently massaged the area around his eyes and temples. In spite of his great love for fishing these waters, he was glad the season had come to a close. The ensuing months would be well-spent repairing and repainting the source of his income.

"Well, old girl," Perry said to his craft as it gently swayed in the afternoon waves, "I do believe I need a rest almost as much as you do."

Perry glanced over his shoulder and saw his older son Sean approach from the direction of the school. He thought to himself, "That boy sure does move slow... even for an islander. And when he does move, it's usually at the direction of his mother."

When the lad got within ear-shot, Perry spoke: "What does your mother want this time, Sean?"

"She says you better go over to Mr. O'Riley's place. Mrs. Doherty called Mom from the hotel to say he didn't show up for work today."

"When did Mrs. Doherty call?"

"A few minutes before I left this morning, Pop... Why is that important?"

Perry squinted up at the grey, cloud-packed sky, put on his sunglasses, smiled faintly, and shook his head. "The kid," he thought to himself, "went to school without telling me and is only now getting around to it." Then speaking out loud: "Never mind, Sean. Go home and tell your mother you delivered her message."

"Yes, sir..."

"You probably shouldn't volunteer you did so *after* school... unless, that is, you want some extra chores. But if she asks you, I better find out you told her the truth. Understood?"

"Got ya, Pop."

Perry watched as his son turned and began his amble home. "If it ain't one thing, it's another..." he muttered. "This 'You take care of it, you're the township supervisor' business is for the birds."

Even so, Perry was glad for the distraction. He'd been putting off motoring over to Harbor Springs all day. Now, Ruth Doherty's phone call gave him a solid reason not to.

"Waldron's Boat Shop will just have to wait until tomorrow. Besides, I just might be able to take my head with me by then."

Perry started down the length of the dock and decided to go see Mrs. Doherty first. "Something else must be going on," he thought, "for her to have called my house. Man alive! That woman wouldn't bother to phone-in a fire alarm."

Perry entered the hotel lobby and saw Mrs. Doherty wasn't at her usual spot — behind the service counter with her nose pressed into one of her romance novels. He called out to her: "Mrs. Doherty?"

"Down here, Supervisor Whitney."

"She's in the basement?" Perry silently wondered. "What is she doing down there?"

He soon found out. The museum looked as if renegade antique hunters had assaulted it. Display items were everywhere: on the countertops; on the floor; stacked on chairs — in essence, everywhere.

The two turned to look at one another as if checking to make sure what they were seeing was real. Perry knew a look of astonishment must be plastered across his face.

"I imagine that's just what *my* face looked like this morning," Ruth deadpanned. "What are you going to do about this mess, Supervisor Whitney?"

Without answering, Perry bolted from the basement of the King Strang Hotel taking steps two at a time. He heard the words, "I'm not cleaning this up!" fade past him as he flew by startled guests waiting for Mrs. Doherty to return. Perry's hangover was quickly forgotten; replaced by something far, far worse: "Oh, man… let me be wrong about Bill!"

He ran down the street to his friend's apartment building. In the process, Perry almost knocked over Sean who was going in the same direction. Sean had to do a double-take to make sure the man who just passed him was his father. It was, and it was also the first time Sean had ever seen his father running.

Perry reached the building's main door which opened into a vestibule-like space. The stairway leading to the second floor apartments was located here along with the lower central hallway leading to the building's four ground-floor units.

He paused… partly to catch his breath and partly because he wasn't sure he wanted to do this. Bent over with his hands on his waist and with his lungs and legs screaming at him, Perry noticed his knee-high rubber work boots were on the wrong feet. Under different circumstances, he might have laughed at his alcohol-induced cluelessness. Instead, he ignored the error and thought: "What if I'm right?"

As if providing the answer to his own question, Perry straightened up and cast his gaze through the glass door and onto the stairway. Then he voiced his confirmation: "Well, tough guy, there's only one way to find out."

Perry opened the building's main entrance and went up the stairs. He came to William's apartment and strained to listen for any sound coming from within. Hearing nothing, he knocked.

~ ~ ~ ~ ~

April was gathering the last of the papers associated with the Mansfield Estate when Anthony Munoz announced his presence by clearing his throat. She looked up with a start saying, "Tony, how long have you been standing there?"

"Long enough, April. Look, I don't mean to pry... you know what, yes I do! I just gotta know... didn't your mother ever make you clean your room? How in heaven's name do you manage this chaos?"

April smiled and considered her reply. She liked Anthony — who was only three months her junior. They both had been hired around the same time but had taken different paths to get to the Detroit Institute of Arts.

Anthony had married his childhood sweetheart while they were both still high school juniors. Angelina gave birth to their first child, a daughter, about three months after they graduated.

Many young men crumble under this sort of pressure. But, the need to provide for his family turned Anthony into a responsibility machine. He continued to hold down the full-time job he had while in school — auto and truck mechanic — but also made money as someone who painted elaborate designs on the vehicles he repaired. Completely by chance, his reputation for design and color on metal came to the attention of an art professor at UCLA.

This new father soon found himself in possession of a full academic scholarship to the premiere art school on the West Coast. Though he had never dreamed of going to college, Anthony moved his family in with his parents and latched onto this incredible opportunity with both hands.

By the time he was in his final year, Anthony was fielding job offers from all across the country. His dream as a boy had been to play shortstop for the Dodgers. Physical stature ruled that out. Instead, he soon discovered what it was like to work in the major league world of art.

Anthony was smart, streetwise, loyal, and (most importantly for April) passionately in love with his wife. For these reasons, April felt she could be more unguarded with him than with any other man at the DIA. She included Anthony in with some women at the institute who were her friends in the best sense of the word.

If a colleague other than someone from this cohort had mentioned the cluttered appearance of her office (John Risner excepted), she would have impolitely told them where to stuff it. But with Anthony, April just returned her well-considered volley.

"I don't! You know that. It manages me. Besides, I'm providing an important community service here. Without this," she said as she swept her arms around the room, "the rest of you *clean freaks* might never know why it is you are so obsessive."

"Uh, right, April. Remind me to submit your name for employee of the month."

"Did you come in here, Señor Munoz, for the Mansfield material, or just to abuse me?"

"Abuse *you*? I should get hazard pay for merely stepping in here. But, I'll be content to escape with the Mansfield manifest, if you please, Ms. Smith."

April rolled her eyes and put on her best disappointed-looking face. She dropped the last manila folder into the cardboard storage box, set the lid, took hold of the box, and came out from behind her desk. Anthony took a step toward her and reached out for his next assignment.

"I was looking forward to cataloging Mary Mansfield's collections of miniature cast-iron gargoyles," she pouted. "But, now you get to have all the fun."

"Yeah, some fun... I heard Risner gave you a special project which involves a stolen artifact. Now, *that* sounds like fun. What's it all about, April?"

"Well, you know about as much as I do, Tony... so far. I haven't had time to review the client's file yet. One thing I do know is Mr. Risner wants to keep this thing quiet. I don't imagine I'll be able to tell you — or anyone — much about it. Hey, Tony... Seriously now, would you do me a favor?"

"Of course, April. Just name it."

"Keep Tom off my back about this. I can usually tolerate his cheesy come-ons, but this investigation is new ground for me, and the last thing I need is for him to be snooping around here trying to be my 'good buddy.'"

"Done... Anything else I can do for you?"

"Yes," April hissed. "Do you know where a girl can go to get someone's kneecaps broken?"

"What!" Anthony exclaimed as he kicked her office door closed, and deposited the file box on a nearby chair. "You'd better be joking, April, cause you know I know guys like that. Is Tom becoming *that* obnoxious?"

"No," she laughed as she rubbed her now tired eyes, "it's not for Tom, and yes, I'm joking… sort of. More like blowing off steam. This thing," she said lifting up the Riley folder, "is keeping me out of New York City for a while. I just wanted to show my new client how much I appreciated it, but the thought of buying him a Hummel figurine seemed a bit over the top."

"Remind me never to get on your bad side."

As she waved him goodbye, a relieved Anthony opened the door, took hold of the file box, stepped through the opening… and decided he would buy Angelina some flowers on the way home from work.

~ ~ ~ ~ ~

Perry Whitney, professional fishing guide, Supervisor of St. James Township, and avoider of all things remotely smelling of trouble, opened his friend's apartment door fully expecting Bill to be lying dead on the floor. What he saw was William sitting on the floor in his front room next to a coffee table with his back to Perry.

Relieved, Perry called out, "Hey, Bill! Got a minute?"

William, without either speaking or turning around, weakly motioned his friend to enter. Perry stepped into the hallway and shut the door. As he moved past his friend's bedroom, he noticed the bed was unmade and thought: "That has to be a first." Then speaking, he said, "So, what's up, old bud?" Perry said hoping that he sounded relaxed.

William was surrounded by a number of family photo albums, and was quietly leafing through one of them. Perry took a quick glance into the kitchen and saw dirty dishes stacked in the sink. Now Perry did relax. "At least the guy is eating something," he concluded in silence. "That has to be a good sign."

Perry found his way to the sofa, sat on it, and asked, "What's going on, Bill? I just came from the King Strang and..." Perry was struck silent because though William's eyes were dry, a deep sadness poured from them.

William cleared his throat and spoke just two words: "It's gone."

Perry took that in and waited for the rest, but the rest never came. So he asked, "What's gone? Has someone died, Bill? What in blazes are you talking about?"

Suddenly Perry was looking up at William who seemed to have been launched off the floor as if by some hidden spring. William placed the photo album he'd been holding on the coffee table, and, with great difficulty, looked Perry in the eyes. He said, "I'm glad you're here, Perry. I was going to walk over to the marina... that's where Joyce said you were."

"You called my house?"

"Actually, Joyce called me around noon. I guess she was worried about me after having spoken to Mrs. Doherty..." William's voice trailed off and he looked at Perry with a sheepish grin. Then he changed subjects: "Can I get you some apple cider?"

"Yeah, that would be great."

Perry got up and followed William into the kitchen. He thought to himself, "Bill is more complicated than I ever realized," and watched as William chose a half-full gallon of cider from the fridge. William poured two tall glasses and handed one to Perry.

As Perry finished swallowing the first mouthful of the cold, sweet liquid, William said, "The tapestry is gone, Perry. Vanished... I have no idea where it is."

Perry heard William, but it was like an echo bouncing off some dark corner of his mind. He was still trying to absorb what he'd heard when William brushed past him, walked over to the sofa, and sat down.

He followed experiencing the odd sensation that three aces were somehow involved. Perry thought he already knew the answer, but felt curious enough to ask the question anyway: "What tapestry? You don't mean *the* tapestry, do you?"

William nodded slowly as Perry sat down at the dining room table. Finally it all made sense to Perry: The mess at the museum; his friend's odd behavior; and the disaster which was William's usually well-maintained apartment. These oddities were all the result of one missing piece of old linen.

And then — just as suddenly — the sense vaporized and Perry exploded: "Bill! It's just one stupid item out of thousands! You mean to tell me half this island is worried sick about you because you can't find that old rag? Damn, Bill, I came over here thinking you might be dead!"

"Well, I might just as well be dead considering how I've let everyone down... especially you!"

Perry's usual, easy-going demeanor now returned as he asked his friend, "What do you mean by that?"

William looked at Perry as if the guy was having trouble adding two plus two. He replied, "You're the king now since your dad retired from office last year. Have you forgotten? If we can't find that needlepoint document by next April, you can kiss your royal office goodbye. The only things I can't figure are who took it, how they got into the museum, and how did they remove it from that desk..."

As William was speaking, the hazy image of his own hand pulling out a gold-stitched cloth flashed in Perry's brain. And with that latent memory returned the hangover which, until recently, had been caged by more pressing matters. Perry groaned because those matters and his hangover were crashing on him like large waves against the side of a boat. Perry sank his head into his hands and tried to forget the truth he thought had been just a bad dream.

"See, I knew you would understand. That's why I've contacted the authorities," said William with a returning sense of resolve.

"What? You called the police?" asked Perry as an entirely new pain suddenly slammed into him.

"No, — sorry for the confusion — I called John Risner at the Detroit Institute of Arts." William saw that his words meant nothing to Perry, so he attempted to translate: "You know this guy, Perry. You took him out on your boat three summers ago."

Perry blinked a few times trying to find an emotional safe-harbor in which to take refuge. He wasn't having much success.

"You must remember him: Lake trout; Penn Championship reel; Thompson ultra-light; four-pound test…"

"Yeah, yeah… ok, now I got him!" Perry said finally. "Not a bad fisherman, just a bit out of practice. Dad did mention something about someone looking at the Strang, but I wasn't paying much attention back then."

"Anyway, I'm going Thursday morning to meet with him and some other guy down in Detroit. He suggested I bring with me a list of visitors who've been to the island in the last month so we can compare it to their list of people who are known to traffic in stolen art."

"We're talking art thieves, here? You mean that old rag is worth stealing?"

"That *old rag* as you call it — besides its use every first day of April — is worth around half a million dollars. At least, that's the number John said was its appraised value."

Suddenly it was Perry who wished he were dead. As if to signal its agreement, his face turned an appropriate shade of pale.

"This day just keeps getting worse and worse," he thought to himself. "I really have to stop playing poker altogether. Damn! Now I remember... that guy drew to a full house, and me with three *bullets*. What *was* his name?"

As he was rolling the events of Sunday night over in his head (as far as his head would let him) Perry watched William resume his perusal of the photo album. Something William said crept back into the fore-front of his consciousness. He rose from the dining room table and sat down next to William on the sofa.

"Bill, did I hear you say you're going to Detroit?"

~　~　~　~　~

April sat in her office looking through the history of the Strang Tapestry for the second time. The first time she read it, it had seemed like a joke. "There had been a Mormon king on Beaver Island?" April asked her otherwise empty office.

Even more amazing to her was there had been a Mormon king and President Franklin Pierce agreed to support James Jesse Strang's unilateral decree with all the power and legitimacy of the United States Government — albeit secretly.

April was sure this was something neither she nor her schoolmates ever read about in any American History course. And, it wasn't difficult to understand why. The political drama of the events leading up to the American Civil War provided all the cover this weird, presidential capitulation ever needed.

"There's not an American politician," she sat there thinking, "at any level of government could ever admit their part at bringing into existence North America's first and only legal monarchy — and expect to remain in office. Now, pair that with a volatile subject like polygamy… and voila! I present to you, friends, the perfect recipe for a disgusting dish called 'conspiracy of silence.'"

She lifted the two photographs of the Strang Tapestry closer to her face and carefully examined them. If it weren't for the history recorded in silk threading, this sampler would not have been one at which she would have looked twice.

"The craftsmanship is fine, as far as that goes…" she deduced. "The linen seems of good quality and in excellent shape — except for that stain."

In truth, it was no better than the other nineteenth-century American samplers April had evaluated. Even so, she understood the value of the artifact and the need for its recovery.

"This is far more than a piece of needlecraft," she whispered, "it's also a legal document."

April had come to the realization that the theft of the Strang Tapestry was as serious for this William Riley person as the disappearance of the Declaration of Independence would be for the head of the National Archives. April noted something else out of the ordinary: in all the papers before her, she had yet to come across any reference to the Strang Tapestry having been insured.

"I suppose it is difficult to insure something which isn't supposed to exist in the first place," she said under her breath. April exchanged the Strang photos for one of William Riley which was also part of the client's profile. "Serves you right, Mr. Riley," April said to the droll image staring back at her. "You should have donated the Strang to us three years ago like Mr. Risner suggested. Now what have you to show for all your efforts at keeping your strange secret hidden?"

In spite of her personal feelings, April was determined to give this new client her best efforts at recovering his missing artifact. "But," she told herself. "I'm only taking on this project because John Risner asked me to." April resolved to be polite and professional regarding her new client, but no more: "You look like an attorney, Mr. Riley," April again said to the image before her, "and that's strike number two!"

~ ~ ~ ~ ~

"You haven't spent a night off the island in, what... twenty years," Perry opined.

"Twenty-one," William corrected him. "You of all people should remember. These are the pictures," he pointed out; lifting an album Perry's way, "of the trip our families took to Mackinac Island. Look! Here is that photo of the Mackinac Bridge from underneath. I'm always impressed every time I see it. And there... there's the one of your dad's old fishing boat, *Majesty*. What was that pet name he used to call her?"

Perry smiled at the fond memory as he took hold the photo album. "The 'Wretched Wreck,' but he was the only one allowed to call her that. I called her by it once in his presence and paid dearly for it."

"If I recall, it sank during that freak summer squall in 1982," William continued.

"Yeah," Perry sighed. "My father actually cried. Even after the Irish Boat Shop built him a replacement with the insurance money, he used to say fishing just wasn't the same anymore. If my mom hadn't loved that old tub, too, she would have divorced him for carrying on the way he did. Say, what's with the stroll down memory lane?"

"As you were so helpful in pointing out, except for the occasional day-trip to Charlevoix, it's been two decades since I stepped foot off Beaver Island. I was just thinking back to that time and then I remembered my folks left these albums with me. To tell you the truth, I'm not looking forward to my trip to Detroit with any great enthusiasm. You might recall my last time off the *Rock* was a near-disaster."

"That's right!" Perry shouted as he closed the album and then slapped his friend on the back. "You got lost. I almost forgot about that."

"I did not get lost you royal idiot!" William shot back. "I hid from my parents because they wouldn't take me up to the fort again. Anyway, by the time I came out of hiding, the rest of you had gone to the police station. So, I waited in Marquette Park and counted horses until my folks found me."

"Man, oh, man... if I'm forgetful, you're out to rewrite history..." Perry scolded William as he reopened the album and began to thumb through the pages. "Let me see... I know that picture's in here somewhere... your mother showed it to me once. Ha! Here it is," he said as he pressed the page under William's nose.

The print was of William at six years of age. Sitting next to him was a very young and very pretty girl. Perry continued, "Your mom reminded me how this family found you wandering around crying your eyes out. The father took *this* photo of you and his daughter together because she was the only one who got you to stop crying. What was her name?"

~ ~ ~ ~ ~

"What's the kid's name?" Jeremiah Wheeler asked no one in particular.

Margaret Smith looked over at the young attorney who was standing by a display of photographs on the Smith's baby grand piano.

"What is who's name, Jerry?" she asked.

"He's looking at that picture of Jim and Rachel's kid with April, honey," her husband interjected.

"Billy O'Riley," Margaret said. "That photograph was taken on Mackinac Island back on Memorial Day Weekend in 1979. April had just turned four the month prior. Wasn't she the cutest toddler?"

"I never remember that kid's name," Richard offered. "But, he sure was the weepiest boy you ever saw."

"Wasn't there some couple named O'Riley you played golf with last week?" Jeremiah asked.

"Yeah, that's them: Jim and Rachel O'Riley," Richard confirmed.

"We play a round of mixed doubles with them just about every Wednesday," Margaret added.

"So, you've known them for a long time, then, Dick," Jeremiah concluded as he continued to sip his scotch whisky on ice.

"Well, yes and no," Richard began to say. "After meeting them on Mackinac, Margaret and Rachel exchanged Christmas cards for about fifteen years. Then, about six years ago, Margaret invited them down here to see what life was like in sunny Florida. Jim retired in '94, and a year later, they bought a place about two blocks over and moved down here permanently. Since then, we do a lot with them socially. Now, tell us, son," Richard said changing the subject of their conversation, "how's it going with you and April? She's so wrapped up in her job that we never hear about her social life."

"Yes, Jerry," Mrs. Smith added, "have the two of you started to go out?"

"To tell you folks the truth," Jeremiah responded, "that's the reason I stopped in this evening. I can't seem to get her to commit to a date with me. She has a head full of excuses, and I was wondering if she's said anything to you about me. You know... 'He has terrible body odor...' or something like that."

"Jeremiah," Margaret offered, "it's useless to ask April's father about this sort of thing. She wouldn't say anything to him... even if you were a raving lunatic. On the other hand, April does talk with me, but she hasn't said anything about you either good or bad."

"So, what's going on?" Jeremiah asked Margaret. "Is it something I said or didn't say? I wouldn't bother to ask, except I really like her."

"Damn!" Richard blurted. "It used to be…"

"Richard Smith, watch your language," his puzzle-absorbed wife calmly stated. (Jeremiah smiled to himself at this revealing inter-play.)

"Yes, sorry, honey… As I was about to say, it used to be so easy for men and women to meet, court, and get married. When Margaret and I were younger… well, let's just say the rules seem to be very different today."

"Rules?" Jeremiah began. "There are no rules anymore. There's no logic to any part of my social life. That's the thing I've always appreciated about the law: it's so predictable."

Richard looked at Jeremiah as if he were crazy. Jeremiah saw this and tried to explain his remark: "What I mean to say is that in a court room, there's always going to be a winner and a loser. I may not know which side I'm on in that regard, but I can always count on there being some sort of resolution. As for relationships… that's another matter altogether. I never know what the hell… heck — sorry ma'am — is going on. I'm thirty and ready for that next phase of my life to begin, but it isn't happening." With those words, Jeremiah lowered himself into one of the Smith's easy chairs, and waited.

After a moment of awkward silence, Margaret put down her crossword puzzle, rose from her chair, and eased over to the frustrated young man.

"Jerry, dear," she said as she placed her hand on his shoulder, "Dick likes to believe he *engineered* our marriage from the first day we met until now." She paused and turned her attention to her husband upon who's face rested an angry scowl. She turned back to the distraught lawyer and continued: "But, let me tell you something, he got lucky. And so will you, but love is like a hat you always hold in front of you upside down by the brim — you never know when the right person will drop their coin and take their chance with you."

"In other words," Jeremiah said, "be patient."

"That's probably why God made you a lawyer, my dear," Margaret teased as she patted his cheek. "You have that rare talent of being able to drive right to the heart of the issue."

Jeremiah looked over to his mentor who shook his head and reburied his nose in the newspaper: "Don't look at me!" Richard said in his defense. "You *want* to marry into this family. Like she said — I just got lucky."

~ ~ ~ ~ ~

"I don't remember," said William. "I think their names are Dick and Meredith Smith. I saw the girl just that one time. My mother got the

Smith's address and wrote them a thank-you letter. Later that year, they sent us a Christmas card. After that, the two of them kept in touch. Of course, you know about my parents moving down to Clearwater."

"These people saved your life and you only *think* you know their names?"

"Don't get weird on me, Perry. They did *not* save my life. Besides, I've tried my best to forget about that whole sorry episode. If my folks want to have a relationship with these people… fine! Just don't ask me to pay any attention to it."

"Geez, old bud," Perry said with raised hands, "take a chill-pill. Ok, change of subject: So, tell me about this trip to Detroit. What's this Reasoner fella going to do for you, anyway?"

"Risner… his name is John Risner. What was that about remembering names? He himself can't do anything, but he has a member of his staff with a background in criminology. That guy is going to help me track down this son-of-a-bitch and have him arrested. At least, that is the plan so far."

William's response reminded Perry that he had an important (albeit unknown) role in this crisis; and also that he needed time to think about what he should do. Like the kid who dented his dad's car, Perry knew he had to leave before he confessed to his complicity. So, he downed the last of his cider and got up from the sofa, saying, "And it sounds like a good plan at that. If there's anything I can do for you, old bud, just say the word."

"Actually, there is. Joyce also mentioned you might be motoring over to Harbor Springs tomorrow. Do you think you could drop me off in Petoskey tomorrow morning? That's where I want to catch the bus for Detroit."

"Consider it done. Anything else?"

"Yes, pass the word to Mrs. Doherty that I'm coming in later to tidy up. Also, I've got some vacation time coming to me, so I'm closing down the place for a while. Finally, can I ask you to keep this just between us for the time being? I don't want the islanders to panic."

"Count on me, Bill. I won't breathe a word of it to anyone."

"Say, Perry," William noted as his friend began walking away, "did you know your boots are on backwards?"

"Backwards… yeah, I know. It's the story of my life." Perry replied as he resumed his strategic withdrawal.

His royal highness, King Perry the First of Beaver Island, skulked away from his best friend's dilemma, walked down the flight of stairs, and tried to imagine how he was going to get out from under the pile of fish-guts which had justifiably landed on his head.

~   ~   ~   ~   ~

April turned back the bedding and slipped in between the soft, flannel sheets. For her, October usually meant two things: any team but the Detroit Tigers in the post-season and the change to flannel sheets on her bed. She, of course, had complete control of the latter but zero input on the former.

She cast her gaze to the digital clock by her bedside. It read 10:22 p.m., thinking, "She's late tonight. Perhaps I should call her instead."

As she reached for the telephone, it rang. April put the device to her ear and said, "You know, Mama, I set all my clocks by your phone calls… you're late! What gives?"

Margaret laughed along with her youngest child and then said, "My, my… have you been sharpening your wit all evening waiting for little ole me? Nothing *gives*, April. Your father and I just said goodbye to our dinner guest is all."

"Let me see," April reasoned, "Jerry said he was going to be at an industry-wide conference in Orlando this week. Your guest's last name wouldn't have been Wheeler by any chance?"

"Yes, April," her mother sighed, "but you must remember that Jerry was your father's friend before he was yours."

"He is *not* my friend, Mama. He's just an acquaintance. May I assume from your comments that my name never came up in your conversations?" There was a silence on the line; enough that April exploded: "Mother! How could you talk about me behind my back with a man I can scarcely tolerate? Have you no sense of decency?"

"I have scads of decency, dear. What I don't have any of are grandchildren."

"Here she goes again," April thought to herself as she closed her eyes.

"Allen and his wife are almost forty, your sister hates the idea of marriage let alone breast-feeding, and Richie is living in Toronto with his boyfriend." This time, Margaret added a new layer of guilt: "What if I were to die next year?"

"Oh, Mama, the fate of your world does not rest in my womb."

"April Anne Smith!"

"Well, Mama, it doesn't. And for the record, I don't particularly like the idea of breastfeeding either. But, that's not why I'm going to tell Jerry to find someone else to *court*. It figures a lawyer would use that particular word…"

At this moment, Margaret felt sure she was about to gain one more shred of insight concerning her daughter's psyche (and that was no easy task). "Well, what *is* the matter with Jerry, dear?"

"Mama…" April pleaded, "don't you get it? It is *not* about Jeremiah Wheeler… it's about me. I want to feel for the man I marry a greater passion than I feel for my career. If I give in and wed someone like Jerry who is decent but whose presence in my life never distracts me from the work I love, then I will be guilty of using that man as a means to an end, even if that end is a noble one like giving you and Daddy grandchildren."

Margaret was stunned beyond words. There was only one thing she could think to do, so she did it.

"Mama, are you crying? I'm sorry. I didn't mean to make you cry."

"Oh, sweetheart," Margaret said between sobs, "I'm just so happy I have you for a daughter. You are such a *good* girl, but, my oh my, where did you ever get an idea like that?"

"Don't you know? Grandma Porter told me once that you could have been as famous a singer as Aretha Franklin if you hadn't married Daddy. You must have loved him very much. I just want that same feeling for myself, that's all. With Jerry, though, all I get is the decency. I'm sorry."

"Don't be, April. I'm the one who's sorry. I just need to take my own advice and keep my hat out there a little bit longer."

"What was that?"

"Never mind, dear," Margaret said as she regained her composure. "If I know you, you will find that feeling and know it when you do. Good night, sweetheart, I love you."

"Love you right back, Mama."

"One more thing, April... my mother was right about me, and so are you." With that, Margaret hung up and thought to herself that her life just got a lot more meaningful.

~ 3 ~

Perry Whitney crept up behind his wife (she was about to remove scrambled eggs from the stovetop) and lifted her high in the air. Joyce screamed and Perry put her back down.

After recovering her balance, Joyce turned a grinning face to her husband, applied a solid punch to his right bicep, and said, "Well, you're in a good mood this morning."

Perry — his body moving slowly toward Joyce's and never breaking eye contact — hesitated and then pressed his lips to hers. He lingered there for a moment longer than he usually did and then pulled away leaving his wife with a different sort of disorientation. "You betcha, babe! Isn't it amazing how a new day can sometimes wipe away all the crap from the day before?"

Joyce — recovering but still confused — reached for the safety of practical words: "Ok, sunshine… sit down and eat your breakfast. Coffee?"

Perry took a seat, grasped, and then held out his cup as his way of responding.

"So, hon, what's got you so charged up today?" asked Joyce as she poured his coffee and then served him the rest of the eggs.

"Hey... I got me a beautiful wife, two great kids, a job I really like, and I live on Beaver Island. What more do I need than that? Besides..." Perry said, now putting on aires, "...I'm the King! I can be happy if I want to be."

"Well, your highness, unless you want to be *crowned* a second time, don't pull a stunt like that again!" Joyce said while waving the now empty skillet for emphasis.

After ten years of marriage, Joyce Whitney knew her man, and this version of him suggested he had figured out something important. There was only one thing important to her husband — besides his family — and that was fishing.

Their anniversary had been last month, the boys' birthdays weren't until next year — her own, as well. So, with Christmas still over two months off, Joyce guessed her husband's exuberance had to do with his work. Her analysis was spot on, but in a way she never could have imagined.

Whatever the cause, Joyce reflected Perry's happiness. Lately, he had been in a miserable mood and she had been prepared to permanently end his reign as St. James Township Supervisor if he had kept up his dark demeanor much longer.

Joyce would never know it, but the plan came to Perry while he was in mid-stroke with his razor. It was not just *a* solution, it was *the* solution to all his problems. As he thought it through a second and then a third time, Perry realized he couldn't have planned the disappearance of the Strang Tapestry any better if he'd tried.

"Except for the lost value — and what could that guy from Detroit know, anyway — where was the crisis?" Perry asked his foam-caked face.

If the Strang was never seen again, Perry deduced that the worst outcome would be he would no longer be King of Beaver Island. Perry had never wanted to be the king in the first place because being king really meant being St. James Township Supervisor, and he hated that aspect of his life.

"If we can just keep Bill busy looking for that stupid piece of fabric until next April," Perry said to his reflection, "then, pal-o-mine, it's nothing but life on the open water!" Perry closed his eyes and swooned at the idea: "No more phone calls in the middle of the night about someone's dog barking; no more meetings about taxes, water rates, school assessments, or road improvements; and best of all, no more sarcastic remarks ending with the phrase 'your majesty.'"

Last evening, and again earlier this morning, Perry had agonized over what to do about the tapestry. Then it came to him: "Don't do a single thing." It was so simple a plan it had to work. "Don't do anything to help Bill search for it or figure out who took it."

Perry followed this line of thinking and concluded there wasn't a snowball's chance in hell of his friend ever connecting it to those four guys who were here last week.

"Even if Bill manages to do that, by then, it will be too late," Perry thought. "It'll be like an overcast day out on Lake Michigan with your anchor dropped off Waugoshance Point. What can go wrong?"

The most important thing Perry needed to do was to get his friend off Beaver Island before someone blabbed to him about that poker game last Sunday night. But that was an issue he was prepared to resolve… right after breakfast.

~ ~ ~ ~ ~

"Jim! We're going to miss our tee time if you don't hurry up," Rachel O'Riley called out.

"I can't find my lucky, green socks. Did you forget to wash them?"

Rachel entered their bedroom to find her mate rummaging through his sock drawer. She said, "Didn't I say *not* to put them in your golf bag?"

"Oh, right," James said sheepishly. "I'll just put on any old pair…"

"And change them once we get to the clubhouse," finished Rachel. "Yes, that was the plan you came up wth last week. Please, dear heart, if you are going to make plans…"

Rachel let the rest of that admonition fade away. She hated repeating herself, and this was already something which had been said too many times.

"Thirty-two years together," she thought to herself as her husband put on the pair of socks he'd chosen, "and the man hasn't changed by even one degree."

Rachel knew it wasn't really true, but it had the advantage of sounding like she felt. She shook her head in wonderment. If she hadn't lived it, she wouldn't have believed it.

"My mother was right about these O'Rileys," she continued to think. "But he was *so* handsome and he really is a dear heart…"

In less than three minutes, the socks were on and the pair were on their way. In spite of the fact moving to Florida hadn't improved her husband's poor memory, Rachel knew this was one of the best decisions they ever made. When Margaret suggested they come visit them in Clearwater, Rachel was surprised with how little resistance James gave to the idea. And he surprised her again two months later when — back on Beaver Island — he voiced his plan to retire and then asked her what she thought about moving to Florida.

As James drove them to the club where Richard and Margaret were almost certainly waiting for them, Rachel remembered back to that day: "If I had false teeth, they would have fallen from my mouth!" She had been so sure James was never going to leave Beaver Island that at one point she contemplated divorce just to be rid of the place. Instead, within a year after visiting the Smiths, she found herself occupying a wonderful split-level home two streets over from her dearest friend.

A young couple from Ann Arbor purchased their home on the island with the idea of converting it into a bed & breakfast inn. As soon as they had set ink to the sale papers, James — usually a stick in the mud when it came to all things domestic — found a new gear and became the lead partner in packing up the house for the move. Between Rachel's sentimental leanings and her husband's eye for the practical, the O'Rileys swiftly settled on which of their possessions would be making the trip south with them.

Even her only child proved to be less of a problem than they imagined. Although he'd been living on his own for a number of years, William had never known a time when his parents weren't nearby. And yet, he embraced their decision to move and even helped out by agreeing to store some items in his apartment with which they could not bear to part, but — at the same time — did not want to tote down to Florida.

Florida turned out to be everything Rachel O'Riley had hoped it would be: Cosmopolitan instead of provincial; active as opposed to sedate; and warm in a way Beaver Island, even on its sunniest day, could never be.

Rachel was not a native islander — she wasn't even from Michigan. When she was two years old, her father — a tugboat captain plying the waters between Chicago and Michigan City, Indiana — moved the growing Jenkins clan to Charlevoix to take a job as a ferry skipper on the Beaver Island run. Charlevoix was then, and still is, a wonderful place to be a kid. But young Rachel's imagination tended to carry her thoughts to more exotic locales.

The year she turned fifteen, her father got her a summer job on board his ferry. While the work was tedious, it did afford her ample time for her thoughts to wander. To pass the time between runs (after she had finished punching ferry tickets), Rachel would imagine herself sailing off to some tropical island or cruising with her fellow explorers up the mighty Amazon River.

Then one day as the boat was being tied up on the pier in Paradise Bay, Rachel caught sight of a young man helping with the bowline. James O'Riley — as she heard he was called — was tall and handsome, and, to Rachel, appeared every inch exotic as his bare-chested muscles rippled under a sheen of sweat and sunlight.

For young Rachel Jenkins, that was the day her dream of wandering the world dissipated; instantly replaced with one clear, present, and (she soon discovered) available obsession.

It turned out to be much more difficult to connect with James Emerson O'Riley in anything approaching a romantic way. For one thing, this man of her new dreams was nine years her senior. It took Rachel over a year and a half of flirting to finally win over the shy Mr. O'Riley. A year after that and it was apparent to all observers Rachel and James were smitten.

Both sets of parents were concerned about the difference in their ages, with Rachel's father saying, "You can do whatever fool thing you want once you come of age!"

They were joined in marriage on Rachel's eighteenth birthday. At first, it seemed to Rachel she got both her man and her previous dream. James surprised her with a two-month honeymoon galavanting around the country. For two young people in 1968 just beginning their married lives, it was a bracing and profound moment — and one which almost sent them in two different directions.

By the time the trip was winding down, James was eager to get back to the sanity of Beaver Island. Rachel, on the other hand, was sad to leave behind all the excitement they had seen while on the road. Rachel described it to friends like a kid getting only one visit to a bakery: an incomplete and unfulfilling experience.

She wanted and expected to one day get the full experience. Rachel had clung to that hope like lint on wool. But two miscarriages and one successful birth later, she began to believe all her larger hopes had been brushed aside.

Then again, motherhood was a mysterious adventure and Rachel surprised even herself at how much she enjoyed *that* journey. As William grew, it was enough she could travel down that path. Once he attained adulthood, Rachel's unrequited aspirations began to seep back into her psyche.

For Rachel, it seemed before she could even turn around, her life was moving in a direction and at a pace not of her own choosing. She went through days on the island feeling as if she were breathing through someone else's lungs or that her heart was pumping a stranger's blood.

She wondered what had happened to that wild child with boundless energy and an imagination to match. Did someone steal away that part of her personality or did she voluntarily set it aside? No matter the answer, Rachel would attempt to access that part of herself only to find her father's voice telling her she was a fool for marrying so young.

When her husband suggested they move to Florida, it was not just a change of address and scenery as far as Rachel was concerned. James could never have realized it, but he was giving his wife a chance to become reconnected to her own body. And Rachel took it. In the last four years, she and her husband traveled more than at any time since their honeymoon.

Rachel was committed to never letting her husband know just how close he had come to one day waking up wife-less. As she looked out over the suburban landscape of Clearwater flowing past them, she thought to herself: "It would break his heart if I said anything. Besides, when it comes to talking about my feelings, I already have my sounding board."

In Margaret Smith, Rachel, had a frequent ear she could bend. In truth, she and Margaret served in this capacity for each other. What began merely as a cordial exchange of cards had evolved over the years into an intimate friendship. Both women were without sisters but had managed to stumble into just that sort of bond with a person from a completely different background.

It never ceased to amaze Rachel the thoughts which would come cascading from her brain when she was with Margaret. Likewise, Margaret had long since determined there was nothing she could say to Rachel which would place their friendship at risk.

At first, Rachel thought it had something to do with the anonymity which goes with words written on paper or a voice on a telephone. But when they got together in Florida, Rachel realized she was wrong. The truth was far simpler: they just loved being together.

They also shared the hope their husbands would grow to enjoy each other's company. The women, however, were too realistic to expect anything more than this from two *old men* whose only connection was they were both born in Michigan.

That wasn't entirely accurate — both men shared a passion for golf with it being about equally divided between love and hate. The weekly round of mixed doubles the women had initiated three months ago was their most recent attempt at transforming hope into reality.

Rachel knew she and Margaret would be having more success if James could only remember where he kept his lucky socks. Richard, like most engineers, was time-conscious. Rachel, on the other hand, doubted her husband had ever owned a watch. Today, she was using this quirk in James' personality to her advantage.

As they turned the corner into the country club parking lot, Rachel took a quick glance at her wristwatch. James would not realize it until he got to the pro shop, but he was about to be thirty minutes early.

~ ~ ~ ~ ~

At the moment James was coming to the truth of his wife's well-intentioned deception, Perry was placing the finishing touches on his own sleight-of-hand concerning Mr. O'Riley the younger.

The two Beaver Islanders were rounding the break-wall protecting Petoskey's marina. William expected his friend to get close enough to a pier so

William could jump off the boat. He was therefore surprised when a young, long-haired man appeared on the wood and steel structure ready to tie-up the *Morning Glory*.

"I thought you had to go over to Waldron's," William said over the engine's din. "What's going on?"

William dropped his suitcase onto the dock and then followed holding his briefcase. Seeing the bow and stern lines were both now secured, Perry cut the power, but the engine resisted coming to a stop.

"Nothing is going on. Joyce asked me to do some shopping for her since I was coming this way. Bill, say hello to Marty Taylor. Marty, this is Bill O'Riley."

"Hi, Mr. O'Riley… Nice to meet you," said the husky kid.

"Uh, it's just 'Riley,' Marty. I dropped the O part when I was in high school. And it's nice to meet you, too."

"Ok, whatever…" Marty shrugged and moved off in the direction of Petoskey. William looked quizzically at Perry and cocked a thumb in the direction of the retreating mane of blond hair.

"What's wrong with him?"

"Nothing is *wrong* with him. It's just how guys are these days. You would know that if you went off the Rock more than once or twice a decade. Besides, you had better be nice to Marty; he's taking us to the bus station."

William — who had been watching Marty when he heard that — turned to Perry with the look of someone who had just been suckered (which, of course, he had). He screamed out, "You bastard! I knew something was up. You were just *too* quiet on the trip here. What's the matter, afraid I might get lost on my way into town?"

"That thought did cross my mind, you nut, but, no, my reason is much friendlier than that. If we drive to the bus station, there should be plenty of time to buy you a cup of tea. The Horizon Bookstore in the Gaslight District has a small cafe. I thought it would be a nice gesture considering how long a trip you have coming today. I called Marty to ask him to meet us here and to provide the wheels."

"Thanks, Perry," William said as he patted his friend on the shoulder. "It *is* good to know I have a friend like you."

William turned away, picked up his suitcase, and started up the pier. Perry put his palm to his forehead and cringed. "Christ alive! That was too close," he thought. When William was finally out of earshot, he continued under his breath, "Perry, old bud, no wonder you're lousy at poker... you're a terrible liar." He followed slowly after his friend and reminded himself: "There's no rest until William gets on the bus to Detroit."

~ ~ ~ ~ ~

"He's arriving by bus? What's the matter… hasn't he heard about airplanes?"

April looked at her boss in total disbelief. It was obvious to her this *Riley person* (as she referred to her new client when no one else was around) didn't know about the main bus terminal in Detroit. She voiced this concern to John Risner.

"Relax," John replied with raised arms. "He's not coming all the way in. I'm having him get off in Southfield. You will pick him up there. Then, just come into town on Woodward Avenue."

April began to calm down as she processed this new data: "Mr. Riley," she thought, "you had better be worth all this trouble." Now she was going to have to serve as chauffeur and local guide in addition to her other, more professional duties.

"I reserved a room for him at the Renaissance Center Hotel." John continued. "All you need do is to get him there in one piece. Tomorrow morning, I'll join him for breakfast and then I'll bring him here for his meeting with you. Look, I'm not expecting you to entertain him. Just be pleasant. I'm sure he'll be tired after his trip, so he might even sleep on the way to the hotel. In any case, April, please be *nice* to Mr. Riley and get him to the hotel by no later than eight o'clock. Ok?"

The pat on the back her boss gave April reminded her of the kind of gesture her father used to apply. It was a combination of one part affection and two parts intimidation. She got the message:

she was a valued employee, but it would cost her if she fouled up this assignment.

John nodded at April and she returned it in kind. Her boss began to walk away, but then a thought occurred to April and she called out to him: "Excuse me, Mr. Risner, but where *is* the bus station in Southfield?"

The department head seized up as if every bodily joint suddenly lost its lubrication. He turned slowly around, and edged back to his young assistant.

"April, I picked Southfield because you grew up in the northwestern suburbs. Are you telling me you don't know where it is?"

April shook her head to indicate that she didn't.

"Well," John said as he looked at his watch, "neither do I. You have about eight hours to find it." With that, he turned away and tried again to return to his office. "Consider this a warm-up of your criminology skills," April heard him say. "After all, you are going to need every one of them in the next week… or two."

So overwhelmed was April by her boss's parting words that she didn't remember getting back to her own office or even sitting down at her desk.

"Two weeks!" she thought. Then she gave out a small chuckle.

It was funny in a sad sort of way, but the joke was on her. Since the day she got this assignment, she never considered just how long something like this might take to complete. April scolded herself for not even thinking to ask. Most of her work, she knew, was open-ended, but this assignment took the frequent ambiguity contained within many of her tasks to a new level.

"Possibly two weeks of working along side a man I don't know and yet already despise!" she said under her breath.

April opened the folder containing the relevant information on the Strang Tapestry and took out William's photograph. As she looked over the image of a man attired in a three-piece suit, she remembered reading that he operated a small museum.

"Well, at least you and I might be able to carry on a descent conversation," she spoke to the picture. "Ok, Mr. Riley, you get to have another turn at bat. Don't blow it!"

With that, April traded the photo for the phone book, and began to track down the whereabouts of the elusive Southfield bus station.

~ ~ ~ ~ ~

The impromptu get-together Marla Kerschner arranged for some of her needlepoint mavens had been a great success. The impetus was the curious sampler her husband had brought back from his fishing trip. Marla decided she just couldn't wait to show it off at their regular meeting, so she called a few of the more obsessed stitchers over to her home to see it.

The session was winding down and Marla and a few other women were working on the clean-up. Their most senior member, however, was peering intently at the sampler.

"Marla, darling," began Dorothy McClellan, "I must tell you: I have never seen anything like this."

With that statement, the women gathered around the sampler which had been carefully attached to a cork-board and set upon an easel. Marla nodded as she finished her sip of the iced tea she'd been drinking.

"It's why I especially wanted you here, Dot. It seemed puzzling to me as well. Have you read the text? It sounds as if an attorney wrote it. You know, I'm not even sure it is American in origin. Look here," Marla said drawing everyone's attention to an area in the center of the piece, "the text in this section refers to a 'king'. What do you make of that, Dot?"

"Hmmm... Well, Marla, the stitching technique is definitely American and so is the linen. On the other hand, until today I hadn't seen Roccoco threads with my own eyes," said their senior member pointing to the sampler's lettering.

Another member of the group — a woman by the name of Nancy Gerrity — chimed in by saying, "What did Phil say he paid for it?"

"He didn't," Marla replied without looking at her. "But knowing Phil as I do, it couldn't have been too much." This comment produced the intended reaction from everyone.

Nancy spoke again: "My son Chad works at the *Dallas Examiner*. Why don't I give him a call and see if he knows someone there who might be interested in taking a look at this sampler? At the very least, they might suggest some expert you could speak with about it. Who knows, the newspaper may even write an article."

Marla considered Nancy, but now with doubt written across her face. She said, "Oh, come on, Nancy... Who besides a bunch of old biddies like us would be interested in a needlepoint sampler from... what's that date at the bottom, Dot... near the signature?"

"August 12, 1856," Dorothy obligingly replied.

"Well, you may be right," Nancy conceded, "but I think I'll give Chad a call, anyway."

~ ~ ~ ~ ~

The Smiths and the O'Rileys had concluded another eighteen holes of mixed doubles golf. The men were still in the locker room cleaning up and changing into their street clothes in preparation of going to lunch at a nearby restaurant. Rachel — as she had lately been in the habit of doing — was the first to get changed, so Margaret found herself playing catch-up.

As she opened the door to leave, Margaret heard the unmistakable sound of Rachel giggling. Margaret was no snoop. Yet, some internal mechanism calculated that she should close the door quietly instead of letting it slam itself shut. She then eased down the hallway trying not to let her foot-steps echo off the hardwood flooring. When she got to the place where the hallway lead into the pro shop, she paused and peeked around the corner.

Even though her view was partially obscured by racks of golf merchandise, Margaret could see Rachel standing close to and speaking with the facility's recently hired club pro; a thirty-something bachelor by the name of Brett Burton. Margaret knew Rachel had turned fifty back in June — she had been the one to plan her party. Nevertheless, Rachel was as slim and attractive as a woman ten years her junior. Margaret wasn't sure if this was real trouble or just an innocent moment, but she knew just what to do to find out.

Again with quiet care, she went back to the door leading to the women's locker room. Margaret opened it and this time let it return under its own pneumatic power. It clanked shut in that annoying manner she was so used to hearing.

Then, she strode down the hall with her two-inch red pumps echoing off the area's hard surfaces.

When she entered the pro shop and set her eyes to find her friend, Margaret's heart sank: Brett was safely back behind the counter and Rachel was casually looking over golf accessories Margaret felt certain her friend had no real interest in.

"There it is: Rachel's doing a whole lot more than flirting," thought Margaret.

Rachel looked up at Margaret and asked her, "All set, Margie?"

Margaret smiled back and nodded her head. Then she added, "Have the men come through, yet?"

"Are you kidding? Jim says he needs to take a longer shower to help ease his back strain, but if you ask me, I think he just likes to gossip."

Margaret tried to think of something to say which sounded natural, but her friend saved her the trouble by suggesting they wait for their husbands at the club's nineteenth hole lounge. She agreed and then thought to herself, "I need a drink to calm myself and, even more, to occupy my mouth!"

By the time their husbands emerged, Margaret was even more on edge. Her anxiety didn't dissipate until her second cocktail began to disappear. While she sipped and listened to Rachel talk, she was developing a plan. Margaret would keep a close eye on her friend over the next several days. Perhaps it was not too late to prevent Rachel from making the worst decision of her life.

~ ~ ~ ~ ~

April recognized William from his photo. Even without it, she would have been able to pick him out; he was the only passenger to get off the bus in Southfield.

The bus driver had to ask William to move forward from the bottom step so she could get out to find and offload William's suitcase from the bus's storage compartment. April — standing next to her vehicle — watched as he absent-mindedly complied.

She shook her head and thought: "He's a hick! On top of everything else, he is a true-to-life country bumpkin."

April composed herself and began to stride toward her new client, but then paused; unsure if her suburban upbringing and college education had prepared her for a situation quite like this one.

She recalled once reading a poem which spoke of going 'into the breech' and wondered if a stint in the military might have proven more useful to her at this moment than those two creative writing courses she took at NYU. Drawing a deep breath, she resumed her short march.

"Mr. Riley, I'm April Smith. Mr. Risner asked me to take you to your hotel. My car is right over there," she said pointing. "If you'll just grab your bag, we can be on our way."

William reached out his hand and grabbed hers. He shook April's appendage vigorously as he spoke, "Yes, hello! Thank you for meeting me here."

They disengaged and April began to walk back to her car. From over her shoulder, she heard, "Wow! Detroit sure is something, isn't it?"

April stopped in mid-stride and William shot past her before stopping and turning to face his chauffeur.

"This is Southfield, Mr. Riley," April said, enlightening her client. "Southfield is a suburb of Detroit. I grew up just a few miles north of here. Detroit is south of here and much, much larger."

"Really? I had no idea," William said with such a broad smile that April worried his face might split in two. "I've not spent much time off Beaver Island, you know."

"I never would have guessed that, Mr. Riley," April said with a perfect deadpan tone.

"Thanks. Uh, you can call me William or even Bill if you like."

April stared at him for a few seconds trying to determine if he was really as naive as he appeared to be or just having a bit of fun at her expense. She decided she didn't need to decide that just then.

"Well, Mr. Riley, if you'll just follow me, we can get you to your hotel. I'm sure your bus ride was quite an ordeal for you."

April walked to the rear of her car, found the necessary key, and opened the trunk. When no bag was forthcoming, she tapped William on the shoulder. He turned to see what she wanted of him, and with her eyelids raised and a forced smile on her face, April cocked her thumb toward the open cavity.

William gave a silent 'Oh!' and placed his luggage carefully inside. April slammed the lid and almost caught some of William's fingers in the process. Her smile disappeared and the two of them made for their respective front doors of April's car.

The prospect of losing some fingernails had the effect of focusing William's attention onto his beautiful escort. He found April to be exotic but couldn't immediately articulate why this was so.

"Ahhh!" he realized finally. "She's African-American! Funny that I didn't notice that until just now…"

And yet — as William continued looking at April after taking the seat next to her — it was clear that April's allure was due to more than mere skin pigmentation. It was something in how she carried herself; a confidence and an intelligence which wafted from her like perfume.

April noticed him noticing her and said, "What? Why are you looking at me like that?"

William — bringing his mind back from the stratosphere — stammered, "Ahh... you said you were raised around here. Could we drive through your old neighborhood so I can see where you grew up?"

April looked at William as if he had just asked her to strip, and said to him, "Why on earth do you want to see my parents' old house? Even *I* haven't seen it since I graduated from college two years ago."

"Just curious... everything is new to me on this trip. Is that a problem? I mean... we do have some time before I need to be at the hotel, right?"

"Look, Mr. Riley..." April began, but was cut off.

"It's William or Bill, even. Besides, aren't you the least bit curious about how the current owners are keeping up the place? My folks sold their house to a young couple..."

"Mr. Riley..."

"Please, call me William," William said sweetly.

"Look, *William*, I haven't had the best of weeks. So, why don't I just take you to your hotel."

"Sure thing... Right after I see where you grew up."

April could not believe what she was hearing. But, she also heard in her head the voice of Mr. Risner insisting that she be 'nice'. So, she smiled and nodded her head, fired up the engine, put the vehicle into gear and made for the parking lot's exit. Checking for traffic, April turned north onto Lahser Road.

In less time than even she had anticipated, April navigated the streets of her old neighborhood to bring William to her childhood home on Mayfair Lane. About one minute later, she slowed her car in preparation of pointing out which house had been hers.

All was going to plan until April realized her old house wasn't cooperating. It was gone. The lot looked the same: same grass; same trees; even the same driveway. But in place of the repository to so many of her early memories sat a residential monstrosity.

April tapped the brakes and the car came to a swift halt. She put the vehicle in park, but did not turn off the engine. William was about to speak — not that April noticed. Instead, she got out and walked over toward the structure with her arms raised high into the air.

William also got out, but shut his door. He walked over to where April stood with her mouth open to a silent scream.

"You didn't have to stop on my account, you know," William told her. "I just wanted to see where you grew up. It's really great, by the way. What a big house! Which window represents your bedroom?"

April turned toward William, grabbed him by the shoulders, and with raised voice said, "This is *not* my house! *My* house is gone, damnit!"

Having expressed herself, April huffed her way back to the car, got back in, slammed the door, and laid down a patch of rubber on the pristine pavement.

William watched his ride vaporize into the wilds of suburbia; April's car screeching its wheels around a distant intersection without so much as a pause. He looked back in the direction from which he and April had come: even if there had been steps to retrace, William doubted that trail might anytime soon lead him to his hotel.

A seat — in the form of a boulder deposited long ago by some primordial glacier — was available by the mailbox belonging to the house which had so offended his beguiling escort. William sat upon this granite sentry and wondered how long he was going to have to remain there orphaned like someone's unwanted pet.

Minutes passed. Whether they were long or short minutes, William could not tell since his only timepiece was stowed in his luggage. Pea-sized gravel lay by his shoes. He scooped up a handful and was surprised to note just how much they resembled the pebbles which inhabited Beaver Island's southwestern shoreline.

He let his eyes come level as he searched for some benign target. One came into view about ten feet away in the form of a small, metal cap protruding from the asphalt. He began to toss stones at it with varying degrees of success.

William was almost to the edge of consistency when a car turned the distant corner — but it was not the one he was looking for. William ceased his target practice as a man in his Mercedes came rolling toward him. When the driver drew abreast of William, he slowed to a stop and lowered his window. William stood, but did not advance toward him.

"Is everything all right, young man?"

"Yes," lied William. "My ride will be here soon."

"You don't live in this neighborhood, do you," the mystery man added.

"No, sir, I live on Beaver Island," said William, happy now at returning to the familiar territory of the truth.

This answer seemed to placate the driver, though William could not imagine why it would. He heard the whirr of the window which rose to define the boundary between their respective worlds, and then man and Mercedes drove off down Mayfair Lane.

As William followed the driver's departure from the scene of his bored target practice, he caught sight of April moving equally slowly toward him. As she rolled closer, William dropped his remaining missiles and dusted off his hands. When her car stopped, he reached out and opened the passenger door. After sitting and securing his seatbelt, April took her foot off the brake and the car began to move forward… which is also where April's eyes were.

William looked down at his hands in his lap and began to chuckle: "You know, Miss Smith, the new homeowners paid me twenty dollars to bring you by here. If you'd like, I could split the money with you… fifty-fifty."

Now a smile broke out onto April's face, and coming again to the intersection, this time obeyed the octagonal sign before her. She then put the car in park and turned to William, saying, "Look, I'm really sorry about that. I was halfway to my apartment in Birmingham before I remembered about you. I guess I loved that old house more than I realized…"

William nodded his head but said nothing. April, however, continued: "Let me try to make it up to you, William. May I take you out to dinner? And, William, I would like it if you called me April."

"Dinner would be just fine, April. Lead on," he replied and then made a mental note to thank John for providing him with such an interesting driver.

~ ~ ~ ~ ~

Joyce Whitney was about to break up what sounded to her ears like a wrestling match between her sons. "Perry must have gone outside for a smoke," Joyce thought as she began moving toward them. It was the only explanation she could think of since her husband usually didn't tolerate rough-housing inside their home.

As she transitioned from the kitchen into the dining room on her way to where her two pre-teens were in the living room, Joyce was stopped in her tracks by the sight of her husband sitting at his work desk in the far corner of the room. She looked at her sons and saw they actually appeared to be getting along. She shifted her gaze back to her husband who must have been deep into whatever papers he was hunched over.

"What is going on with him?" Joyce wondered. "Usually the least little turmoil from them makes him roar like a startled bear." It did not escape her notice just how out of character Perry had been acting as of late. "And now this…"

She recalled this morning's breakfast ambush and then another shocker when he got back from dropping off the *Morning Glory* in Harbor Springs: Perry had returned with her favorite cheeses and dried tart cherries from Symon's General Store in Petoskey.

"What is that man doing?"

Joyce knew Perry would likely tell her what was going on if he were pressed, but she hated to push him in that manner. Yet, her curiosity also needed to be sated. Then a wry smile formed at the corner of her mouth.

"Perry, you'd better do something about your sons before they damage something we can't replace," Joyce voiced with feigned irritation.

"What? Oh, yeah… Right!"

Like she expected, Perry rose from his desk and stormed into the family room. He barked to his sons, "Sean, Nicky! If you two have that much energy, I want you outside, *now*, to cut firewood. We still need over five cords stacked before the snow starts flying."

While her husband was occupied with their boys, Joyce eased over to the desk where Perry had been making marks on two calendars. Underneath every date, Perry had penciled in another number. For January 1, 2001, that number was "90," while the date after that had "89" under it.

"What's he counting down?" she asked under her breath.

It was now clear to Joyce her husband was preparing for something to happen around April 1, 2001, the day when the strange numbering stopped. That date had a large, red circle drawn around it and the entire calendar for April was festooned with exclamation marks.

Joyce looked at Perry who was continuing to scold his sons while he helped them put on their coats and hats. She again smiled, thinking: "He really *is* going to make them cut wood…"

Joyce — like every other Beaver Islander — knew the significance of the first day in April. What she couldn't figure out was why her husband was suddenly so excited about it. She knew how reluctant Perry had been to take over the title of King of Beaver Island from his father. But, when his older brother Art died of a sudden, massive heart attack, Perry also knew he would be expected to nominally run for and accept the position of St. James Township Supervisor.

Joyce returned the calendars to the orientation they'd been in when she began looking through them. She returned to the kitchen to finish washing dishes and marveled that after all their time together, Perry was still able to surprise her.

~ ~ ~ ~ ~

April closed the front door to her apartment and shed her gloves, scarf, and coat. She was smiling to herself as she thought how wrong she sometimes could be about people. William Riley was nothing like she thought he was going to be.

"Yes, he's naive," she decided. "But he's no country bumpkin… and did that man know his art and art history!"

Parts of their conversation — especially their disagreements about art — reminded April of her days at NYU. It turned out they shared many of the same interests. April so enjoyed her time with William she almost didn't get him to the hotel by eight o'clock. She stole a glance at her wristwatch, and thought, "Almost time for mother's nightly gossip call."

By the time her telephone rang, April was ready for bed. She put down the trade magazine she had been reading and picked up the phone next to the chair in which she was sitting.

"Hello?"

Pause...

"Yes, Mama, I'm feeling much better today. Thank you..."

Pause...

"No, I'm sorry. I forgot to tell you. I'm not going to New York City next week. I've been given a new assignment. What?"

Pause...

"Well, Mama, I can't tell you too much about it. But I did meet my new client today and I think we'll get along."

Pause...

"Thanks! I really appreciate your support. Oh, I have some bad news..."

Pause...

"No, it's not about me. Will you please just listen? I went by our old house today, and..."

Pause...

"You knew? Why didn't you tell me?"

Pause...

"I am *not* overly sentimental... And even if that's how you see me, you and Daddy still should have told me. Does Ritchie know?"

Pause...

"Last year? Mama, just because I'm the youngest shouldn't mean I'm also the last one to find out important things."

Long pause…

"Ok, I love you too. Give Daddy a kiss for me. Good-night…"

April set the handset back in the cradle, rose from her chair, turned off the lights, and went into her bedroom. She then removed her robe and hung it over the back of an easy chair.

After turning down her bedsheets, she picked up an old and well-worn stuffed rabbit. Looking at it, she said, "Misty, you don't think I'm *overly sentimental*, do you?" Hearing no response, she added, "I didn't think so."

~ 4 ~

Chad Gerrity looked at his wristwatch. Marla Kerschner was late and her lateness was about to affect his own ability to be on time for a 9:30 a.m. meeting.

The newspaper's lobby was bustling with activity and Chad wondered if she had somehow slipped past him unnoticed. As he was finishing that thought, he saw her at the information desk just inside the doors. He hurried over to her and called out: "Mrs. Kerschner! I'm Chad. Perhaps you remember me. Your husband and sons used to take me along on some of their fishing trips."

"Yes, I remember, Chad, but that was a few years ago and you're all grown up now."

Addressing one of the security men behind the desk, Chad said, "It's ok, Bruce. She's with me," and took hold of the visitor's badge the guard handed to him. Then turning back to Marla, he said, "Please put this on and follow me. I'm taking you to Larissa Johnson's office. Mrs. Johnson is our Variety Editor. She told me she's excited about seeing your sampler."

Marla nodded but said nothing; so overwhelmed was she by the scene before her. She followed Chad who was moving at a brisk pace down corridors and up escalators, and, finally, to a large open expanse of cubicles central to glass-encased offices lining the building's exterior walls.

An old garment box containing the sampler was held by Marla as if it were a life preserver. Suddenly, she found herself standing outside the office of Larissa H. Johnson. Chad knocked on the open door and motioned for Marla to enter.

"Welcome to the asylum, Mrs. Kerschner," beamed the newspaper woman. Marla turned to say a "Thank you" to Chad, but he was already gone.

"Are you people always in such a hurry around here?" asked Marla as Larissa motioned for her to take the chair by her desk.

"Actually, Mrs. Kerschner, today is what we call in the business a 'slow news day'. It's the reason I was able to see you on short notice. Frankly, I have been frustrated by the poor selection of story ideas at my disposal. I'm hoping your sampler will change that for me. May I see it, please?"

As Marla placed the box containing the sampler on the woman's desk, Larissa took the opportunity to balance her eyeglasses at the end of her nose; eyeglasses which — up to then — had been dangling around her neck.

Rising from her seat, Marla lifted away the top of the garment box and set it to the side. Then she removed the strange linen sampler and spread it before the curious woman.

Larissa squinted and began to examine the item. Marla could see her shake her head and wondered as to what that might mean. As far as Larissa was concerned, the gesture was to confirm what Chad's mother had told her, "The text is arcane and perplexing — not at all what one might expect from a nineteenth century sampler."

Then Marla broke Larissa's concentration with a question: "Do you know who Franklin Pierce was, Mrs. Johnson?"

"I'm sorry, whose name did you say?"

"There," Marla continued, pointing to two specific places on the tapestry. "That name appears at the top and then again at the bottom of the piece. Right... here and... there."

Larissa looked at the name and then at the overwhelmed housewife. Without responding, Larissa picked up her telephone and dialed a four-digit extension number.

"Jim? Yeah, it's me. Look, you need to see this sampler I told you about..." There was a pause as Larissa listened to his response. "Can't you slip away for just one minute? This could be something. Wait! Better yet, I'm coming over to you. It might help if your entire department saw this thing." (Marla could hear that the man was speaking but could not understand what he was saying.) "Ok, but I can't promise to keep it that short," said the newspaper woman as she hung up the phone. She looked intently at Marla, then said,

"Mrs. Kerschner, come with me, and bring your sampler."

~ ~ ~ ~ ~

William yawned and looked out at the city skyline from the comfort of his hotel room. He had been given a room on the twenty-second floor of the Renaissance Center Hotel complex located adjacent to the Detroit River. Alas, his vista did not include either it nor Windsor, Ontario beyond.

Instead, below and to his left stood what he learned last evening was the Joe Lewis Arena, or *The Joe*. William had of course seen pictures of Detroit but decided none of them had done the city any justice.

At least, that was his determination after what had been a mostly sleepless night. William had counted no less than fifteen sirens going off at various times. But, it wasn't city noise which had kept him awake. The insomnia he attributed to adrenaline coursing through his bloodstream.

William took a moment to recall the bus ride from Petoskey: All those small towns and forests until — after passing Clare — they were replaced by farmland and natural gas rigs as far as he could see. Finally, he discovered that Detroit had a different sort of beauty which was awe-inspiring in its scope and wondered if all large American cities shared this trait.

His stomach growled and William rubbed the ache away. That got him wondering what the time might be. He went over to a bedside table and turned the digital clock on it so he might be able to check the hour. It mocked his inattentiveness by displaying 9:21 a.m. in bright, red numbers.

"That can't be right," he said quietly, and then continued wordlessly, "John was supposed to meet me here for breakfast at eight thirty." He picked up the telephone and depressed the button which supposedly connected him directly to the front desk. "Hello? Yes, this is William Riley in room 2212. Has a Mr. John Risner come looking for me?"

There was a pause as the woman on the other end went to find out the answer to William's question. Presently, she gave it to him.

"He is? Please tell him I'll be right down and that I'm terribly sorry. Thank you. Good-bye…"

William hung up and immediately shed the top half of his sleepwear on his way to the bathroom. He splashed some water on his face and examined his chin to see if he might be able to get by with not shaving today. His stubble was barely noticeable, so he picked up his deodorant instead of his can of shaving cream.

He exited the bathroom and now exchanged his pajama bottoms for a pair of tan kaki pants and a button-down shirt. He quickly added a belt and then sat on the bed to put on some socks. He slipped his feet into his boat shoes, put a folded-up tie into his pants pocket, and grabbed his wallet containing his identification, money, and keycard. Lastly, he put on his suit coat, and then grasped hold of his overcoat, earmuffs, and briefcase. Making sure he was properly composed, William exited his room and made his way to the elevator.

When he reached the lobby and the doors opened, William saw John sitting on one of the many couches which dotted the Renaissance Center's lobby. He stood just as William began to speak: "John, please forgive me. I don't know what to say…"

John took his client's hand and shook it slowly saying, "Don't worry, William. I called the institute and they know we are running late. It's good to see you again. How are things on the Rock?"

"Pretty much like they were when you visited three years ago. Oh, Perry Whitney sends his regards and asks if you are going to come back to try your luck again with the lake trout." John frowned as the two men disengaged. William could see he had touched a still-raw nerve. "Sorry… He made me promise to ask."

"It's nothing you've done, William. It's just that fishing for me is like golfing can be for other men: I aspire for mediocrity but have difficulty getting there. Now, change of subject… Do you still want to grab breakfast, or would you rather go straight to the institute?"

"Breakfast, please. I'm really hungry... That young woman you sent to be my driver took me out to dinner, but I think I did more talking than eating."

A smile crept over John's face as he pointed William in the direction of the hotel's restaurant.

"April took you out to dinner? Where did the two of you go?"

William opened his mouth to speak, but paused to think. Finally, he said, "John, I just can't recall the name of the place or even where it was. About the only things I do remember about last night are our conversation and her eyes. Tell me, is she a regular employee of the institute?"

The two men were shown their table and then directed to the breakfast buffet. John noted with surprise April had obviously not told William who she was at the DIA nor that the two of them would be working to recover the Strang. He broke this news to William.

"Let me see if I have this right," William replied, "April's the *guy* who is going to help me?"

"Well," the museum director smiled and said, "when you called the other day, I didn't immediately know which member of my staff it was going to be. So, yes... I believe April is the best-qualified of my people, but she does come with a bit of a temper. Would you prefer I assign someone else?"

"No, that won't be necessary," said William as he slid pancakes and bacon onto his plate. "She seems to know a lot about woven artwork and we got along well at dinner."

For reasons William did not understand, he thought about but purposely did not mention the incident involving April's former home. He followed John back to their table and the two of them sat down. After scooting his chair in place, William added, "I wonder why she didn't tell me we would be working together?"

John thought about this oddity for a few seconds as he chewed on his biscuit and jam. Upon swallowing, he said, "April probably assumed I had already filled you in on that, which — I might add — I should have done. Sorry, but that was my mistake, not hers."

William nodded in understanding between sips of tea, and the conversation faded for a few moments. Finally, John filled the silence: "I'm certain you will find April to be an asset in your search for the Strang... as long as you don't mention New York City."

"Why New York City? What's wrong with New York?"

John leaned in close to William and the young man did likewise. The DIA department head said with a glint in his eye and a wry smile on his lips, "Well, for starters, New York City is one place April *won't* be going to this week. You see... I pulled her from an assignment there — it was important, but not as important as this, so don't worry for her. April will still get to do it, but she was upset to say the least when I broke the news to her."

William leaned back into his seat and processed this information as he ate his meal. After a bite or two of food, he said, "So, what time is my meeting with April?"

John looked at his watch which told him it was just after 9:50 a.m. He replied, "We should be able to get to the institute by 10:15 and have you sitting in her office by no later than 10:30. How does that sound to you?"

"It sounds just fine," he responded. Just to himself, William added, "It will be nice to see April again."

~   ~   ~   ~   ~

April sat quietly in her office. She was at loose ends — being there, as she had been, organizing her notes and ideas on the best strategy to track down the Strang since eight o'clock.

By 8:45 a.m., she felt prepared, and then John Risner called her to say William was apparently still asleep. The meeting which had initially been scheduled for 9:30 a.m. was now not going to happen until much later in the morning — fifteen minutes past ten o'clock at the earliest.

April looked around for some piece of work which she had left dangling. No such loose threads appeared to her. The wall clock silently signaled the beginning of the ten o'clock hour.

"Well, that's it," she thought. "There's just no avoiding it any longer."

The clutter which peppered her office could no longer be denied. April loathed organizing her office. To others, it may have appeared chaotic, but she knew the location of every report and volume.

Recently, John Risner had been one of those *others* who occasionally commented on her disorganized order. April understood this was his way of telling her to bring her office space up to the institute's standards. She was bending at the waist over a stack of books with her back to the door when a voice spoke up from behind her…

"Well, that's a view I haven't seen since my days as a quarterback at Ball State University."

A surprised and embarrassed April stood up and faced Tom Zurakowski. She said with an edge in her voice: "Sweet Jesus, Tom! You know better than to sneak up on a person like that!"

"I'm sorry, April. I didn't mean to startle you. I just dropped by to see what you were up to. How about I lend you a hand? You look like you could use one."

April knew the last thing she needed was to be beholden to Tom. She tried to defer by replying, "Um, thanks but no thanks, Tom. I'm not sure what I'm doing myself so I wouldn't know what to ask you to do."

"Nonsense!" responded her irritating co-worker. "Between the two of us, we'll have your office looking like mine in no time."

Tom smiled at April as he came into her space and took off his suit coat. He unbuttoned and began to roll up his shirt sleeves as April stood there unsure of her next move. She returned a lame smile to Tom and then thought of something: "Say, why don't I call Tony to help, too?"

As April reached for her telephone, Tom replied, "Don't bother. Today is his daughter's sixth birthday. He took a personal day."

April's heart sank as she now remembered Tony saying he would be gone all day. Then the image of throttling William Riley crept into her thoughts: "This wouldn't be happening if you hadn't decided to sleep in, *Mister* Riley!"

April watched as Tom returned books to their correct empty spaces on her bookshelves and knew what was soon to come from this annoying ex-quarterback.

"Ball State!" April thought to herself as she resumed her efforts. "What kind of Michigander goes to Ball State University for football?"

~ ~ ~ ~ ~

Jim Hunsberger and his staff of political reporters were huddled around the conference table examining Marla Kerschner's odd sampler. He straightened up and looked Larissa Johnson's way.

"I don't get it, Larissa," he said in his slow, Texas drawl, "why did you think any of us would be interested in a piece of old needlework?"

Larissa rolled her eyes at her colleague and then said, "Mrs. Kerschner, would you please read the words on your sampler?"

"Certainly," Marla replied; happy to be of some use at last. She cleared her throat and began to do as instructed: "'By Order of the Executive: As Chief Executive of these United States, I, Franklin Pierce, do avow and confirm the following decree:

"'1. That the title of "King" shall be conferred upon the current office-holder and will remain in effect until such time as his natural death, removal from office, or succession by his legitimate issue.

"'2. That both said title and sovereign jurisdiction of this Kingdom comprising the natural limits of Beaver Island shall be maintained by the annual public reading of this decree on the first day of April.

"'3. That if the above is not performed, the title shall terminate and the jurisdiction revert to the state of Michigan.'"

"'4. So Ordered on this, the Twelfth day of August, in the Year of our Lord, 1856. Franklin Pierce, President.'" Marla retook her seat and then added, "That's the extent of it."

"Thank you, Mrs. Kerschner, but you did leave out one item," Larissa said, then turned to her colleague, saying: "Correct me if I'm wrong, Jim, — and I don't think I am — but isn't that a presidential executive order number?" she asked, pointing to the upper right corner of the piece.

As the group returned their collective attention to the sampler, one of Jim's more seasoned reporters chimed in, "You know, Jim, I think she's right. It looks to me as if someone has copied this text verbatim from some other source, right down to that number and President Pierce's signature."

Other voices added their concurrence, but the unimpressionable Jim Hunsberger stood his ground: "Even *if* it is an executive order, it makes no sense." Turning to a colleague who, up to now had remained silent, he asked, "Paul, have you ever heard about there being a kingdom set up on some island in the middle of Lake Michigan?"

The political journalist slowly shook his head and then spoke, "Look Jim, I have a buddy who works at the National Archives. He owes me a favor or two. Give me a couple of minutes and, with his help, I'll find out if there's anything to this document. With this number and date, he can do a search for any corresponding document in their possession."

"Do it!" barked his boss.

Ten minutes later, the reporter walked back into the conference room with an odd look on his face. He said, "Jim, you aren't going to believe this, but that particular presidential executive order still has an active 'Top Secret' seal on it. My friend says no one is even supposed to know the *number* exists let alone the contents of the document itself."

"But it was issued in the middle of the 1800s, for Pete's sake!" a seemingly defeated Jim Hunsberger exclaimed. "When does the seal expire?"

"It doesn't. My source said it was sealed in perpetuity. Not even our current chief executive can unseal it… I asked."

Jim turned his attention to a beaming Larissa Johnson. "I don't know, Larissa. It *seems* like there may be something to this. It may also be someone is playing an elaborate trick on Mrs. Kerschner." Then, addressing Marla, said, "Sorry, ma'am."

Marla buried her head in her left hand as her right one meekly waved away Hunsberger's polite sentiment.

Turning back to his staff, he continued, "Without a way of corroborating the text, this sampler may just be a historical oddity. I mean… how could something like this have been kept hidden from the American public for so long?"

Heads all around the table nodded in agreement, except for Larissa's.

"Regardless," she replied, "it might make for an interesting read for the Sunday Magazine, Jim. Anyone on your staff want to help me write it?"

Hands from half the people in the room shot up.

~ ~ ~ ~ ~

From time to time, April would glance over in Tom's direction and could see a smirk on his face. April decided that in spite of Tom's arrogance, he really did know what he was doing when it came to organizing an office. She had needed his help, or at least the help of someone like Tom but without his particular set of expectations. And her office was indeed beginning to look a lot like his.

April also had to admit she was going to enjoy not having to walk around and over top of clutter on her way to her chair. She checked the time. It was now just past 10:20 a.m. John Risner and the frustrating William Riley would be coming through her door at any moment. But even here, the timing couldn't have been better, for the two of them were almost done. Then again, completion also meant an unpleasant consequence was in the offing...

April stood and replaced the last two books which had been on her office floor for many weeks. She looked around to see where Tom was and was startled to find him standing right next to her with a broad smile on his chiseled face.

"I believe we're done," he said. "Is there any other way in which I may be of assistance to you?"

"Um… no, Tom… I believe you have helped me plenty. Thank you." April squeezed her right hand in between them.

Tom cradled it in both of his, but cast to her a hurt look with his eyes. He said, "I was hoping for more than just a handshake. Why don't you let me take you out to dinner and then we can go clubbing. I know some places with great music. You owe me the pleasure of your company for *one* evening at the very least, don't you think?"

April pulled her hand back through Tom's resistant grip, and replied, "I think I need to go to the ladies room. Please excuse me."

Before Tom could respond, April was out her office door and moving quickly down the hall to the women's restroom. She entered it and, to her relief, found it empty.

"Why can't you tell that smug son-of-a-bitch where he can stuff his cutie-pie smile and puppy-dog eyes?" she demanded of her reflection.

April heard the outer door open, and a woman she had never seen before entered the room and then accessed one of the stalls. April turned on the water and washed her hands trying to remove the last traces of Tom Zurakowski from them.

Soon, the toilet behind April flushed and the woman emerged to complete her washing up.

April turned off the water and pretended to check her hair and makeup. The woman dried her hands, threw out the paper towel, and left the restroom having failed to acknowledge April's presence.

Meanwhile, back in April's office, Tom had finished rolling down and buttoning his sleeves. He had also put his suit coat back on and checked his tie as he said to himself under his breath, "She's not going to wriggle off my hook this time!"

He was straightening the cuffs on his coat when he heard some movement and looked in the direction of the open office door. His boss had entered with another man whom Tom did not recognize.

John looked at Tom, scanned the recently cleaned space and then rechecked to make sure he and William were in the right place. The nameplate said he was, but it certainly didn't look like April's office. John asked him, "What are you doing here, Tom? Where's April?"

"She went to the ladies room for a moment, sir. I was waiting to speak with her about something."

"Save it for later. Mr. Riley here has a meeting with April. Have you finished putting together the curriculum for that junior high art symposium?"

"Yes, sir… Your secretary has it."

"Great! That means you can get started on your next project a day earlier than you initially expected."

Tom took this less-than-subtle hint and replied, "Of course, sir... I'll be going. It was nice to meet you, Mr. Riley. Have a good meeting..." With that, the chagrined assistant made his exit.

John turned to William and directed him to take one of the two leather chairs in front of April's desk. He took the other one as they waited in silence.

At that very moment, April exited the ladies room and made her way back to her office with a renewed resolve to face down her crude colleague. As she stepped into her space, she said, "I think you really need to leave now, Tom... Oh! I'm sorry, Mr. Risner. I didn't know you were here."

April's boss and William both stood and John said, "No reason to apologize, April. I'm just sorry Tom wasn't here. It sounded like the beginning of quite a speech. I'm glad you finally decided to give it to him." April looked at her boss as if to say, "You knew about all that?"

John smiled and continued, "Well, the two of you have already met, but please allow me to formally introduce you. April, I would like you to meet Mr. William Riley, curator of the Beaver Island Historical Museum. William, this is Ms. April Smith, Assistant Procurement Officer here at the DIA specializing in woven artifacts, fabrics, tapestries, and such. William, April is one of my most capable assistants. I am going to leave you in her hands and allow the two of you to get to work. April, please let me know if you need anything."

"Yes, sir," said April, who now was returning John Risner's coded smile.

John passed April on his way out of her office as she went to sit at her desk chair. William, who up to this moment had been quiet, spoke: "You have a nice office, April... very tidy."

April — who at that precise moment was allowing her body to be enveloped up by the chair's cushioned covering — slowly closed her eyes and thought to herself, "Oh God... not another one!" Instead of voicing that errant thought, she said, "Thank you, William. How would you like to begin?"

William responded by lifting his briefcase to his lap, opening it, and pulling out a raft of paperwork. He said, "I have a list containing visitors to Beaver Island since the first day of September. It's not a complete list because some visitors come to the island and stay with friends or relatives. This list has only the names of the people who were registered at our hotel or in one of the bed and breakfast inns — we have three, now."

April took a copy of the list which William handed to her and quickly flipped through the hand-written pages. She asked him, "Why only since the first day of September?"

"Well, you see, I have been in the habit of examining the Strang Tapestry on the first working day of every month. It isn't a regular display item in our museum. It was about eighty years ago, but someone spilled tea on it, so it was removed to a locked desk drawer in the room housing the Whitney Family Collection."

April nodded and William continued, "There is a good chance someone on this list knows where the Strang Tapestry is. At least, I thought it might be a good place to begin."

April took all this in and then asked a question she hoped would not offend William: "What makes you think the Strang was stolen by a visitor? Why not suspect one of the local residents?"

April noted with approval this question did not seem to offend William. He merely listened and nodded his head as he heard it.

"Yes, I considered that possibility as well. The thing is, Beaver Island is a close-knit community. Most of the residents are people whose family roots on the island go back generations. They have a vested interest in the preservation of our history. Besides, you can't spit on The Rock — as we call it — without everyone else knowing where it landed. If a resident took it, I would have heard about it."

April laughed at this last comment, and then said, "So, does this mean the islanders know why you're here in Detroit? That might make our task a bit more difficult."

"Well, I did tell Perry Whitney... he's the Supervisor of St. James Township... that is to say, he's our current king. I haven't told anyone else;

and I asked him to keep the news of the Strang's disappearance to himself for the time being for just that reason. Mrs. Doherty — she manages the hotel — Mrs. Doherty knows something is going on because she saw the mess I made in the museum on the day I discovered it missing. She's also the island's chief gossip; which means by now everyone suspects something big has happened."

"Ok… We'll just have to hope for the best on that front. Now, who besides you had access to the desk drawer you mentioned a while back?"

"As far as I know, I have the only key. However, the desk is old and the lock is not very sophisticated. A determined and experienced thief would have no problem picking it without leaving a trace of his actions."

There was silence in the room as April considered all this information. Then William broke the quiet: "What do you believe the chances are of recovering the Strang Tapestry, April?"

April slowly shook her head and replied, "To tell you the truth, William, I just don't know at this stage. Not very good, I would imagine. That is to say, it may take years to get it back. About our only hope is if the artifact comes up for sale somewhere. The institute has, of course, already alerted the major auction houses and art dealers to be on the lookout for an unusual nineteenth century American needlepoint sampler. However, if the Strang is exchanged in a private sale or lands in someone's personal collection, it could be many decades before it comes to anyone's attention."

April saw that she had just about crushed William's hope. It was a very sad and somewhat mean thing to have done, but the truth is not always a kind messenger.

"Look, William," she continued, "I have to say these things to you. Otherwise I'm not doing my job with integrity. This is what happened with thousands of pieces of artwork stolen during World War II. But, not a year goes by that some painting or sculpture taken from a murdered Jewish family doesn't come into the light of discovery and is returned to the nearest living relative. So, don't lose hope. It just may take longer than you want to get the Strang Tapestry back."

"Thank you, April. Thank you for being honest with me. I guess I was hoping you could just check my list of visitors against a list of known art thieves."

"Well, we aren't the police," April said with a smile. "So we don't have a book filled with art thieves' mug shots. Neither are we like a casino; we don't have people looking at video monitors checking certain faces in the crowd. Although, come to think of it, that's not such a bad idea... Look," April said regaining her train of thought, "I'm here to help you find the Strang Tapestry and to get it back, if possible, and *that* is what I am going to do... to the best of my ability. I can't make any promises beyond what I just expressed, but the Detroit Institute of Arts wants it recovered almost as much as you do. After all, we still hold out hope that one day you will donate it to us."

This final quip made William smile. Then he said, "Ok, April, what did you have in mind?"

~ ~ ~ ~ ~

"Well, honey, what did you have in mind?" Rachel asked her husband. "If you don't want to go to the Smith's dinner party, how do you want to spend Saturday evening?"

Almost as soon as James voiced his reluctance, he knew he had made a mistake. He looked up at his wife from the comfort of his favorite easy chair and smiled saying, "You know what, on second thought, having dinner and conversation at the Smith's house sounds like a great way to spend the evening."

"Fine, then," responded his wife. "Why don't you phone Dick and let him and Margie know we'll be there... That's seven o'clock, Jim... understand?"

"Understood, dear."

Rachel walked from the study and James leaned back into his chair. He looked at his hands resting on each of the chair's leather arms. "This is the finest chair I've ever owned," he thought to himself as he passed his palms over the cool, brown surface.

He allowed his eyes to lift away to take in his immediate surroundings. He saw his desk set at an angle in the far corner of the room in front of the built-in bookcases which lined his light-infused sanctuary. The chair he was in and the desk had been recent gifts from Rachel.

"I have all my books here," he continued thinking, "and every trinket small and large which holds some special meaning to me. I have more quiet and comfort now than at any other time in my life. What are a few hours of chaos one night every other week?"

In spite of Florida's consistent climate — or because of it — James Emerson O'Riley often asked himself what he was doing here. His life was now measured in ways totally alien to him: By weekly golf outings; meals taken in fancy restaurants; trips to Mexico, the Bahamas, or to wherever his wife's interest pulled her; and by dinner parties at the Smith's home. Wherever he was, the Smiths were never very far behind — or ahead.

James sat in that precious space and permitted his thoughts to wander. He had to admit he really did like Dick and Margaret. For over twenty years, they had been in his wife's orbit of friends, but all that changed when they moved to Clearwater.

It had been years since James had had a friend such as Richard Smith. African American visitors to Beaver Island were rare when he was growing up, but he had formed friendships with quite a few black men during his time away from home.

Friendship with Richard was helped by the fact both men enjoyed playing golf and reading just about anything which passed before their eyes. James, though, sensed their different career tracks were the biggest barrier to a deeper friendship. The truth was that Richard's technical mind compared to his own more cerebral attitudes kept them apart far more than the amount of melanin in their skin. It helped that both men understood this; and from this realization flowed their mutual respect.

Nevertheless, James longed for Beaver Island and the change of the seasons which came with living in that northern latitude. He dreamt of quiet days and nights. He yearned for more time spent with his nose buried in a book. Most of all, he wished for more time spent with Rachel.

As he continued to sit there, he pushed those selfish thoughts back where they belonged: deep under the promise he had made to himself to provide his wife with the lifestyle she craved, but — until recent years — could not give her.

James was in Florida because he had had *his* way for their first twenty-seven years of marriage. Now, it was her turn. Coming here was his undeclared gift to his wife and would always remain so. Rachel must never suspect how he truly felt about their new surroundings.

"Yes," James thought as he closed his eyes, "I'll take it to my grave. Besides, I have my study... my sanctuary of sanity."

And it wasn't that he hated to travel. It was simply that he'd done so much of it prior to meeting Rachel. Like his spouse, James had the urge to see the world. When he turned eighteen in 1959, he enlisted in the merchant marines and served on ships plying the length and breadth of the Great Lakes.

Just before he began to crew these freighters, the Saint Lawrence Seaway had opened and foreign-flagged, ocean-going vessels began sailing on the lakes for the first time in history.

An opportunity presented itself, and for more than two years, James served on ships venturing all over the world. He traveled from Singapore to Stockholm; from Hong Kong to Cairo; from Perth, Australia to Scotland's Firth of Fourth.

By the time he was twenty-five, his traveling itch had been thoroughly scratched. He came back to Beaver Island where his father would soon be retiring as curator of the island's history. While he waited for that day to come, James hired-on as a dockworker for the local ferry service. Soon after that he met Rachel. Suddenly, memory of his recent promise to his wife flashed in his mind.

James reached for the telephone resting on the lamp table to his right and punched in the number for the Smiths and waited.

"Hello, Dick? Yeah, it's me. Hey I was calling… What? No, it's much better, thank you. Rachel put some of that warm/cold roll-on stuff on it. Hey, I was just calling to let you and Margaret know we'll be there for the dinner party this Saturday. That's at seven, right?" There was a pause as James listened to his friend. "She will? Good, it will be nice to see her again." Now he let loose with a round of laughter. When James finished, he continued: "She's not that bad, Dick. Ok, we'll see you Saturday."

James returned the phone to its cradle. He rose from his chair and walked over to the bookcase to grab something from his modest collection of classics. He chose a volume of Longfellow's works containing *The Song of Hiawatha*, returned to his chair, and attempted to recreate his previous life.

"Yes," he said under his breath as he opened the book, "I will make the best of this life as much as I can. After all, there's no point in any of this if I'm miserable."

~ ~ ~ ~ ~

William Riley lay back on his hotel bed, his fingers interlocked between the pillow and his head, thinking, "What a day!"

It felt to William as if he had received a semester's worth of information and instruction in one afternoon. What April was able to do with a computer impressed him greatly. He sat next to her transfixed as she sent email messages whizzing across the country asking others like herself if they had any information about the Strang.

With his list of names — about one hundred and fifty, only some of whom came with addresses — April was able to pinpoint where many of these people lived. With these locations identified, the two of them would be better able to monitor the sale of an unusual artifact like the missing sampler.

By the end of April's work day, they had made a surprising (to William) amount of progress, though no clear leads emerged. In their mid-afternoon conference, April offered, "The best course is to eliminate as suspects as many of these visitors to Beaver Island as possible."

William concurred.

She showed him how to go about finding and collating as much information on these people as might be obtained in the public domain. It both amazed and worried William just how much data that turned out to be.

William lay on his bed with his eyes riveted to the ceiling replaying in his mind — like a video feed from a Wimbledon match — every serve and stroke coming from April's hands. He was captivated by her ability to whittle down his list to a more manageable one hundred and seven names.

What really stuck with William as he lay there was the fragrance April wore; it's remnants triggering his thinking: "It's too potent to be mere memory." When William drew his shirt closer to his nose, he realized it had absorbed at least some of what had wafted from her. He closed his eyes and breathed-in another sample.

Only seconds into enjoying this experience, William's eyes opened as he remembered why he was in Detroit. He shot up from the mattress like a drop of water from a hot skillet and began removing his tie and shirt.

Twenty minutes later and all his evening toileting behind him, William slipped under the sheets with April's scent still fresh in his mind in spite of his efforts to mask it with more pressing thoughts.

~ 5 ~

April sat behind her desk and prepared for another day at the computer playing cyber-detective. She had long since come to see it as just another tool at her disposal, but William's naïveté about computers reminded her they were indeed one of the miracles of the modern age.

As she waited for him to arrive, she recalled how surprised she was that working with William was, in fact, an enjoyable experience: "He's focused," she thought, "but not too serious; he's knowledgable but knows enough to ask questions; and his lack of an over-active ego is refreshing."

Then April smiled to herself recalling how skilled William was at giving her a genuine compliment, as he did concerning her abilities as an investigator.

William, she decided, possessed that rare gift of being able to sit close to someone without invading that other person's space: "At least, he didn't invade mine," she continued. "Or, if he did, it was in such an innocent manner that I didn't mind it."

As she organized the raft of papers before her, April wondered if it was his attention to the job at hand which kept his nearness from bothering her. But almost as soon as that idea came to her, April discarded it. She had worked closely with others — men like Tom Zurakowski, for instance — and along with their attention to work most of them gave off sexual vibes like a blaring stereo speaker. William, April concluded, gave off something entirely different: friendliness.

And yesterday when April looked into William's eyes, *it* wasn't there: April could tell when he looked at her that William saw her as a woman of competence in her chosen profession. That realization alone was enough to drive away any lingering anxieties April might have had about William's proximity.

Then a thought swept into April's mind she had never before considered. It was a thought so revelatory she opened her mouth in shock: "That's the reason I'm so put-off by Jerry!" she spoke in a whisper. "When he looks at me, all he sees is a young, attractive *black* woman! The only things about me that smug attorney values are my skin color and my gender."

Anger and disgust rose in April in equal measure. She understood now as never before how racism was like some cursed virus which spread from mind to mind without regard to an individual's origins. Then — like a space heater being unplugged — April's flaring rage dissipated into pity: "Even the Jeremiah Wheelers of this world can become infected with it and unknowingly spread this poison among their own people," she said to herself.

April's thoughts turned back to William and she wondered how his mind had been able to remain untainted by racism. Whatever the reason, April was grateful that he seemed free of it. If nothing else, it would make the goal of recovering the Strang that much easier to accomplish.

~ ~ ~ ~ ~

Perry stretched out his arms and tried to shake the lethargy from them. Then he pressed his right hand under his chin, tilted his head, and pushed his jaw sharply upward. A sound resembling a stick drawn quickly across a picket fence echoed ever so softly off his house above and behind him.

He rotated his head around to see if his attempt at self-adjustment had succeeded at easing the pain in his neck and shoulders. Satisfied with the results, Perry reached for his pack of cigarettes and popped one half the way out. He grasped the naked tip with his lips and — with mere muscle memory — replaced the pack in his left hand with his butane lighter. Seconds later, the new day's first dose of nicotine was entering his bloodstream. He paused his breathing and looked out from that hillside over the waters of Lake Michigan east toward Cross Village and Good Hart.

"Day one hundred and seventy-seven," he said loud and proud to no one but himself. Perry so liked the sound of that number that he said it again, but then added, "Less than six months, and I'll be free of this stupid title."

Perry exhaled and pale blue smoke from his habit curled around his head like a cat in the calm, cool morning air. He looked across the landscape and noted how dew covered every unheated surface. The sun's nascent rays made it appear to Perry like shimmering lacquer. To his fisherman senses, it was one more sign of the coming change in his routine.

He continued down the hill to the pole barn he and his brother Art had built near the shoreline. It housed most of his fishing equipment and served as the winter storage unit for the *Morning Glory*. But his boat was, at that moment, in Harbor Springs having her engines serviced. Today's task was to see to it she had somewhere to go once that work was completed.

Reaching the grey structure, Perry paused to take a final draw or two from the cigarette. (He never smoked indoors.) He released the butt and watched it float into a bucket of sand where dozens of previous ends had already met their end. In spite of the lingering odor of tobacco, Perry noted the crisp scent of pine in the air.

From a spring-loaded, metal spool-like contraption on his belt, Perry drew out a set of keys. Finding the one he needed, he inserted it into the heavy padlock securing the side door. After opening the lock and pulling it free from the galvanized steel u-bar, he rotated the L-shaped plate aside, and set the padlock back through the u-bar to dangle there uselessly. The keys he carefully let retreat back to their coiled perch.

Perry was under no illusion such a meagre security system was going to keep anyone from stealing equipment: it was about dissuading all but the most desperate of thieves. Experience had taught him that while his fellow Beaver Islanders could be trusted, no structure this close to the water was safe from mainland criminals.

As he opened the door, Perry thought about how far William was from knowing where the Strang might be and with whom: "So far, so good," he said to himself. The one thing which kept Perry from completely enjoying the progress of his little conspiracy was the question of what his father would say to him when he found out: "There certainly will be hell to pay," he concluded in silence.

Perry hoped for nothing more than a verbal dressing-down from the island's previous monarch, but even with thirty years of being the man's son, he had to admit his father was as unreadable as ever. Perry looked around the boat-less interior, flicked the light switch to illuminate the mess, and said, "The first order of business is garbage detail."

As Perry began to pick out the real trash from the stuff which only appeared to be worthless, he decided his own course would remain unchanged no matter how his father might react. In spite of her rich history, Beaver Island needed to be free from her kings.

"You owe at least that much to your sons," Perry said to his reflection as he caught his image in a cracked and smudged mirror.

~ ~ ~ ~ ~

For someone supposed to be retired, Phil Kerschner still managed to work too many hours at his old profession: certified financial planner. The only difference was now he was called an *independent consultant*. His son Russell — who had taken over his old firm and even some of his old competitors — would call him in from time to time to speak with clients who insisted on learning about tax shelters. This had been Phil's specialty, but the golden era of tax shelters had passed and most of Phil's consultations consisted of trying to talk these clients *out* of going in this financial direction.

Phil had been doing a lot of talking this week, and for once he was happy to have the distraction. It had been an unnerving week at home, and he wasn't sure how much more of Marla's good mood he could take. For Phil, the obvious solution was to be found this weekend at a fishing cabin he often rented down Corsicana way. "If I can just get through the rest of today..." he thought as he entered his home.

As she had done every other day this week, Marla greeted her husband with a kiss and a hug which he both dutifully and warmly returned, asking his wife, "How was your day, Marla?"

"Oh, Phil! The newspaper has agreed to do an article about my sampler," she effused as Phil removed his overcoat and shoes and placed them in the hall closet. "Now, it won't be in the Sunday Magazine as they first thought," Marla continued. "But, that's because it is going to be a much bigger article."

Phil picked up the daily newspaper from a hallway table and made his way into the living room all the while thinking: "This is going to be a long one."

Marla followed behind him spewing on about photographs and column inches while he found his favorite chair and took it. Phil had the presence of mind to smile and nod his head at appropriate places.

"I believe they said it was going to be published in their paper next Wednesday or perhaps Thursday, but I'm not sure. Oh, Phil! Isn't this exciting? And I have you to thank for it, dear."

"It sounds like something to celebrate."

"That's just what I was thinking. I'm going to host a party here and invite our closest friends. The boys and their families will be here, too, of course. The ladies from my needlepoint circle have already volunteered to help me with the food and beverages. Let's see… have I forgotten anything?"

"Do you want me to be here as well?"

Marla looked at him with a twinkle in her eyes and replied, "Phil, you are such a kidder. You will be the 'man of the hour'. If you hadn't bought me that sampler, none of this would have been possible."

Phil Kerschner smiled and wondered if he could get his cabin reservation extended through *all* of next week…

~ ~ ~ ~ ~

Another day of searching for the Strang had come and gone and William Riley seemed no closer to figuring out where to look for the tapestry let alone where to find it. April was doing a great job, he knew, but he also knew they were searching for a needle in a haystack without knowing the location of the haystack.

Speaking of location, William marveled at how much he had learned about the one he was in just by doing some old-fashioned people-watching. He pressed his back against the park bench in Hart Plaza next to the Ren Cen (as the locals called it), took another bite from his coney dog, and looked on as Detroit sped past him like one of its iconic muscle cars.

"And, boy oh boy," William mused, "do these people know how to move for effect…"

He had never before seen so many adults in so much of a hurry. They drove, rode, and paced past him with unrelenting purpose. It was, in fact, the unrelenting part which really caught William's eye. There were hardly any interactions between them — unless they happened to be traveling with someone. Those traveling alone pulled their coats around themselves like cocoons and strode to the beat of some inner metronome.

Then a thought formed in Williams's mind which was, by turns, first funny then sad: "Most of the people I see here seem to be more isolated in their world than I was back on Beaver Island! Back there, a five-minute walk might take an hour — depending on whom I might encounter."

It came to him that he understood as never before the phrase 'hiding in plain sight.' William was sure there were many reasons why people gravitate to a city the size and complexity of Detroit.

"Some of them must be here so they can fade away into the background."

As William chewed the final bites of his evening meal, he wondered from what source of sadness or fear these people were hiding. Then he trained that thought inward: "Who am I to accuse anyone else of hiding from the world? If it weren't for radios and newspapers, I would be a complete outsider in my own culture. As it was, it took a near catastrophe to get me to interact as much as I have. What fear has kept *me* isolated all these years?"

William tried to think of what it was he feared. He knew some folk feared the unknown. But, that hadn't been his recent experience. On the morning he left Petoskey, any apprehensions he might have had vanished like the exhaust from the bus' tailpipe as he was carried south.

To his pleasant surprise, William found himself eager to see what might be around the next bend in the road. Far from being afraid of the unknown, newness unfolded before William like the turning of a page in an exciting book.

"All right, then. Something rules my heart and it isn't fear. So, what is it?" he asked under his breath.

He sat there determined to uncover the answer. He would not have been able to say how long it took, but the answer did eventually come. To William's horror, he realized it was something far more destructive than fear: complacency.

"I got burned by my first girlfriend, so I created my own world and have ruled it like a monarch. It's a predictable and manageable little space from which I draw just enough energy to keep myself alive, but no more than that."

At the tender age of twenty-seven, William Riley had figured out that he wasn't living: he was surviving on a self-designed and self-maintained life support system. He rose from the bench and began making his way back to his hotel room. He felt exposed — as if his thoughts and feelings had become words captured in conversational balloons floating over his head. Young Mr. Riley had just discovered an important truth about himself and he didn't like it.

"Will I be able to change?"

The front entrance to the Renaissance Center loomed before him in much the same way the missing Strang Tapestry had done before his departure from Beaver Island. As he entered the hotel and walked over to its bank of elevators, William did something that a week ago he would not have thought possible: he sent to heaven a small sentence of gratitude for the Strang's disappearance. He still wanted its return, but its theft had knocked him out of his neat, little world.

"Even if I don't find the Strang," William said under his breath, "perhaps I'll discover something else just as valuable — like an identity which makes sense."

~ ~ ~ ~ ~

James saw Richard's mother standing alone across the living room and waved to her, thinking to himself: "She looks as bored as I feel." James genuinely liked the old girl, so he mostly ignored Richard's apologetic attitude about her. "She certainly has more personality than her stuffed-shirt son!" he continued thinking as he made his way over to her.

James recalled the only other time the two of them had met: when Richard and he were coming back from the club and his friend had to get something from his mother's place. Not sure how Vera's memory was these days, he reintroduced himself.

"Oh, I know who you are, Mr. O'Riley. I never forget a face or a name. My body may be ninety-five years old, but my mind is younger than yours! Margaret tells me your kin are from Beaver Island. Is that right?"

"Yes, ma'am, it is. Have you ever been to Beaver Island, ma'am?"

"If you call me ma'am one more time, you'll never find out! Just call me Grandma... most everyone else does."

James laughed out loud and said, "Ok! So tell me, Grandma, have you ever been to Beaver Island?"

"No, but I hear tell I'd fit right in. Nothing but old ways, old cars, and old people!" Again, James let loose with a great belly laugh and this time Vera joined in by cracking a smile. She continued, "My family was from Saginaw — so was Dick's father. That's where we met. Did he ever tell you his father's kin were some of the earliest negroes to settle in Michigan?"

James shook his head in real interest as he sipped his cocktail. This served to galvanize Vera who decided that for once she was in possession of an interested audience.

"They came in before the war," she went on, "and by that I mean the *Civil* War. They weren't slaves, neither. Well, at least the Smiths weren't. Old Mrs. Smith — mind you, I never met her — but I know on good authority she was an English negress... born a free-woman. So, what about you, Mr. O'Riley? How far back does your family go in Michigan's history?"

It was always such a delight when people asked James about his family history. For one thing, it happened so rarely. For another, it was a subject about which he actually knew something. "Well, Grandma, I think we might have you beat. The O'Riley family goes all the way back to 1856 on Beaver Island."

Vera considered this for a moment and then said, "So your people kicked the Mormons off the place, did they?"

This bit of reasoning impressed James: not many people knew Michigan's history to Vera Smith's degree of detail.

"That's right! My family had help, of course, but you certainly know your state history."

"I'd better," the matron replied with a gleam in her eyes, "I've lived through enough of it myself." This time, it was Vera who broke out laughing as James stood there too stunned to do anything more than smile.

Rachel appeared suddenly at her husband's elbow saying, "You two seem to be having quite a bit of fun over here. What's your secret?"

"Honey, I'd like to introduce you to Richard's mom, Vera Smith. You hereby are on notice to address her as Grandma. Grandma Smith, this is my lovely wife Rachel."

"Oh, Jim! I've met Vera many times. Margaret and I have taken her out to lunch on countless occasions."

"Oh, I see... I believe I've just been had," replied Rachel's mate.

"Not really," answered Vera. "While it is true I've spoken to your wife about family, it was always about *her* family, not yours. I prefer to get family histories from the most accurate source available."

"Right... I should have known. Dick did tell me once you were the family historian."

"Are you sure he didn't refer to me as the family *spy*?" James's smile betrayed the accuracy of her question as he looked to his wife for support. Vera patted him on the arm and rescued him herself when she said, "That's fine, young man. He can call me whatever he wants to, but I still remember the day when he was thirteen when he fell asleep on the toilet."

This time, it was the three of them busting a gut. James looked in Richard's direction. The gaze which met his eyes could have melted steel.

"Getting back to your family history, Mr. O'Riley," asked the energized Smith family sleuth, "what do you know about them prior to Beaver Island?" Rachel saw where this was heading and chose that moment to make a strategic withdrawal. She patted her mate on the back of his hand and went to look for Margaret.

"Actually, not very much... About all I do know for certain is my two times great-grandfather came from Mackinac Island and that he wasn't Irish."

Now it was Vera's turn to have her interest piqued.

"You don't say! What was he, then?"

"As far as anyone in my family ever knew, he was just your garden-variety Englishman in search of fame and fortune."

"So, does that mean he changed his name to fit in with the others?"

"Yes, he did. In fact, that was the reason our son William gave for dropping the O from our family name. He said, 'If we aren't really Irish, I don't see much sense in keeping it.'" James took another sip from his glass as he let Vera process this latest factoid.

"What was your ancestor's last name if it wasn't O'Riley?"

"It wasn't anything fancy or unusual," answered James. "It was Smith... Peter Edward Smith."

It took a few seconds for that name to bore through all the minutia in Vera's brain. Finally, she realized why it sounded so familiar. Without any warning, she pitched forward into James who promptly dropped his cocktail glass so he might catch the slumping matron.

"Dick! Your mom's not doing too good over here!"

In a flash, Richard was helping to ease his mother over to a nearby sofa asking, "What happened, mother? Is it your pacemaker, again?"

Vera looked up at her clearly worried son and the other partiers now gathering around her. Suddenly she felt every bit as old as her ninety-five years. Vera haltingly replied, "It's *not* my pacemaker, Richard. Let me rest here for a spell while you go get the car ready to take me home. I just need some peace and quiet, that's all."

Twenty minutes later and now back in the comfort of her own four walls, Vera waited for her son to finish his rendition of a mother hen.

"Lordy!" she thought to herself. "I sure hope I didn't act like that whenever he was sick."

"Is there anything else I can do for you, Mother?"

"Yes," said the increasingly frustrated family genealogist. "You can take out the trash."

Richard found the garbage can, but it was nearly empty. He was about to say something, but then remembered that phrase was his mom's code for when he and his friends were making a ruckus inside the house.

Richard walked over to his mother and leaned over to kiss her on her cheek. "Very well, Mother. I'm leaving. I love you, too. Give me a call when you're feeling better. Deal?"

Vera nodded. Only when she was sure her son had left for good did she rise from her davenport to walk over to her antique roll-top desk. She sat on the cushioned chair before it and pulled open the bottom-most drawer. From within it she removed a thick manila folder secured with a large, red, rubber band.

Practically no one else in the Smith family cared a hoot about this history, but Vera knew every inch of it even though she herself had only married into it. She was certain the information she needed was in this folder, and not long after removing the rubber-band, she found it.

With great care, Vera lifted free a marriage certificate and a lithographic print which was nearly the same age. She placed both items on her desktop and stared long at them. The image was of a man and his newly-wed wife — nothing unusual about that except, whereas the woman was dark-skinned, the man was as pale as the White Cliffs of Dover. After a time, Vera spoke to the face of the man staring back at her.

"Peter Edward Smith: Well, you old coot, I finally tracked you down. I bet you thought you could keep yourself hidden forever. Well, mister, you have been found out! So, you changed your name and got yourself a *new* wife. You probably figured your two families would never cross paths. Well, the joke's on you. Tell me, Pete, did your second wife ever know about your first one? Now, there's a bit of irony for you: You helped to kick out the polygamists and you were one yourself! I bet *that* little tidbit never made it into your family history… until today, that is."

Vera smiled to herself in quiet congratulation. She continued to ponder the unexpected nature of this discovery and then her smile became a chuckle as she realized that her son and James O'Riley were fourth cousins.

~ ~ ~ ~ ~

"I wondered if we were pushing her too hard this afternoon," said a worried Margaret Smith.

Rachel thought about this for a moment and then replied, "Oh, I don't know, Margie. She seemed like her usual perky self at lunch. Besides, she's never been shy about telling us when she's had enough."

"Yes, that's true, but this was to be one of those rare times when she stayed on through the evening hours. You know how much she likes to cook her own evening meals." At that moment,

Richard returned. He looked at his wife and smiled. Margaret interpreted it for Rachel: "Well, that's a relief. Dick got back here quickly, which can mean only one thing."

"What?"

"It means Vera threw him out, that's what! If she did that, then she's feeling fine."

Rachel returned her friend's grin and both women moved off to interact with the other guests. Before Margaret began another conversation, she stole a quick look back toward Rachel. There was no hint now of the giggly school-girl Margaret had seen on Wednesday — except for the new dress. The three of them, as they often did on Saturdays and Mondays, met for lunch and then did some shopping.

If it hadn't been for the incident she witnessed at the pro shop, Margaret wouldn't have given a second thought to Rachel's choice of attire. But in light of it, Margaret realized her friend's fashion sense now bent to emphasizing her slim figure.

The fact Rachel had worn the dress tonight supported something else Margaret suspected: Rachel hadn't yet crossed the line into actual adultery. Instead, the dress reflected a new attitude about herself. The not-so-subtle attention she was getting from the young, handsome golf course employee was making Rachel feel younger, too. Margaret hoped she was wrong about her friend, but she didn't think she was. The signs pointed to Rachel about to go skydiving without a parachute.

"Right now for Rachel, it's an exhilarating feeling," Margaret mused. "But that feeling won't last forever. Her actions, if permitted to play out to their natural conclusion, will almost certainly have severe consequences."

It would be those consequences — like the impact at the end of a long, glorious free-fall — which would kill her.

Margaret looked at Rachel, smiled as the woman caught her eye, and thought to herself, "I wonder if she would accept a parachute if I offered her one?"

~ 6 ~

Something about April was different on Monday morning but William couldn't quite decipher what it might be. Since arriving at her office, she seemed, by turns, either aloof or distracted. Sensing she wanted to be left alone (and because he was thirsty), William had gone looking for some hot tea.

Now he was back and stood in her doorway with tea in one hand and a cup of coffee for April in the other. She was sorting through a stack of papers, but instead of placing them back in their original piles, she was setting them on other stacks of papers that had — for some days now — been growing in size next to her desk.

Over the last five days, in fact, William had a front row seat as April's office took on the appearance of a place where puppies might be trained. At first, he considered it to be just a natural consequence of their work. By Saturday, he began to suspect some other dynamic was at play. And now, with the new week laid out before them, William was persuaded their work to recover the Strang had very little to do with the clutter scattered before him.

April rose from her chair and saw William standing in her doorway holding two drinks and smiling.

"What's so funny?"

William heard the irritation in April's voice and tried to respond in an appropriate way by saying, "Here's some coffee for you... black, no sugar."

"Thanks," April intoned as William moved toward her. "But, why were you smiling?" she asked without looking at him.

"It's nothing really. Only that standing in your doorway just now reminded me of the mess I made in my museum right after I discovered the Strang was missing. Before I cleaned it up, I briefly toyed with the idea of chucking the whole lot of it into the garbage."

It was instantly clear to William that April did not find his comments to be funny. The effect was like an icy curtain being drawn across the space between them. William retracted his smile and found a place on April's desk to deposit her beverage. An awkward silence filled the next several seconds.

During this time, William took his own seat and a few sips of the steaming liquid staring up at him. Then he cleared his throat in preparation of taking a more direct approach to the problem.

"April, I apologize. I'm not sure what I've done or said to upset you, but I seem to have put my foot in my mouth."

April blew out a breath and retook her chair. She stared at William, but then — before speaking to him — reached over to activate her computer. "Forget about it. It's not your fault. Look, let's get to work, ok? We have fifteen or sixteen places to contact this morning. Have you been able to eliminate any more people from that list of yours?"

"A few," William replied totally stunned by the tone of frustration in April's voice, "but I'm hoping to narrow it down even further by the end of business today."

"Good…" April said, and then William heard her continue speaking under her breath: "…get this thing done as soon as possible."

For William, it was like he was now working with a completely different person. Gone was the woman who would crack wise with him and share in the weirdness of their quest. In her place sat a disinterested stranger.

Whether April was being honest about him not being the cause of her change in attitude or not, William got the message: she was going to be all business today. He was scheduled to have lunch with John and would ask him about this abrupt alteration in April's personality.

~   ~   ~   ~   ~

Margaret set her cordless phone down onto the kitchen countertop and thought to herself: "Well, that was a strange conversation."

Rachel had called to explain why she was not going to be able to go out to lunch with her and Vera today. Yet the woman's excuse was almost too thin to be believed: "A pedicure…" Margaret repeated; wondering if it sounded as silly coming from her own lips.

After a moment's reflection, Margaret reached for her purse and car keys which were both next to the phone, but pulled her hand back. She stared in silence at the three objects — letting her gaze play from one to the next in quick succession. Then she swore under her breath and jerked the purse and keys away.

"This is *so* stupid," she said out loud. "I would never tolerate Rachel doing this to me!"

Two minutes later, Margaret was parked along the street four houses up from the O'Riley residence. Rachel's car was still parked under the carport. A minute after settling in, Margaret saw Rachel emerge from her home wearing one of her newer dresses. Margaret thought it easily made her friend look ten years younger.

Rachel backed out the drive and began to move away from Margaret's vantage. When Margaret felt enough distance was between them, she pulled out and began her pursuit. She calculated the odds Rachel was going to meet her blonde hunk to be no better than even money. That changed the moment it seemed Rachel was headed for the club.

Margaret kept the vehicle in sight just enough to know if it turned into the club's parking lot. When it did, she felt something like nausea sweep through her body.

An opening appeared in the lane to her left and Margaret eased over to it in preparation of turning into a strip mall directly across from the golf course. By the time she found a parking spot from which she could have an unobstructed view, Rachel was already out of her car and walking toward the pro shop. Margaret noted how the club parking lot was virtually empty.

"It's 10:30 a.m. on a Monday... what's going on here?"

Monday was maintenance day at the club, but there would still have been the vehicles belonging to the staff parked in the far corner of the lot. Yet, even there, the cars were few.

"Of course! It's Columbus Day. Most of the staff have the day off. Smart, Rachel...very smart."

While Rachel was entering the glass doors leading into the pro shop, Margaret was putting her car into motion. As one of those doors closed behind her younger friend, Margaret was already halfway out the parking lot on her way across the road. She chose a spot away from the pro shop, turned off the engine, grabbed her purse, got out of her car, and began walking toward the same entrance Rachel had just gone through.

Margaret stole a glance into the shop through one of the windows. The lights were off and it was empty of people. Redirecting her gaze to the road, she thought: "This is none of my business. I could still walk away."

She shook her head ever so slightly as she pulled on the handle. The door came toward her in complete silence.

"Woman," said Margaret under her breath, "you just broke the first rule when having an affair: always lock the door behind you."

It was more evidence her friend was new at this. After quietly closing the door she set the dead bolt. For what she was planning, Margaret didn't want to risk an interruption.

It came to her as an indistinct noise from the hallway leading to the men's and women's lounges. Before heading that way, Margaret took one more glance around to make sure no one was following *her*. Confident she was both alone and undetected, she removed her pumps, laid them aside, and began heading toward…

"That's no mere noise," she realized. Margaret was familiar with *that* sound and named it.

"That's what oozes from a woman when she's being sexually aroused!"

With care, she opened the door to the women's lounge. Even so, it caught near the top causing a distinct grating of metal on metal, but the other sound easily overwhelmed it. After entering, Margaret eased the door closed without further incident.

She made her way toward the far left of the lounge and snuck a peek around the corner. Rachel was sitting in a chair with her head thrown back and eyes closed tight. Her mouth was open and her dress pulled down at the top. Brett Burton was massaging her friend's left breast through her bra as his head began to disappear under Rachel's new dress. Margaret cleared her throat.

The effect was like someone had applied an electric current to Rachel. Her eyes flew open and the words, "Oh my God!" erupted from her throat. She shot up from the chair knocking Brett backwards. Margaret noted her friend's face to be an almost comical mixture of orgasmic bliss mixed with shame as she tried to put her dress back into place. The self-satisfied employee slowly got to his feet and considered Margaret like a card shark looking for his next *pigeon* to pluck.

"Get yourself together, woman," spat Margaret, "and wait for me out in the shop. Don't leave; we have to talk." Margaret waited for Rachel to acknowledge this and — when she was convinced she understood — let her move past her without further hinderance.

When they were alone, Brett said, "Hey *brown sugar*, don't be so impatient. There's more of me to go around. You could have waited for me to finish off your friend. I have time to do you, too."

Margaret laid out her sweetest smile and ambled over to the gigolo. With her left hand she reached out for him and ran it over his chest. She dropped her right hand to her side and quietly opened the side pocket of the purse which was hanging from her shoulder.

As she was doing this, Brett reached out and put his right arm around Margaret. She let her left hand wander south and Brett began to close his eyes in anticipation of her manipulations. With a swiftness he hadn't anticipated, Margaret grabbed the man where it counted and before he could utter a scream, Brett felt the tip of what could only be a blade at his throat.

"Do I have your full attention, *pretty boy*?" asked an empowered Margaret.

It was all the shocked man could do to hiss out: "Yes…"

She continued in a low voice, "Good, now listen up. You've got quite a reputation… I know, I checked around. As I see it, you have two options: death or unemployment. Assuming you live through *our* little affair, there will soon be any number of husbands who will want a piece of your hide. I'll see to it personally. The alternative is to clear out today… and if you are real smart, you won't leave a forwarding address. Got it? Now, git!"

Margaret released her grip, but kept the knife poised. Brett rubbed his aching groin and looked with unconcealed anger at Margaret as he slowly backed his way out of the lounge. Margaret matched him step for step. She could see in his eyes the briefest of thoughts about going for her knife, but then the realization form on his face that this woman was, in fact, capable of killing him.

Opening the lounge door, the jilted man turned and ran down the hall, past the still-stunned Rachel in the pro shop, and — after unlocking the door — out into the parking lot. A moment later, the sound of screeching tires could be heard.

Back in the lounge, Margaret closed the switchblade and put it back. Her dad had given the blade to her when she was a teenager forced to walk home from Pontiac High School. Until this moment, she had never opened it in anger.

"Life is *so* funny…" she said to herself.

Margaret checked her appearance in the lounge's full-length mirror, turned off the lights and left. When she emerged into the pro shop, Rachel was standing by the front entrance with her head in her hands… weeping. Margaret picked up her shoes and slipped them back on her feet.

She approached her friend and again opened her purse. This time Margaret took out a handkerchief and handed it to Rachel. "Here, take this and wipe your eyes. You look like shit."

With the sound of that four-letter word, Rachel looked up at Margaret in surprise and said, "I thought you didn't approve of swear words."

"I don't, but it sure got your attention, didn't it!" Margaret said while cracking a smile. "Now, come on, let's pick up Vera and go to lunch." The women left the pro shop and walked over to Margaret's car. She spoke again: "Leave your car here. You're in no condition to drive. We'll get it on our way home."

Rachel nodded meekly and got in on the front passenger side of Margaret's car. When both women were seated and Margaret had begun driving, Rachel asked, "Are you going to tell Jim about this?"

Margaret replied but kept her eyes forward. "Well, that depends on you."

"What do you mean?"

"Look, it depends on whether this was a one-time fling you promise never to repeat or if this was one in a long line of men. Which is it?"

Rachel blew her nose into the cloth and said: "Margie, I swear I've never done anything like this before. I'm not even sure why I agreed to meet Brett today. I lost control of my senses, but, I'm not making excuses. I wanted that man. If you hadn't shown up... By-the-way, how did you know?"

"That you were in there? I followed you."

The look on Rachel's face reflected the tectonic nature of Margaret's words. She began to ask, "But I still don't understand how you…"

Margaret sighed and cut off her friend. "Rachel, you're not the *only* woman ever to have an affair."

Rachel thought about this for a moment and then understanding kicked in: "You mean…"

Margaret glanced at the sniffling Rachel and nodded. Then she said, "My only regret is someone didn't intervene with me like I did with you. One week of ecstasy followed by thirty-five years of shame…"

With anger in her voice, Rachel spat, "I feel like such an idiot. One look at me and Jim will know."

Margaret checked the traffic behind her, pulled the car to the side of the road, applied the brakes, and put the car into park. She turned to her friend and took a deep breath.

"Rachel, if you give Jim so much as a hint of this then you really are an idiot. Listen to me, sister: We are going out to lunch with Vera like we do every Monday. We are going shopping and you are going to buy some sexy lingerie. I want you to gather all that passion and focus it on your man. Forget about that brainless gigolo. He won't be around here after today, anyway — I convinced him it was in his best interest to move on. Finally, you will take your guilt and bury it deep within you. You will hide it from the world — even from yourself if you can — and take it with you to the grave."

"In other words, pretend like today never happened. Is that fair to Jim… or to Richard?"

Margaret reached over to place her right hand on her companion's left shoulder and replied, "It's more fair than ruining three good decades of marriage over three minutes of stupidity — or in my case, six days. My affair happened because I was angry with Dick for working long hours while I was stuck at home with two young children. I resented what my life had become and thought I deserved something more. I was wrong on all counts. After the sixth day, I realized how selfish I was being. Whatever *your* reasons, Jim deserves to think of you as being his faithful wife. You've already hurt yourself. Don't magnify your sins by torturing him with your guilt."

Rachel considered her friend's words as she looked out the passenger window at a central Florida thunderstorm building over the Gulf of Mexico. A moment later, she sighed and said, "Ok… Let's go get Vera. How do I look?"

"Better," replied her co-conspirator, "but there's a mirror in your visor. Fix your makeup."

Rachel rotated the visor down, noted the smudged nature of her lipstick, and reapplied it accordingly. As she did so, Margaret pulled them back into traffic and added another bit of advice: "One more thing… Vera is very observant. If you can make it through shopping and lunch without arousing her suspicions, Jim will be a breeze. Trust me on this… just act natural."

"That's easy for you to say… My heart is racing!"

"So's mine," she shot back. "I almost did surgery on Brett back there!"

As Rachel gave her friend a questioning look, Margaret reached into her purse while keeping her eyes on the road, pulled out the switchblade, and opened it.

A shocked Rachel smiled and said: "When you said you persuaded him to move on, you weren't kidding, were you." And with that, loud laughter echoed in the car.

~   ~   ~   ~   ~

Loud laughter echoed to the right of the checkout register. John and William looked at each other and the department head cocked his head leftward to an area of the cafeteria without as many chattering patrons.

It didn't take long for William to work his concerns for April into their conversation. John was apologetic: "Perhaps I made a mistake assigning this project to April. I'm sorry, William."

"No, John, that's not the problem… I can't imagine anyone doing a better job. It looks to me like there is something in her personal life is bothering her. It's like she can't wait to finish looking for the Strang. I mean… I want it recovered more than anyone, but all the fun we had last week looking for it has disappeared. I'm concerned for *her*, not for myself."

John nodded as he listened to his client describe working with April. Then the explanation came to him. He allowed a thin smile leak from his face and said, "I know why April is so out of sorts today. Remember how I warned you not to mention New York City to her?"

"Yeah," responded William drawing out the word in one, long ascending inflection.

"Well, today is when April was set to go there. I'll have a word with her. She shouldn't be allowing her professional disappointments to seep into your project."

"Do me a favor."

"What?"

"Don't say anything to her, ok?"

"Are you sure?"

"Yes, look… I've had my own share of dis-appointments lately. I understand what she's going through. Besides, April shouldn't be reprimanded just because she won't laugh at my jokes anymore."

There was a denouement and William used it to get back to his meal. Then John's voice broke the silence: "Was there anything there to laugh at to begin with?"

William's fork-full of meatloaf froze at the entrance to his mouth as he looked at John sitting there staring at him with piercing eyes and pursed lips — one side mischievously up-turned.

It began as a chuckle rolling up from William's gut. As he laid the fork back onto his plate, it morphed into the same kind of noise they had so recently sought to escape. After a minute, William caught his breath enough to speak.

"Touché, John. Touché!"

~   ~   ~   ~   ~

The three shoppers had just settled into the cushioned seats around their table. The fourth chair served as the weight-bearer to their coats and packages. Clearwater has many good restaurants and this one was Vera's favorite.

Not more than a minute from the time they had been shown their table, a young, uniform-attired woman appeared with menus in hand. Margaret recognized her, but there seemed to be no such reciprocity in the waitress's face.

Having distributed the menus, the girl proceeded to recite those lunch specials which did not appear in print. Goblets of water were offered and accepted. She forced a smile onto her face and promised to return in a few minutes to take their orders.

Margaret stole a glance toward her mother-in-law. Vera had been unusually quiet since being picked up at her apartment... so much so that Margaret was certain even Rachel had noticed this. This odd solemnity had continued right through two hours of shopping, and Margaret was beginning to worry.

"Vera, have you recovered from that fainting spell on Saturday?"

Vera took a sip from her water glass and smiled coyly at her companions. She answered, "Yes, but I had good reason to faint, Margie. I found out a secret which concerns the two of you."

Rachel gasped and then exclaimed, "My God! How did you find out about that so quickly?"

Likewise, Margaret looked at Vera in horror and asked herself, "Is there nothing she can't uncover?" Then speaking, said, "How did you know about our secrets? I mean, Rachel's just happened this morning."

Vera set her glass back down and said, "*Your* secrets! I don't believe we are talking about the same thing, ladies."

Hearing this, both Margaret and Rachel tried to calm themselves. Vera was neither fooled nor placated. She considered these younger women, thinking to herself, "There are only two crises capable of sending this kind of panic through a woman... and the illness of a child would not be kept a secret."

"All right!" Vera said in a commanding voice. "What happened this morning? Is it the reason why we got a late start?"

Margaret noticed that Rachel looked as if she were ready to melt into a puddle of guilt and grief. She was, therefore, about to respond to Vera but was interrupted by the return of their waitress.

"What may I get for you ladies, today?"

"Three whiskeys, no ice," Vera responded without looking her way.

The startled girl nodded and moved off. As she did so, she repeatedly looked over her shoulder at Vera. Margaret finally spoke in a quiet voice: "Vera, Rachel almost made the biggest mistake of her life today. Please don't say…"

"You mean like that *mistake* you made back in 1965, Margaret?" Vera interjected.

Margaret's hands covered her mouth and tears began to well up in her eyes. Nothing was heard save for the ambient sound of more pleasant conversations. Vera — noting the waitress's return — cleared her throat. Rachel and Margaret both set about composing themselves.

The waitress returned and distributed their new drinks. Before she could ask for their respective orders, Vera spoke: "Give us another minute, my dear. We're not quite ready… are we girls?"

Her companions nodded their heads but did not make any verbal reply. The waitress smiled and moved over to another of her tables. The alcohol soon disappeared from Margaret's tumbler. The burning sensation going down her gullet reminded her that she still had functioning vocal cords.

"You never said anything. Why?"

The matriarch looked upon her daughter-in-law with compassion, took hold of her hand, and replied, "Because, you came to your senses and did the right thing in the end. Now, we'd better decide what we want to eat before they throw us out of here."

Vera picked up her menu and opened it. Rachel looked at her friend as if to ask, "What should I do?" Margaret answered Rachel by picking up her menu even though she felt like she had lost the ability to eat.

Five minutes later — their orders taken — Rachel said to nobody in particular, "I still feel like a fool…"

"Good!" spat Vera. "That feeling will help you keep your mouth shut. You must never tell Jim. Margaret, that goes for Richard, too."

"I know. But maybe he already knows about it…"

"I doubt it. My Richie is the kind of man incapable of hiding his feelings. If he knew you had an affair, you would never hear the end of it."

Somber silence enveloped the trio until the spell was burst by the bringing of their food. Rachel began to eat just to occupy her hands and was surprised to find that the act of eating actually calmed her down. She spoke up: "Vera, if you weren't referring to our... *mistakes*, then what were you going to tell us?"

After she chewed on both this question and her salad, Vera responded, "I don't know if I should tell you, now. Heaven knows we've all had enough surprises for one day."

"Come on, Vera," Margaret teased, "drop the other shoe. You know the old saying: 'A few more tears can't make a rainy day any wetter.'"

Vera thought about it for a few seconds and nodded her head. "Fine, but like that *other* business, this is something you can't share with your husbands... least ways, not yet."

"This sounds serious," Rachel commented. "Is it?"

"It may be for them," Vera responded. "It depends on how well they get along."

"Well, what is it?" asked an increasingly curious Margaret.

Vera looked at her companions and said, "Your husbands are cousins... fourth cousins to be exact. They are both the distant progeny of one Peter Edward Smith of Bristol, England!"

Rachel and Margaret looked at one another with mouths hanging open as the rain shower which began when they arrived at the restaurant immediately doubled in intensity.

~   ~   ~   ~   ~

The telephone chirped and April — reclined in her bed reading — looked over at the digital clock next to it. It read 8:53 p.m.

"Mom's early, tonight," she thought to herself. She reached over, lifted up the device on the third ring, and said, "Hello! You're early, tonight."

John Risner paused to consider April's enigmatic greeting, and finally replied, "Actually, April, I thought I might be calling you at too late an hour."

April sat up in bed embarrassed, now, at the realization of to whom she was speaking. "Oh, I'm sorry, Mr. Risner. My mother usually calls about this time of night. Is something the matter, sir? I don't believe you have ever called me at home before."

"You're right. I believe this is the first time. At least it's for a good reason."

"The Strang has been found, sir?"

"No, it's nothing that dramatic. Still, I think you'll find it just as fulfilling for you. William told me earlier this evening that he's decided to go to New York City to speak with some people there about the Strang. He then asked me if you might be able to accompany him. I told him it would be fine with me, but that I would call you to see what you wanted to do." April was silent for so long that John had to ask, "April, are you still there?"

"Yes, sir, I'm here. I just don't know what to say. I mean, of course I would love to go to New York. It's just something I didn't expect to have happen this week. When would we be leaving?"

"That's why I'm calling you tonight. William booked seats on a flight leaving Metro Airport tomorrow morning at ten o'clock. I recommended he contact the Stratford on the Park Hotel. They are one of several places the institute uses when staff are in Manhattan on business. Just in case you said yes, I told him to reserve two rooms. I thought if you wanted to go, you would probably like to have time enough to pack a few things before the morning."

"Yes, Mr. Risner," April replied, "I would be happy to go with William." Then she thought, "This explains his flurry of activity this afternoon." She almost didn't get to ask her next question, as her boss was in the process of saying his goodbye to her. April interjected, "What about my original reason for going to New York City, sir? Do I have your permission to look into that matter as well?"

John took a deep breath and spoke carefully to his young assistant, "April, your first priority is to help William recover the Strang. If we can find it, we might be able to convince him the tapestry belongs with us. Acquisition of the Strang Tapestry would be a major coup for the institute... and for you, as well, I might add. You are scheduled to return on Thursday. So, yes, if you complete the work concerning the Strang, and if you have time left over, then by all means take care of as much of that other business as you can. Otherwise, the answer is no, April. Is that clear?"

"Very clear, Mr. Risner."

"Good! I'll call William and tell him you'll be going. Pick him up at the Ren-Cen by 8:00 a.m. That should give you plenty of time to make your flight. Good night, April…"

"Good night, sir," April replied and then pressed the button to turn off the phone. It rang again as she was reaching over to put it back on its base. She pressed the same button and said, "Hello?"

"April?" Margaret Smith said, "Your line was busy. Is everything ok?"

"Yes, Mama, everything is great. I just now got off the phone with my boss. He was calling me to tell me I'll be going to New York City this week after all."

"So, you finished your mystery project."

"No, I'm going to New York as part of that project; and I'm not saying anything more about it! How was your day?"

"Well, my dear, about all I can say is I hope never to have another one like it again."

"Was it that bad or that good?"

"I can't say, yet. About all I can say is it was one very strange Columbus Day. If Christopher Columbus' days were all as weird as this one, he may not have discovered the New World."

"Now who's being mysterious?" April teased.

Her mother did not respond in kind. Instead, she turned serious, "April, I would love to talk in detail with you about it, but I am bound by one promise and one act of compassion to remain silent. Just send up a little prayer for all of us down here in Clearwater."

This rarely seen side of her mother troubled April, and that feeling came out in her next question: "Mama, are you all right? This doesn't at all sound like you. Please tell me the truth."

"I'm fine, but some of my friends here aren't. Now, when do you go to New York City and how long are you staying?"

April was reluctant to leave off this line of conversation, but her mother's firm tone left her little choice.

"I leave tomorrow morning. That's why Mr. Risner called me this evening... so I could pack for the trip. The client and I get back on Thursday. I don't know what time of day, so I may not be here when you call Thursday night."

"In that case, I'll call you Friday evening to see how your trip went. Be safe, dear, and have some fun in that Big Apple of yours!"

"I will, Mama. Give my love to Daddy."

"Good night, April... I love you."

April threw back the covers, put back the phone on its base unit, and began the process of packing for a three-day trip to New York City. As she did, she pondered her day. Like her mother,

April couldn't say if it had been a good one or a bad one. Whatever it had been, she hoped her mother was doing some praying of her own and sending at least a few of those holy lines northward on her youngest child's behalf.

~ 7 ~

"**D**id you not sleep well last night?" April asked a quiet William.

The focus of that question continued to watch metropolitan Detroit pass by as April drove Interstate 94 west toward Metro Airport.

"No, I'm just thinking…"

"About what?"

"Sorry!" said William; suddenly aware of his distracted state of mind. "I was thinking there's so much I haven't done with my life, and I'll be thirty in a few years."

"I guess you'd better get started, then," said April in a teasing tone.

"I have. If someone had told me a few months ago I'd be going to New York City, I would have laughed at them."

"Have you ever flown before?"

"Nope! Never have," William retorted. "Then again, I'd never been on a bus until last week, so…"

"Well, it's a good thing you were. Otherwise today's trip might be too much of a shock to your system."

William shook his head at April's jibe and thought to himself how nice it was that *old* April had returned from whatever dark place she'd been of late. William wondered further if she knew how much of an open book she was.

"She has to be. I don't have much experience reading women's emotions," he noted in silence. "Of course, it helps having John giving me inside information…"

William tried to think of something to say before she caught him staring at her again. Then it came to him: the truth.

"I *am* nervous about flying."

"Well, in that case," replied a still-precocious April, "I'll be happy to hold your hand."

William again shook his head but this time added a doleful pout to his face.

"What's the matter…" she continued, "too embarrassed to hold a girl's hand?"

"Nope… If you can stretch it out over three rows, I'll take it."

"We're not sitting together?" April asked in genuine disappointment.

"Sorry, it was the best the airline could do on short notice. At least the tickets didn't cost very much…"

April's expression changed from disappointment to surprise.

"*You* bought our tickets? Isn't the institute paying for this trip?"

"No, I made it clear to John this was my idea instead of something you were recommending. Also, I knew he wouldn't have agreed for you to come with me unless I paid your way — and I really wanted you to come with me."

"Why?"

"Look, this entire project is your area of expertise. I'm completely out of my element here."

"But you arranged our meetings, didn't you? And you took care of our flight and hotel reservations," April pointed out to him.

"I made a couple of phone calls, that's all. But, even if I was more competent, I still would have asked you to come with me. I need a friend, right now, April. You've been a real friend to me. I know it's a selfish reason, but on some level, I *do* need you to hold my hand. I hope you aren't angry with me for dragging you along."

April sat there digesting Williams's words and tried not to allow them to become a distraction to her immediate task. She noted that the airport exit was little more than a mile away, signaled a lane change, and eased on over to the far right lane.

"I *am* angry, William," April finally replied. "I'm angry with myself. For someone you consider a friend, I haven't been very nice to you."

"Sure you have."

"Ok, but not always... Let's see... I hated your guts for the two days before you arrived in Detroit; I left you on the street in my old neighborhood; and lastly, I was nasty to you yesterday. I believe that about covers it. Some friend I am! I apologize, William."

April took the ramp leading to the airport and then came to the gate for 'Long Term Parking' before William responded.

"You really don't need to apologize to me, April. You were disappointed, and believe me when I say I know what that feeling can do to a person. Besides, I take your hatred of me as a kind of compliment."

"What! Why?"

"Because," William replied as they pulled into a parking space, "I believe it's only possible to genuinely hate a friend."

April turned off the car's engine and stared at William with incredulity written across her face.

"So, if I'm hearing you correctly, you are saying a person is able to feel hatred only for someone they're emotionally close to?"

"Something like that."

"What about a stranger who…"

"Look, I'm not saying we can't feel negative emotions toward strangers, all I'm saying is actual hatred, like real love, is an intimate thing… that it takes a close connection."

April unlatched her seat belt and opened the driver's side door — all the while looking William in the eyes.

"I don't know if I agree with you, but in the meantime, come on, *friend*, let me introduce you to New York City."

~   ~   ~   ~   ~

Marla hung up the telephone in the front hall and found herself shaking with excitement. She said: "Phil! That was Mrs. Johnson from the newspaper. She is going to publish the article about my needlework piece in Thursday's edition! I'm calling the women from my stitching group and telling them the party will be on Thursday evening. Phil, I checked your appointment book. You don't have any excuse not to be here."

Phil grimaced and returned his attention to the sports page. While it was true Marla's disposition toward him of late was improved, this party promised to be too much of a price to pay.

"That reminds me," Phil mused. "She had her pride and joy framed and placed under special glass which retards the sun's ultra-violet rays... all for the low price of $250." Phil added that amount to the fifty dollars he *didn't* get in that poker game and decided not to think about it anymore. "Let her have her fun," he continued to himself, but now under his breath. "It will all be over in a few days. Then, the weekend will be here and Russ might be persuaded to drive us down to Galveston Bay to try our luck."

Fishing had become for Phil the one thing Marla didn't complain about anymore. He thought: "That alone may be worth the three big ones I'm out."

~   ~   ~   ~   ~

Joyce Whitney opened the side door to her husband's pole barn and called out for Perry.

"I'm under here, babe. What's up?"

"Nothing, honey... I thought you might like a fresh thermos of coffee. Want some?"

"Sure," Perry said as he continued scrapping Zebra Mussels from the hull of his boat. "You going to join me?"

"I didn't bring mugs... just the top from the thermos," she responded as she poured the steaming liquid into the lid.

Perry crawled out from under the vessel, jumped to his feat and dusted off his overalls. "I can share, Joyce. As I remember it, we used to share a lot of things when we were younger."

Joyce smiled at her husband and handed him the coffee. Perry took both the plastic cup and a sip before finding a spot to park both parts of the thermos.

With deliberateness, Perry reached out and drew Joyce to him by the stamped leather belt on her jeans. Then he reached around her back and drew her body to his. The couple poured themselves into each other until both remembered they needed to breathe.

Perry's left hand came around and cupped the right side of his wife's slender neck while his lips continued their wet assault on Joyce's left earlobe.

"Oh, Perry! What's gotten in to you? Ever since Bill left the island, you've been in a really strange mood. Not that I'm complaining…"

Perry smiled as he removed Joyce's windbreaker. "You *sure* you're not complaining? Cause if you are, I could stop seducing you and get back to work."

"What's going on between the two of you, and where is he?" Joyce continued in spite of Perry's oral assault of her neck. He answered her between each kiss.

"I have… no idea… where… Bill is right now. Nor… could I… care less!"

Perry noticed Joyce was wearing one of his faded flannel shirts. He began unbuttoning it.

"Besides, I just remembered something I haven't shared with you… yet!"

He freed one more button, slipped his left hand beneath the soft material to discover she had chosen not to wear a bra. Perry played his calloused fingers lightly across his wife's right nipple. Joyce felt herself begin to go weak in the knees. Before she collapsed, Perry pulled her close and kissed her full on the mouth.

Joyce threw her arms around her man's thick neck and let the passion wash her senses away. Then she felt herself being lifted off the ground. Perry carried her over to a ladder which was leaning against the side of the boat. He began climbing it. After effortlessly taking Joyce over the side-rail, Perry set her on her feet again.

"Have you ever made love on a fishing boat?"

Joyce smiled coyly and shook her head. Perry reached to his right and opened a long storage container. From within it, he pulled out a large blanket.

"Well, gorgeous," said the amorous fisherman, "today's you're lucky day, but we have to hurry before my wife catches us."

"She already did, you nut!"

"Oh... ok..." said Perry as he unfurled the covering.

~ ~ ~ ~ ~

"You know what thought just came to me?" said William as the taxi he and April occupied sped them over the East River and onto Manhattan Island.

"No, what?" replied April.

"It just now occurred to me that going from Detroit to New York City is about a magnitude level greater than going from Beaver Island to Detroit. Here I thought Detroit was big, but this place is huge! I mean... I've seen pictures and all, but nothing can compare to actually seeing New York City with your own eyes, can it?"

"You got that right, buddy!" replied the cabbie as April and William smiled at each other. "So, this would be your first time, am I right? You two here for the ALCS? As for me — I'm hoping for a subway series. Anyway… you ain't seen nuttin' yet! The Yanks are going all the way!"

"Actually," April began, "I went to college here, but yes, this is my colleague's first trip. But no, we are here for business not baseball."

"Well, then, kids, sit back and enjoy the ride. I'll get you to your hotel in one piece and see to it you enjoy the experience."

True to his word, about fifteen minutes later, the driver pulled up to the curb in front of their hotel and got out. William — seated curbside — opened his door and stepped out. Before April could follow he said to her: "Wait here one minute, please."

William walked around to the rear of the taxi where the cabbie was busy removing their luggage. April could see William's lips move, but couldn't decipher any actual words. He returned to the open passenger door and said, "April, I'm going to take our bags and check in at the front desk. I've spoken with the driver and have asked him to take you where you need to go."

"What are you talking about?"

William leaned into the cab and tapped April's briefcase saying, "I'm talking about what's in here. Go take care of that project which made you get so angry when you weren't able to do it. John told me you would be bringing your paperwork in case you had some extra time. The heck with that! Go have some fun. I'll meet you back here later on."

Before April could even think up a response, William had closed the door and the driver was pulling back into traffic.

"Where to, miss?"

~ ~ ~ ~ ~

"So… I took a long bubble bath. Then I found a book I began to read about a month ago and joined Jim in the study. How about you?" Rachel asked Margaret — who was on the other end of this phone call.

"Well, after speaking with April, I tried to watch a little television, but then realized I needed something to occupy my hands, so I found some crossword puzzles and finished them. I took them to bed because I was afraid if I began speaking to Dick I would just blurt it all out!"

"I know what you mean, Margie. I was feeling the same regarding Jim. But I think I overdid it."

"How so?"

"One time he looked up from his book to say that *my* book must be good because I was so quiet. I just smiled at him, but in truth, I almost peed myself! Hold on… here he comes… So, Margie, how's April doing these days?"

James passed by his wife holding in one hand a salad plate with a toasted onion bagel with cream cheese, and in the other, a mug of decaf coffee.

Margaret played along, but was relieved to be speaking about something else. "Actually, I'm glad you asked. She's in New York City today."

"Really? But I thought you said that trip got postponed."

"It did. *This* trip is connected to her mystery project."

"So, she still hasn't told you anything more about it…"

"No, she hasn't. She's amazingly tight-lipped for someone her age. I'm going to ask her how she does it — I need a refresher course in keeping secrets."

"Speaking of keeping secrets, I tried calling Billy three times on Sunday, but he never picked up the phone. It's been over a week now since either Jim or I have heard from him."

"Are you worried?"

"No, Billy's famous for his long periods of monk-like silence. I thought of calling one of our old neighbors on the island, but Jim jumped all over me."

"No kidding," gushed Margaret. "Mild-mannered James blew his top?"

"He sure did!"

"Did you write that down on a calendar?"

"No, but I actually thought about doing just that," replied Rachel with a chuckle. "You know me so well, sister."

"Well, I certainly know you better now than before…"

"Yes, and when it comes to our son, Jim has my number, too. He told me to stop smothering him."

"Typical man's attitude…"

"Perhaps, Margie, but in this case Jim's right; I do tend to *over* mother my only child. Jim thinks if we leave him alone, Billy might actually get a life for himself."

"Hmmm, I tried that on my children with varying degrees of success. Seems to me there ought to be some sweet spot right in the middle between kicking them in their hind quarters and ignoring them completely."

"I'll let you know if I find one on Billy. Now, tell me, how are your other children?"

"Fine as frog's hair," Margaret sighed. "But, I don't think any of them know what sex is for. I'm going to be sixty-six on my next birthday, and I *still* don't have a single grandchild! I thought April might be the one to break this drought, but now I wonder if she'll ever let a man come between her and that career of hers."

"Now, there's something I can sympathize with you about," Rachel commiserated. "Billy hasn't had a girlfriend since high school and Beaver Island isn't exactly crawling with eligible prospects. And now, that job of his has become his entire life. I believe he's destined to remain a bachelor."

"Couple of stellar mothers we turned out to be…" Margaret lamented.

"Hey, there, Margie… don't beat yourself up. We did what we could. Now, it is up to our kids to finish the job. That is just the way of it."

There was silence on the phone for a few seconds, and then Margaret spoke.

"Still doesn't get a grand-baby in my arms; but, thanks for listening… again."

"Any old time… Hey! I'd better be going. See you tomorrow?"

"Probably… bye, Rachel," concluded the now-somber Margaret.

~ ~ ~ ~ ~

The taxi stopped in front of April's hotel. She paid the driver and got out. Surveying the sidewalk, she found and then chose a path through the throng with the best chance of safely crossing the ten feet to the hotel's front entrance. The doorman did his job and seconds later, April found herself in the lobby of the Stratford on the Park. She looked toward the front desk and saw the clock. It read: 5:14 p.m.

A middle-aged gentleman — the manager or perhaps one of his assistants — saw April and asked, "May I help you, miss?"

"Yes, a colleague checked me into my room earlier today. My name is April Smith. I would like my room key, please."

"One moment, Ms. Smith," the man replied. After accessing the appropriate computer screen, he again spoke: "Yes, your'e in room 522, and according to my screen your luggage has been delivered."

"Thank you," April replied. She followed the clerk's hand from the keyboard to the pigeonhole for room 522. There was a note in the slot in addition to the key. The man dutifully handed both items to April, then moved on to the next patron.

April strolled toward the bank of elevators, pulled the note card from the unsealed envelope, and began to read: "Dear April, I hope you had a good day. I finished most of what I set out to do here, so I decided to go to the Museum of Modern Art. You may meet me there if you want to. I'll head back to the hotel if I don't see you by 6:00 p.m. Best regards, William."

April reversed her steps and renewed the clerk's attention.

"Excuse me, sir, but could you tell me how long it might take for me to get to the MOMA from here?"

The man considered April's question, said to her, "One moment," and then motioned for a female assistant to join them. "Terri, this young woman would like to know how long it would take her to get to the MOMA at this time of day. Could you enlighten her?"

"Sure, Mr. Aaronski... Well," the girl said looking up into empty space and then to April, "forget the taxis; they're too slow during rush hour. You better stay off the subway lines, too. Between the regulars and those going to the Bronx for the game tonight, it'll be a zoo. The quickest way I know of is to take a M1 through M5 bus... they have their own lanes. There's a stop up at the next corner," she said pointing in that direction. "Any one of them should get you there in about fifteen minutes. I believe the stop at 53rd Street is the closest to the MOMA."

"Thank you very much," April beamed.

With that, she went back to the elevators and took the next available one to her floor. Five minutes after placing her briefcase on the bed and freshening up, April was back on the sidewalk in front of the hotel and walking toward the bus stop.

~ ~ ~ ~ ~

William was sitting on a bench in front of a Seurat work entitled *Evening, Honfleur*. His fingers were interlocked behind his head and he had a dreamy look on his face. His long legs were stretched out before him and every so often he had to retract them to enable other art lovers the ability to pass by. William hadn't felt this relaxed in a long time.

April had been watching William for about two minutes before she walked over and stood next to him without speaking. She gazed at the image which had so captured his attention and smiled. William noticed her and sat up straight.

"Oh! Hello, April. Have you been standing there for a long time?"

April didn't answer his question. Instead, she sat down next to him, pointed to the painting, and asked, "Does it remind you of home?"

William smiled and turned his attention back to the Seurat. He said, "Yes, it does. So, did you just get here?"

"About five minutes ago... I asked one of the docents if he'd seen a man fitting your description, and he sent me over this way."

William nodded and began to rise from the bench, but April placed a hand on his arm. He sat back down and focused his full attention upon his seat-mate.

"William, why did you do it?"

He shifted on the bench to face her and rested his left arm on the back of the bench. A look of uncertainty crossed his brow.

"Do you mean this morning when the taxi stopped at the hotel?" April silently nodded her head. "Well, it occurred to me after I spoke with John last night that you needed a friend, too. You know... some person who's there for you and not just using you for his — I mean my — own purposes. I once heard it said, 'If you want a friend, then be a friend.' That's what this morning was about."

April placed her left hand on top of his right one and cleared her throat: "But, you aren't telling me everything. If I'm really your friend, you owe me the complete truth. What else is going on here?"

William looked at April shocked he could be read so easily. He stood up and paced around the area in front of the Seurat, but never took his eyes off April. Finally getting hold of his thoughts, he spoke.

"What I said a moment ago is completely true, April, and I meant it. But you're right: there is something else going on, and I owe you that as well. I'm sorry I've kept it from you, but it's only come to me in the last two days."

April braced herself while William drew in a deep breath. She wasn't at all surprised it had finally lead to this

"Here it comes," she thought to herself. "Men are so predictable. Show them the smallest affection and they are ready to drag you into bed."

This time, though, April was ready.

"I don't care about the Strang anymore! There, I actually said it," proclaimed an elated William with arms raised in glorious triumph.

April looked at William stunned both by what he said and what he hadn't said. But, it was the latter which propelled her up and sent her right hand arcing toward the beaming left cheek of her client.

The slap caught William squarely, and it seemed to him every nerve ending in his face was suddenly on fire. His toothy grin was transformed into a hollow opening as he watched April storm from the exhibit room. Only after she turned the corner and disappeared from view did William think to bring his left hand down to rub his stinging cheek.

~ ~ ~ ~ ~

April had taken a seat on a bus going back toward the hotel before she realized why it was she had smacked William. A crimson, twisted glob of shame rose within her. It took all her remaining strength not to burst into tears. She felt like a child.

"Well," she scolded herself in muffled tones, "you certainly reacted like a child who'd had her favorite toy taken from her!"

April nodded her head without any thought of the people seated near to her.

"That's it, exactly," she continued, but now in silence. "I was *so* ready to hit him with my witty sarcasm and *so* disappointed he didn't set himself up for the kill-shot. When he didn't meet my expectations, I punished him but good."

It had been over a decade since April had hit anyone in anger. The pain coming from her right palm reminded her that acts of violence always carried their own punishment. April massaged the throbbing appendage. Fortunately, nothing seemed broken save her sense of common decency.

"What must William think of me?" April screamed in silence. Then another thought shocked her in a different way: "Some part of me is dis-appointed he isn't in-love with me! It's my most vain part, no doubt."

April sat back in the seat and closed her eyes. She thought about the men — black men, white men, young and old men — all of whom had at one time or another been sexually attracted to her. Over the last few years, the trend had become so pervasive she had come to assume *all* men wanted her in a sexual way.

"Some part of me wanted William to be sexually attracted to me, too, but he's only interested in being my friend. I have so few real friends to begin with, and now I've gone and driven one away out of what… vanity?"

April brought her face down toward her hands… no longer able to stem her tide of tears. An elderly man of Asian extraction saw this.

"Miss, are you all right?"

April looked up, startled by his question.

"I'll be fine, sir. I just did a very stupid thing… I hurt a friend of mine."

"Well, if she's a good friend, then I'm certain she has already forgiven you."

"My friend is a guy. Nevertheless, I believe you may be right. I'll see in a little while. By-the-way, I've lost track of where we are. Please, could you let me know when we're getting close to the Stratford Hotel?"

"Do you mean the Stratford on the Park?"

"Yes."

"It's a good thing you said something. It's coming up at the next stop."

April smiled and patted the man's arm in a gesture of thanks for his alertness, but even more for his kind words. By the time the bus came to a rolling stop, she was by the pneumatic door as it opened. April stepped off the bus and ran down the sidewalk making for the hotel's front entrance. She held her emotions together until arriving at her room.

When she shut the door behind her, April threw herself on the bed and finished the flow first begun on the streets of her favorite city in the world. It was, in fact, a weep worthy of the Big Apple.

~ ~ ~ ~ ~

As he made his way out the museum's front entrance, William's attention was drawn to the red MOMA banners fluttering gently above him like giant stationary butterflies. He looked for April among the scattering of faces nearby, but saw no sign of her. He buttoned his coat, pulled out his earmuffs from a coat pocket, but kept them in his right hand.

While he thought April might be puzzled or even mildly upset about his change in attitude concerning the Strang Tapestry, William hadn't anticipated her strong reaction to the news.

"Did I miss something?" he silently asked himself. "Does she think I'm wasting her time?"

Tall structures cast shadows thickly onto the street-level, making it seem much closer to dusk than it actually was. William wondered as to the time and then remembered he had his watch on his wrist. He pushed back the coat sleeve on his left arm and saw it was just past six o'clock.

"Could it be she thought I brought her to New York for some kind of sexual encounter?"

He looked around to see if those around him could detect the confusion and sadness which seeped from him like water through a levee. He immediately banished that thought for the self-centered trope which it most certainly was.

William merged into the pedestrian sea before him and allowed himself to be carried by this tide of urbanites. With his mind in neutral and his senses at a minimum in terms of interpreting his surroundings, William was not surprised to discover — when he emerged from his zombie-like state — that he had no idea where he was. He walked over to a large window behind which was some kind of fast-food pizza shop. It reminded him of something.

"I was going to ask April if she knew of any good places to eat in this part of town. Well," he thought, "I'm not hungry now anyway…"

William looked around and marveled that every few seconds, more people walked passed him than stepped foot onto Beaver Island in a year. And it amused him to observe — even in this big, sophisticated city — shops festooned with Halloween decorations. The holiday was still weeks off, but William half-expected children to come up to him asking for treats.

"Sinatra called New York 'the city that never sleeps', but I am tired," he whispered into the chilling air.

William's case of Strang fever had broken… the obsession had run its race in and through him. The only thing left was the exhaustion. That it all had been internal to William mattered not in the slightest, and his still-burning cheek reminded him he had lost more than the will to carry on this desperate search.

"I lost a friend, today," he whispered.

William brushed his fingertips across his bruised cheek and then looked at his hand. It was clammy and shaking. He made a fist to arrest the tremor, but fatigue sapped even this solitary show of strength. He set free the strain and let his hand drop to his side.

Threading his way through the crowd, William stepped to an open section of curb and hailed down a taxi. When one pulled over for him, he quickly opened the door and clambered in.

"Stratford on the Park Hotel, please," he said with relief at being able to remember the name of the place. Not one part of the next twenty minutes seemed familiar to William save the final moment when he experienced a powerful dose of déjà vu.

Minutes later, William tapped on the door to room 522 not sure if he wanted April to be there or not. He certainly had no idea what to say to her if she was. After a moment, the door drew back and April appeared — and appeared also to William's eyes to have been crying. He opened his mouth to initiate an apology, but before the first syllable emerged, April stepped forward, wrapped her delicate arms around his neck, and resumed her weep.

The only response William could think to do was to place his own arms around her and pat her on the back. She let him go and stood before him.

"What happened?"

"Please come in, and I'll do my best to explain."

William eased past April who closed the door. He found the room's only chair and took it. April remained standing, but shifted her weight back and forth from one foot to the other with her arms folded tight to her chest.

"Do you want to take your coat off?"

"In a moment, April," he said. " First, I want to…"

"No, William, I believe I know you well enough to guess you are about to say you're sorry. Please don't."

"But, I must have offended you deeply for you to hit me across the face!"

"William," April said as she sat down on the end of her bed, "believe me, the offense was mine. I wasn't expecting you to say what you said to me."

"Right! I kept my feelings about the…"

April surprised William by falling to her knees in front of him and cradling his lower jaw in both her hands. "Shhh! Don't speak just now, William. I'm not doing a very good job of explaining my actions and I need you to listen for a moment. Ok?"

"Ok."

April let her hands fall away, rocked back onto her feet, and then returned to the bed. "Look, I would be lying if I said I wasn't surprised by what you said about not caring if we recovered the Strang Tapestry or not. But, William, I was expecting you to say you were in-love with me, and I guess some part of me became enraged when… when you *didn't* say it. I am *so* sorry I hit you, William. I haven't struck another person in a long time."

William nodded his head in understanding, and when it was apparent she had finished her apology, said, "Thank you for your explanation... it clears away some things. But, April, I have to ask: Are you in-love with me?"

"No! At least, I don't believe I am. It's just... I'm not used to a guy who only wants to be my friend. They all say that, but most of them want to be something more — if you know what I mean."

"Well, April, you *are* beautiful, so I can imagine that would be a common... uh, problem for you."

A flash of deep satisfaction passed through April at hearing this, but she let it go in favor of her next question: "Are you in-love with me, William?"

William wanted to think about this question, but not for a second longer than necessary. "No, I don't believe I am. I mean... I like you a lot, April, but we've only just met... and we're from such different backgrounds..."

"Yeah, I'm black and you're white..."

"True, but I was thinking more along the lines of: You're from the big city and I'm from the fringes of civilization itself..."

April laughed and then said, "William, you are too cute!"

"You know," he continued (trying to ignore her remark), "I was also thinking — while I was walking around the city — maybe you felt I had tricked you into coming to New York with me so I could get you into bed… or something like that. But you have to know, April, that's just not my style."

A visibly relieved April rose from the bed. She said, "Will you accept *my* apology, William, for slapping your face, and worse, for imagining you to be a lesser man than you are?"

"Already done!" William returned April's smile and got up from his seat. They shared another hug before he continued, "Now, I don't know about you, but I just found my appetite. What do you want to do about getting something to eat?"

"I know just the place! It's a short taxi ride from here, but William, I insist on buying."

"Fine by me…"

As April grabbed her coat and hat, and they exited her hotel room, she finally got the chance to ask him that *other* question which had been plaguing her.

"Now, tell me, what did you mean when you said you didn't care about finding the Strang Tapestry anymore?"

~ ~ ~ ~ ~

William held open the large, wooden door to a French restaurant and then followed April into the establishment. He was expecting the place to be as crowded as the rest of the city. It wasn't. A young woman approached them, took their autumn wear, and placed the items in a coat-check ante-room.

Moments later, the maître d led them to a booth about midway down the left side of the room. Their table — draped in pressed, white linen — was carefully pulled away by a garçon to permit the couple access to the cushioned bench located against the outer wall.

William waited for April to sit and, as she did, noted with awe the cool, brown leather upholstery. He, too, sat and after the table was moved back into place, the waiter laid out their service: crystal water goblets; the finest silver cutlery William had seen outside of his family's Easter dinners; more linen in the form of napkins folded to resemble blossoming flowers; a slender, glass vase holding a solitary red rose; and lastly, a short, smokeless kerosene lamp.

Focusing his attention on this last item, William noted the accomplished manner in which their waiter removed the glass top with his left hand, lit the wick with an old-fashioned lighter in his right, and replaced the lid. If it had been any faster, William would have had to call it magic.

April took her napkin, unfurled it, and set it on her lap. William, however, let his astonishment wander around the room. Where the leather of the booths gave way, the wall was clad in mirrored glass up to the top of what must have been twelve-foot ceilings.

The ceiling itself was likewise appointed with mirrors, but these were segregated by thick, oak beams. And within every quadrant so defined hung a chandelier — paired, it seemed to William, with an inverted twin. The overall effect was to make this space (which in reality could not have been more than twenty feet in width) seem enormous to William.

The garçon returned bringing with him both ice and water for their goblets, and, of course, their menus. He also placed upright between William and April another, much smaller menu which matched the style of its larger companions.

April touched William's arm and pointed to his napkin. William quickly opened, and then sank his sail. In so doing, he realized it was easily twice the size of any napkin he'd ever used. Looking at April, William could think of only one thing to say to her.

"Wow!"

April smiled at her companion's single-word assessment and took an opportunity to herself look around the establishment.

"Yeah, it's some kind of amazing venue, huh? I discovered it back when I was a senior at NYU. Well, actually a friend of mine back in Detroit suggested I come here at least once before the semester ended. But, she gave me lousy directions, so I had to do some searching before I finally found it."

William nodded his head and replied, "I'm sure that only made you treasure your first experience here all the more."

April — who by this time was opening her menu — closed it again, looked with surprise at her table-mate, and said, "That's right! It did. But you're the first friend I've shared this place with, and that makes tonight feel even more special."

"We're really friends, then, are we? I like the sound of that, April. You're a good person to have as a friend."

"Am I? Considering how I've treated you since we met, I don't know if that's as true as you believe it to be. I thought I was mean to you before today... You've certainly seen me at my worst, William... and I mean my very worst! Did I hurt your cheek?"

William shook his head and was about to say, "Not as much as my heart," but thought better of it. Instead, he said, "No, not too much." Then he picked up his own menu and opened it. Scanning the items listed within, he was startled to see everything was written in French! He looked at April with his mouth open but found himself unable to speak.

"I'm sorry," she said between giggles, "I should have said something before, but I wanted to see your expression when you opened your menu. Thank you for — this time — exceeding instead of destroying my expectations!"

"You're welcome... I think. But how am I going to order my food?"

"Let me, if you please. I speak fluent French. Besides, they have this delicious-sounding seafood sampler entree I've always wanted to try, but it always seemed too big for my appetite. If I order that for you, then I can snitch some. You like seafood, don't you, William?"

"Well, living on an island, as I do, I've had my fair share of fish... and I ate the planked whitefish at *Juilleret's* once when I was six. Does that count?"

"Sounds like a French restaurant to me. Yeah, I think you are ready for this place."

Now William broke into a chuckle and April looked at him with a wounded expression. "What... did I miss something?"

"Not really, but remind me to take you to *Juilleret's* one of these days. Once you see it, you'll understand my reaction. I will say this: it, too, is a great place to share with a friend."

The garçon appeared and April immediately began to place their orders. William noted how her voice took on an even more lyrical quality as the Gallic language flowed across her lips. The young man responded in kind and William could tell he had asked April a question even though William understood nothing else of what was being said.

April reached for and opened the smaller menu and turned to William saying, "He wishes to know the kind of wines we want served with our meals. Do you have a preference?"

"No."

April turned her attention back to the waiter and finished making her selection. After he departed, she said, "I ordered a bottle of chardonnay; it's less expensive than buying it by the glass." April saw a curious, little upturn on William's mouth which made her question her decision. "Is that ok with you?"

"Whatever you get for us I know is going to be fantastic, April. I was just thinking, if I've seen you at your very worst, then I've also seen you at your very best."

April smiled at William as if to say, 'thank you,' but said instead, "I hope not, William. I *really* hope not."

Three hours later, April closed her hotel room door, flung the key-card onto the low dresser, and watched as it slid to the base of the TV. She shed her coat and scarf and hung them in the small closet near the bathroom. Entering the bathroom itself, April turned on the light in preparation of taking a much-needed soaking bath.

She bent over into the tub and secured the drain plug before engaging the large, metallic knob which both turned on the water and adjusted its temperature. The water came out too hot, so she dialed it back to a more pleasing setting.

Earlier that day, April had spied on the countertop next to the sink a small wicker basket containing a selection of bath salts and beads. She looked through the options and chose a lavender-scented one, opened it, and added the crystals to the quickly filling tub.

Five minutes later, her clothes were laying across the bed and April was lying back being comfortably enveloped in that warm, fragrant pool. As she soaked, she permitted all the stresses of the day to seep from her body.

To insure that she account for them all, April replayed the day's events in her mind as best she could remember them. As frowns and smiles traded places below her closed-eyes, April came to one thought which seemed to sum-up all that had passed between them: like William, she enjoyed the sound of being able to call him a friend and have it not be a euphemism.

Dinner with William had again been a thoroughly wonderful experience. As she brought some of the warm water up to her face, it occurred to April that in the last week, she had been out to dinner with William twice and also shared lunches with him on three occasions.

"Five dinner dates with the same guy in one week's time," she mused. "That must be a record for me."

An even more surprising thought for April was that William was white. She had never been out on one date with a white guy let alone five.

"But, these weren't actual *dates*, were they?" she asked herself. "We've just been working to get the Strang Tapestry recovered. Besides, tonight sure didn't *feel* like any date I've ever been on."

When they said their 'good-byes', there had been no kiss on the cheek and not even the expectation of one. There was only a friendly wave at the door and a mutual wish for a good night's sleep.

"It wasn't a date... it was an experience shared with a friend," April concluded.

But even as she arrived at this place in her thinking, April knew it to be an inadequate description of what she and William were to each other. Yet, they really were friends now — a fact which made easy the conversation when it came time for William to explain why he no longer cared about the Strang.

As April listened, William told her how much of a shameful shock it had been to discover the tapestry missing. It was by far the most valuable item in his museum's collection, and the key to Beaver Island's unique status within America.

He told her how the islanders considered themselves Americans, but how they also had a special pride which was reflected in the things they did and did not permit to come onto the island.

April recalled William saying that when he first arrived in Detroit, he was bent on the Strang's recovery. As the days came and went, though, it began to seep into his conscious mind just how much he had *not* been living an authentic life.

She remembered sympathizing with him as he characterized his last five years as being a 'life-support' kind of existence, and shared with him a similar time she once had while in college. William told April that the longer it took for them to find the Strang Tapestry, the more unfulfilled he found his life to be.

While on the taxi ride back to their hotel, April asked if he had made any progress in either of these quests. William explained that if nothing else, his time spent in New York City meeting with curators and impressing upon them the national treasure nature of the Strang had been invaluable. It was a message which could only have been done in person.

As for his more personal journey, William told April he was making progress there as well. When William thanked her for her assistance with both projects, April remembered that moment as perhaps her most-favorite of the day. As she thought back to it, her face responded accordingly.

"Yes," echoed April's voice off the humid surfaces around her, "William isn't a colleague against whom I sometimes compete, and he's no longer merely a client I have to placate. William is a friend in need of my help."

~ ~ ~ ~ ~

April's friend decided he liked showers. It was one of many luxuries William had encountered since leaving home, but so far, the only one he wanted to take back with him. As he lay on the too-soft mattress after his latest one, he also reflected upon his day. Unlike April, he was tense because he kept returning to a question April had asked him hours earlier, 'Are you in love with me?' At the moment she first asked it, William had answered truthfully, but now he wasn't so sure.

"She brings to mind the title from one of James Herriot's books: *All Things Bright and Beautiful*. April is both. She's also black. I can see myself falling for her, except for…"

He wasn't a racist. William knew plenty of people who were and he despised them for that attitude. He simply assumed, because of this difference between them, that falling for April Smith wasn't going to happen.

William failed to appreciate that this same assumption was responsible for bringing him to the edge of the most intimate relationship he'd ever experienced. The accuracy of his answer was now moot. What both young people failed to appreciate was that seeds of their mutual affection had already been quietly and abundantly planted. Whether or not those seeds might blossom into actual love between them was now just a matter of time… and timing.

~ 8 ~

"**Y**ou seem stiff in your follow-through, Jim. Is your back giving you problems already?" asked a genuinely concerned Richard Smith.

James had just launched his ball from the third tee and had to concede his friend's observation: his lumbar region was protesting a lot more than usual. "Dick, it is. But, you wouldn't believe me if I told you why."

"What's the matter, Jimmy... Rachel too rough on you last night?"

James left his tee in the ground rather than exacerbate his condition further by trying to retrieve it. He turned his smiling face toward his golfing buddy and whispered, "Not just last night... the last *two* nights!" Their wives were fifteen feet in front of them preparing themselves for this par four hole. They either couldn't hear or didn't care what their husbands were talking about.

Richard chuckled and then replied, "You want I should spot you a few strokes since it looks to me you're all *stroked-out*?"

James joined in with his friend's cheesy humor, but his laughter stopped when it caused yet another muscle spasm.

"As much as I enjoy these Wednesday golf outings, Dick, I'm going to bow out this morning. I'll go tell the girls."

"No, you get into the cart. I'll tell them we're *both* calling it quits."

"We can all go back to the clubhouse, Dick," said Rachel a moment later.

"Yes, dear," agreed Margaret, "if Jim's not feeling well, we can enjoy the lounge for an hour or so."

"There's no reason for you to give up being out here this morning just because of us. No, you go ahead and finish the front nine, at least. Jim and I will be fine by ourselves. Just don't talk about us too much."

Both women smiled and waved him away. On the trip back to the clubhouse, Richard continued speaking as he operated the cart.

"If you were a museum director, how the hell did you come down with a bad back?"

"Not that I didn't have to do any lifting, but my career wasn't to blame for this. I was in the merchant marines for seven years after high school and did a lot of heavy, stupid lifting in that span of time. You know the routine: young buck trying to impress the old salts and all that bull. Well, by the time I was twenty-five, I had the back of someone twice that age."

"Seven years, eh? Were you only on the Great Lakes, or did you go international?"

"I did a little of both, but mostly on the lakes. I even made the Lake Superior run in November… once. Well, half of it anyway. Believe me, Dick, making that trip in the summer was bad enough. Sweet Jesus… what a monster she is in the fall!"

"Why only half? Was it as bad as that Gordon Lightfoot song?"

"Worse… Those guys on the *Edmund Fitzgerald* actually had a fighting chance of making it to the Soo: they were riding low in the water with a full cargo stabilizing them. They sank because two wave crests lifted the bow and stern but exposed the middle. Their own unsupported weight split them in half. They were victims of bad timing more than bad weather."

"So, what happened to you?"

"Well, I was crewing this ship with a rookie captain who thought he knew more than he did. He took us through a squall as we were heading west toward Duluth. You understand, Dick… we were empty which meant we were riding high. That ship was pitching on the water for more than eighteen hours; and buddy, let me tell you… After that, I knew what a flyswatter looked like from the fly's perspective. First thing I did when we docked was to hitch a ride back home. I wasn't the only one, either. Some of those fellas were ten-year men."

Richard pulled behind the last in a line of parked carts with a new respect for his seat-mate. He turned the key to the off position, but left it inserted in the ignition. James had climbed out and was about to take hold of his golf bag.

"Whoa, there, Jim! Let me take it. Just focus on hefting yourself today."

James nodded and followed his friend up to a porch area where their bags joined a kaleidoscope of others waiting for their respective owners to put them to use or put them in some near-by trunk. Richard did his best to keep up the banter as he opened the outer door to the men's locker room.

"So, if I'm hearing you, Jimmy, you were ready for a desk job."

"Something like that. It was that, and — I think I told you this before — it was a job my father expected me to take over from him. When we got back from our honeymoon, my dad literally handed me the keys and walked away. But, I made a mistake in agreeing to do it. I should have told him to forget it. I mean, for me it wasn't too bad."

Richard found his locker and began changing into his street clothes. In his estimation, he hadn't been out on the links long enough to warrant taking a shower. He watched as James eased himself into one of the more comfortable lounge chairs scattered around the locker room. His friend would take the opposite tack, albeit for a far different reason.

"It was only when Bill was born," continued James with his eyes closed, "that I understood my mistake: someday he might feel compelled to do as I had done and continue the tradition. And that's exactly what he did. But, it's no life for any young man, and I'm to blame for him being there. He's better than that damn job."

"Why don't you say something to him?"

"What could I say? For me it was a paycheck, but to Bill it's a damned religion! No, for him to make that kind of change in his life, it's best if he figures it out without any help from his father. Know what I mean?"

"Yeah, but if what you say is true, it's going to take something pretty special to motivate him."

James nodded as he slowly bent over to remove his shoes and lucky socks.

"Or someone," he grunted in pain.

~ ~ ~ ~ ~

William rinsed his face and checked in the mirror for any stray stubble he may have missed. Satisfied, he looked at his watch which told him he had about ten minutes before he was due to meet April in the hotel lobby and then join her for breakfast.

This was the seventh morning of waking in a strange bed and eating in strange spaces. And over this span, not so subtle changes had taken root in him. The most notable, besides the awareness he was living a dull life, was his new-found preoccupation with time.

On Beaver Island, William sometimes went days without putting on his watch. At home it was more decoration than it was a useful tool. But in the last week, William found himself relying on it almost constantly.

William at one time held the notion that a watch was the modern equivalent of a slave's shackle. After one week away from the island, that conceit now seemed comically pretentious. If he somehow lost his timepiece, he would be forced to purchase another or else feel as panicked as a hiker lost in a forest without a compass. As he finished putting on and adjusting his tie, William decided he didn't need *that* kind of crisis in his life. The missing Strang Tapestry was crisis enough. Then there was April…

William had awoken to unsettled feeling toward her. He had become April's friend, but now that friendship felt like it was getting away from him.

"Ok, Bill," he spoke to his reflection, "now you're going to keep April as your *friend*! Don't talk about your feelings and don't ask about her's. Finally, don't tell her how pretty she looks."

William exited his bathroom and grabbed his coat, scarf, gloves and earmuffs. He turned off the lights and looked around for anything else he might have missed. Drawing in a deep breath, William repeated in his head the rules he had just come up with.

He exited his room and went to call an elevator. As he waited for it, William took the opportunity to do some more deep breathing. When the lift's door opened, he was relieved to find it empty. William stepped forward, turned, and pushed the button for the lobby.

Moments later, William was delivered to his destination and saw April standing near the entrance to the hotel's dining room. She was wearing a cotton calf-length dress with a purple floral print and purple flats. She smiled when her eyes caught sight of his tall frame. William's face was similarly festooned.

"Goodness, April," William heard himself say, "that dress and you sure were made for one another!"

"Do you really think so? I hoped you might like it. It's one of my favorites, too."

As soon as she said this, William felt as if his heart had suddenly become lodged in his throat.

"This is going to be a lot more difficult than I thought…"

April led the way into the seating area for hotel patrons. William caught up to her, pulled out her chair, and watched as she floated onto the blue, cushioned seat. He sat opposite her and found himself struggling to find a more neutral line of conversation to engage in. He resorted to the obvious.

"Did you sleep well last night?"

"Like a baby. How about you?" April's voice sang in reply.

It was so clear even a deaf person could have understood it: April hadn't a care in the world. Those dulcet tones were still echoing in William's ear when April jerked him back with a repeat of her question, "William, did you hear me? I asked if you were feeling all right."

"What? Oh, sorry... Yes, I'm feeling fine. I just didn't get as good a night's sleep as apparently you did. That's all..."

She glanced down at her menu and asked, "Is it worry about the Strang?"

"The Strang!" William screamed to himself. "Of course, get her to talk about the Strang Tapestry."

"Yes," he now voiced, "I'm worried. With each passing day, the trail gets a little colder, doesn't it? You know... I thought the thief might try to ransom it, but we would have heard a demand by now, wouldn't we? It would have driven me nuts, but at least I would have known. But, now..."

"Well, let's not think about that today. Today, I thought I might help you with your *other* quest."

"What do you mean?" William asked between sips of water. "Don't you have to finish your oriental carpet project?"

"Nope! I got it all done yesterday... thanks to you. I hope you don't have any meetings scheduled for today."

"Only one, but it's not exactly what I would call a *meeting*."

"Well, what is it?"

"The director of the Guggenheim said I could accompany him as he walked to his lunch at some restaurant around the corner from his office. The woman I spoke with told me he was a fast walker, so I had better be a fast talker."

"I know about him. He's famous — or should I say, infamous — for that sort of thing. If that's the case, you're better off having Mr. Risner's boss give him a call." Leaning in closer to William, she continued in a whisper: "They're in-laws, so they have to speak to each other."

Straightening back up, April continued: "It sounds to me like we are off the company clock. So, sit back, Mr. Riley, and let your good friend April be your personal tour guide to the Big Apple. We're going to have so much fun today, you may not want to go home tomorrow."

William smiled at April, but within himself he was beginning to doubt if his *rules* were forceful enough to withstand the kind of day he was about to experience.

~ ~ ~ ~ ~

"Well, Margie," said a beaming Rachel "our plan seems to be working."

"It certainly does. Now I'm sorry we didn't think to do this two years ago."

"The guys do seem to be getting on much better lately," Rachel added.

The women were seven holes through the back nine. Rachel suspected what lay behind her husband's early exit but felt only a small pang of guilt. After all, they both had thoroughly enjoyed themselves.

"Even if Jim's feeling pain now — with massage therapy, he'll be as right as rain," she reasoned as she watched Margaret line up her ten-foot par putt.

Rachel made a mental note to thank her friend at some point during the day. Margaret had advised her to purchase some alluring sleepwear and Rachel had to admit it had been just the thing to rekindle her husband's interest.

That purchase, though, had been made on Monday evening instead of Monday afternoon. After their lunch with Vera, the three women went back to Vera's place to examine the Smith Family genealogy.

Rachel was impressed that Vera was able to compile so much information. Vera explained how most of it had been collected by earlier generations. Much of her work these days consisted of keeping the history up-to-date.

There had been, in fact, only one glaring gap in the data: the fate of Peter Edward Smith. Apart from him, the Smith Family's record in America was well-documented — until, that is, one tried to delve beyond the birth of the slave ancestors.

Margaret, of course, had seen most of this material before, but she now looked at it with renewed interest. So, when Vera pulled out the lithograph of Peter and his young wife (whose name was Elizabeth), she and Rachel both gasped.

The resemblances were as uncanny as they were unnerving: In the faces of this couple, Rachel and Margaret each could see shadows and suggestions of their respective children. In Peter, Rachel saw the eyes and nose of her son staring back at her; while in Margaret's estimation, Elizabeth could have been April's twin. Both women voiced these thoughts to Vera who nodded in understanding.

Together, the Peter Smiths made a handsome couple — decked out as they were in what must have been their finest attire. Vera was long-familiar with the proud and satisfied faces which the primitive image could not obscure. Now, so too were Rachel and Margaret. In truth, even a casual observer could see it: The couple was saying, "We are two people very much in love and not at all ashamed to let the world know about it."

"Vera," asked Rachel, "what more is known about them? Where were they born?"

Vera carefully drew forth the Smith's old, but well-preserved marriage certificate. It showed the date of their union; August 2, 1849; the names of their respective sets of parents; their ages; and whether or not either of them had been married before (neither had) or were legitimizing any previously born children (they weren't).

Vera went on to explain that there was correspondence showing the Smiths were forced out of England because they were a mixed-race couple.

"Before leaving England, Peter wrote to a family member living in Canada talking about settling in Michigan. That letter eventually got back into his hands; probably when they passed through Windsor. Now I have it here somewhere."

She continued by describing how Michigan before the Civil War was still a rough and tumble frontier only a few decades removed from Indian raids perpetrated by the British-aligned Chippewa Tribes.

For a few years, it appeared the couple enjoyed great happiness and celebrated the arrival of two sons. But, by 1854, Peter began receiving death threats from white settlers. In order to protect his family, he relocated his wife and children among a small black community living near present-day Saginaw. After about a year, Peter disappeared never to be seen again.

For over twenty years, Elizabeth Smith received money and correspondence from her absentee husband. In 1876, the letters stopped coming. She never discovered what had happened to him or where he had been living; nor had their sons or any other family member found out his fate... until last Saturday.

"Rachel," asked an inquisitive Vera, "how much do you know about Peter Smith cum O'Riley?"

"Not much... About all I do remember about him is that he died on July 4, 1876: America's one hundredth birthday,"

"Well," Vera sighed, "that explains why he stopped sending money to Elizabeth that year."

Their perusal of the family history complete, the women sat back and turned the conversation toward Vera's son and James O'Riley. After considerable deliberation, it was decided the wives would tell their husbands about their common ancestry — just not yet.

Margaret and Rachel explained to Vera how their husbands were still trying to come to terms with one another as golfing buddies. They weren't sure how the news they were cousins might affect that relationship.

"That sounds about right to me, ladies," Vera confirmed. "The right circumstance for telling them will present itself. It's just a matter of time..."

"And timing," Margaret added.

"Time and timing," Rachel thought to herself as she watched Margaret launch her ball high and long down the center of the fairway on the seventeenth hole.

Margaret bent down to retrieve her tee, but Rachel saw how it had been decapitated by her friend's driver. Margaret flicked the broken shaft off to the side and both women made for the cart.

"Is today the right time?" Rachel wondered silently.

A similar thought was passing through Margaret's mind as she sent the electric cart into motion.

"What about telling them after we get back to the clubhouse?" Margaret asked herself. Then she recanted that thought. While it seemed the two of them were getting along better in recent weeks, Richard still complained about James being a *closed book*.

For completely separate, but equally valid reasons, the golfing duo returned to the first idea they had settled on with Vera.

"Who knows… perhaps the men will be ready by Christmas."

~ ~ ~ ~ ~

After a day spent touring New York City's most iconic sights, William had come to the conclusion being guided by April was like going on a mini around-the-world tour. Manhattan was, he quickly understood, a place without a distinct cultural or ethnic core — unless that core was searched for within the island's great diversity.

He was prepared for the vast throngs of people. What he wasn't ready for was the immense diversity in the kinds of people who made up that throng.

April made certain William saw most of the major landmarks: They had taken the ferry to both Ellis and Bedloe Islands; and April took him on a 'B' Line subway up to 145th Street and back. They also walked down Broadway through Times Square, had lunch at the *Wild Blue Restaurant*, and ended the day's activities watching the sunset from the Empire State Building's observation deck.

In those ten hours of touring, April never once let go of William's arm. On only three occasions he could recall did someone look at them askance: An elderly man on the subway, a middle-aged caucasian woman in front of Tiffany's, and a young boy of indeterminate lineage in Central Park.

Of all the places they went, Central Park impressed William the most. Here in the heart of this urban Colossus was a good-sized slice of paradise. The trees still carried most of their leaves and the leaves still bore most of their coloration. Waterfowl darted across tranquil ponds. Squirrels were either chasing or being chased by their rivals as they were searching for but never finding that last nut to bury. Then there were the people…

By the time they got to the park, William had become inured to the diversity that was New York City. What was new in Central Park was the variety in the ethnic pairing: couples and families of mixed races were all over the place! And when these folk looked at them strolling together, William saw smiles of support in their faces instead of disgust, anger, or indifference.

For these regulars, the park was a place they could come and make the world play by their rules. It was their sanctuary and the others like them fellow members of a large and very diverse congregation.

In this space, whatever hesitation William had about being with April evaporated. She was his friend and he would never again permit disgusting social expectations — either written or unwritten — get in the way of this simple truth.

For many long stretches of time, April was far more quiet than he had expected her to be. While she always pointed out important places and gave William background information, there were also long periods when all they would do was walk with arms linked in silence. It was as if they were both operating by that ancient monk's admonition to, 'speak only when it improved the quiet,' and since they couldn't, they didn't.

It was nearly nine o'clock when they entered the lobby of their hotel and glided over to the elevators. Arms still entwined, they entered the next one which opened to them. William was closest to the buttons, so he pressed the one for the fifth floor where April's room was located.

When they arrived at her door, William finally let go of April's arm. He cleared his throat and said, "That was perhaps the best day of my life up to now. Thank you very much."

"Really? You're welcome. I enjoyed it too. I've always liked New York City in the autumn, but I especially like it when I'm sharing it with a friend because it's like seeing it again for the first time, but through their eyes."

"I can understand that. I felt the same way about Beaver Island when a cousin of mine came there for the first time."

"So, William, were you interested in doing anything else tonight?"

William shook his head slowly and took in a deep breath of air.

"April, I'm beat! I'm so tired I'm not even hungry. Besides which, that pretzel we ate was a meal in itself."

April chuckled, nodded her head, and replied, "Yeah... I might order something from room service later, but you're right: it's time to stop. I'll see you tomorrow morning. Oh, please remind me again... what time does our flight leave from La Guardia?"

"Two forty-five, I believe," William responded as he removed his earmuffs and slipped them in the pocket of his overcoat. "We're set to get back to Detroit by around 4:30 p.m."

William watched while April did some quick calculations in her head. Then she frowned.

"Rats! Tomorrow is pretty much shot. We'll need to leave here by eleven o'clock at the latest. That means we won't have much time to do more than eat breakfast and get checked out of our rooms. And by the time we get back to Metro Airport, we might as well just go home. Well, in your case William, that means going back to the Ren Cen."

"About that… I need to speak with John about finding me less-expensive accommodations. I appreciate the institute paying for my stay in Detroit, but…"

"William, I really wouldn't worry about that if I were you. It's our pleasure to do it."

"If you insist, but, I *am* sorry for the mistake with our airline tickets. That was nothing but inexperience. If there's a next time, you can make the reservations. Deal?"

"It's a deal. Good-night, I hope you have a better night's sleep."

"Thanks. After all the walking around we did today, I believe I will. Have a pleasant evening, April…"

April inserted the room key, opened the door, and waved to William as he returned to the elevator. The door closed. She let out a sigh and said, "Well, I needed a day like that."

As she sat down on the bed and began to pull off her shoes, April thought about how William was such a pleasant companion. In her experience, men could be so gabby... and far too many of them went on and on about themselves.

"William, though, is different," she pondered in silence. "It's not that he's simply more quiet than most other men. It's that he knows when to say something and when not to."

Even though there was no way to connect what they had done today with the recovery of the Strang Tapestry, April marveled at how their tour of the city again did not feel like being on a date. She was searching in her mind for a better word, but couldn't come up with one. Instead, she tried describing it.

"The problem is the word *date*. It's too impersonal. What William and I did today was more intimate."

As soon as that last word passed through her consciousness, April was brought up short by an apprehension which immediately burst forth from her mouth: "Did I just say what I think I said?"

"Yes," replied her inner voice, "you said intimate: i-n-t-i-m-a-t-e, and it means..."

"I know what it means, damnit!" she said as she collapsed back onto the mattress. "It means trouble..."

~ ~ ~ ~ ~

The elevator door opened to the seventh floor. William stepped off and thought to himself that having April for a friend wasn't going to be as much of a problem as perhaps he first imagined. While they had a wonderful day in each other's company, he had felt no pressure to give her a kiss good night or do something else designed to propel their relationship to that next level.

"So she held onto my arm," he thought. "It was a cool day. It would have been silly not to take advantage of each other's body heat."

William then considered April's smile.

"That was about the joy of sharing New York with a friend… nothing more. She isn't falling in love with me, so don't fall in love with her, old bud," he told himself out loud.

It seemed to William a simple plan: just don't fall in love. He reasoned about it the same as a man might also say to himself, "Don't fall into that large, deep pit of fire you are walking toward." But, as simple as it might seem, William's plan failed to consider one important element: the force attracting him to April was more akin to a moth's instinct than it was to a man's intellect.

He came to his hotel room, found the key, and opened the door. He could see the bed had been freshly made and a mint lay on the pillow. William shed his overcoat, but instead of hanging it up, he draped it over the room's only chair. His suit coat was next to be added to the pile.

He kicked off his shoes and sat on the bed. In turn, he lifted each foot and gave it a quick massage. Then he loosened his tie and popped the top button on his dress shirt. He unbuttoned his shirt sleeves and rolled the cuffs back up his forearms. Spying the remote control for the television set, William grasped it.

"Here's something I hardly ever do," he thought. "I'll watch some TV and find out what's happening in the world. Perhaps I'll find an old movie..."

He tossed the mint to the side-table, gathered the pillows in a pile behind his back, and congratulated himself:

"You are over the hump, old bud! Tomorrow, we go back to Detroit and continue our search for the Strang. If we find it, great! If we don't, then I go back to Beaver Island and let everyone know it has been lost for good."

One thing William now felt confident about was that in those now-familiar spaces of the Detroit Institute of Arts, he could maintain his friendship with April without worry until he had to leave. There would be no further opportunities for his feelings to go in a romantic direction.

"Now," he asked out loud, "how the heck do you operate this thing?"

~ 9 ~

The bite of pizza in William's mouth was hot, chewy… and completely tasteless. He lifted his napkin and discreetly transferred the offending food into the crumpled paper. April detected this sleight-of-hand and furrowed her eyebrows.

"What's wrong?" she asked through a pepperoni and cheese-filled mouth.

"How can you eat this garbage?" William asked in wonderment.

April tried laughing as she chewed, thought better of it, and switched to merely smiling. She swallowed before again attempting to talk.

"Poor William… you're just not cut out for airport food, are you?"

The object of her glee slowly nodded his head as he switched to drinking his equally tasteless tea.

LaGuardia was a perpetually moving can of sardines at this early afternoon hour, and the pizza kiosk had been the only place without a long line in front of it. It was now glaringly apparent to William why this had been the case. As if eating unpalatable food wasn't bad enough, he had to do it standing at a chest-high table inches away from the airport's conveyor belt of travelers.

April looked at her watch and sought confirmation from the digital display hanging from the ceiling of the nearby corridor.

"Finish up. We have about sixty-five minutes before our flight leaves and we still must check in at the gate."

"Are we really in that much of a rush?"

"No, but do you still want to be here for dinner?"

"Say no more!" William responded as he looked around for a trash can. "I'm ready when you are."

Finding his intended target, the receptacle promptly ate what he wouldn't. A moment later, April added her own contribution to the cause. The two young people took hold of their briefcases (their luggage having been checked through already), found an opening, and injected themselves into the chaos. The pair were squeezed almost uncomfortably close to each other as they made their way to the departure gate.

"I don't know about you, but I enjoyed our walk through Central Park more!" said William over the din.

"You know, I'm glad you mentioned that. I was thinking about yesterday myself and wondering if my holding onto you made you feel uncomfortable. Was it too intimate?"

With that question, William realized they were both struggling with the same problem: the nature of their friendship. He also realized April was smart enough to talk with him about it.

"I wasn't offended, if that's what you're asking," he said after a moment's thought. "Look... yesterday was chilly, so being physically close to each other made sense. And, if it felt intimate, April, that's because we're friends. But, if what you're really asking is if it made me feel like taking you to bed... I think I told you that's not my style."

"And just what is your *style*?"

William chuckled at her emphasis of that last word and told her once he stopped smiling.

"Frank Sinatra... but without the cigarettes."

April nodded and then noticed they were about one hundred feet away from their departure gate. She pointed this out to William, along with the fact a line had already formed leading to the ticket counter. Two minutes later, they had taken their places at the rear of the que. Twenty-five minutes more, and it was nearly their turn.

"Watch this!" said April to William as the airline clerk motioned them to come forward. The gate manager gave the duo her best practiced smile.

"Tickets, please..."

April presented them to the clerk asking, "Are there any seats still left in Business Class? If so, I would like to use some of my points to up-grade our coach tickets."

She handed the woman her airline club card and waited for her to check the availability of the seating. During this exchange, William watched in wonderment. After no more than a minute, April got her answer.

"Yes, Ms. Smith, I have two adjoining seats still available. Do you want them?"

"Yes… Thank you very much…"

After another moment, the manager stapled the boarding passes to their tickets and handed the bundle back to April who turned to William smiling and then pointed to a pair of seats still unoccupied in the lounge area to the right of the gate.

"Are you impressed?"

"Very!" William responded, meaning it. He was pensive for a moment and then added, "What did you mean by using your *points*?"

"Most airlines have these programs for people who do a lot of traveling. I signed up back in college when I was flying home between terms. Since taking the job at the DIA, I've continued to accumulate points every time I fly. I just used some of them to move us up to Business Class seats."

"Why?"

"Because," April said slowly, "I saw how you were last time we flew. Business Class has more legroom. I wanted to show my appreciation for allowing me the time to get my other project done."

"I thought that's what dinner at that French restaurant was for…"

"It was, William, it was…" said April in defense of her actions, "What you did was very special to me and even more amazing because you sacrificed some of your own success."

William gave a slight nod of his head, let April's words sink in, and then asked, "Is there any other reason?"

"Yes… My arms aren't long enough."

"What?" William asked, laughing.

"Well, I saw the worry in your eyes the last time we flew. Being together in Business Class means I can give you a hand to hold onto."

"Thanks…"

"Not a problem… That's what friends are for."

~ ~ ~ ~ ~

"That's what friends are for, Marla." Nancy Gerrity said to the nervous hostess. "You just sit there and delegate. Let the rest of us do the work. Here… have a glass of iced tea."

Marla Kerschner plunked herself down at her dining room table and accepted the tall container of sweet tea she herself had prepared the day before.

"Do you think we have enough food?" she heard herself ask after taking a sip.

"Marla," said an increasingly exasperated Dorothy McClellan, "you asked that same question not more than twenty minutes ago. The answer is still the same: yes! We have more food than we need. The only thing you must worry about is whether or not Phil will be here on time."

"He'll be here."

"How can you be so sure, Marla?" asked Nancy. "Everyone knows he hates parties."

"Come on, Nancy, what do you think *sons* are for?"

Laughter filled the room for a few moments. Another member of this stitching group — a middle-aged woman by the name of Pamela Abercrombie — picked up the newspaper article about her friend's unusual sampler. A good-sized color photo of Marla holding it appeared above the story itself.

"Where should I put this?" she asked no one in particular.

Marla furrowed her brow and looked around the dining room for a suitable location. It was Dorothy who found the solution.

"Why not tape it to one of the patio doors and draw the curtains up to act as a kind of frame?"

Nancy and the others concurred as they went about their individual and joint tasks of preparing the Kerschner home for the evening soirée.

Marla rose from her seat and — with iced tea in hand — went over to where the now-framed sampler had been balanced on an artist's easel. Dorothy came and stood next to her.

"For something so small," her friend said, "it certainly has generated a lot of big questions. I wonder if you'll ever discover the answers?"

"Probably not, Dot," shrugged Marla, "but asking those questions sure has been fun, hasn't it?"

~   ~   ~   ~   ~

"He won't tell me what they mean, Becky," Joyce Whitney complained to the person on the other end of her phone. "He just smiles and changes the subject, or he finds some way to distract me…"

Joyce let the ambiguity of that last phrase remain as she recalled the way her husband had distracted her the other day. She smiled at the memory as she listened to her neighbor prattle on. If their sons had not been making a racket coming up the road from school, Perry and she would have had some explaining to do. Becky asked a question, and suddenly Joyce's thoughts were brought back to their conversation.

"Yes, I think that's strange, too," she answered. "He's been gone for over a week and nobody seems to know where he went. Has anyone called his folks in Florida?" Joyce paused to hear the reply, and then added her own point: "No, I guess I wouldn't have the guts to make that call, either. I mean… it's really none of our business, is it. Perhaps Bill just went on vacation? You know, he's never been anywhere. That's probably it: he finally went to see his folks. I know for a fact they begged him to come down last winter."

Joyce paused again as her friend opened a new line of inquiry.

"Well, Bill told Mrs. Doherty he was just reorganizing the museum," she replied. "It seems plausible considering it hasn't been done in years. I wouldn't even take note of it except for Perry's odd behavior. Believe me, Becky, something fishy is going on, and Perry and Bill are in on it. They must have some kind of surprise planned for next April the first, and I for one am determined to find out what it is!"

Joyce listened to her friend's sign-off, added her own 'good-bye,' and replaced her phone on the wall-mount. Walking over to her husband's oddly marked calendar, Joyce noted that she had one hundred and seventy-one days to figure it all out.

~ ~ ~ ~ ~

After stowing their briefcases and coats, April and William began to settle in for the ninety-minute flight to Detroit. April slipped past William on her way to the window seat. He took the aisle seat after she sat down. William noted the space between his knees and the seat in front of him was expansive.

"Compared to that other flight, this is like sitting in my living room."

He turned to April and smiled. She smiled back and then went fishing for her seatbelt. Finding it, she fastened it and took up the slack.

In spite of the added space of Business Class, William could feel his apprehension grow. He was visually searching for a restroom when he felt something cross his lap. Startled, he looked down to see April taking care of his belt, too.

"Relax, William," whispered April, noticing his discomfort, "you're going to be just fine."

William drew in some slow, deep breaths, but the technique wasn't achieving its desired effect. If anything, he was beginning to feel panicked — the unexpected securing of the restraint the likely triggering event. He began to unbuckle himself, but April put a hand on his arm.

"Where are you going?"

"I have to use the restroom."

"I understand, William, but you can't. The toilets are always locked-down while the plane is on the ground. The crew won't open them until we are airborne. Here... give me your hand." William hesitated, but April patiently insisted, telling him, "Come on, big boy! I mean it…"

William complied. He watched as April began to use her two small, delicate hands to gently massage his larger, left one. She took each finger and expertly worked the tension from every joint. She caressed his palm with her thumbs and used her soft, two-toned fingertips to draw lazy circles and other shapes on the back. After about ten minutes, she said, "Next…"

William shifted slightly in his seat and immediately gave her his right hand. When April had finished with that one, she asked, "Feeling better, now?"

Without speaking, William looked into April's eyes and nodded his head. She began to pull her right hand away, but William took it in his left and gently rested both appendages on the armrest between them. April smiled to herself and turned her attention to the view outside the plane. Fifteen minutes later, the jet was airborne. William had made it through both taxiing and takeoff and his grip on April's hand never changed.

As soon as the 'Fasten Seatbelt' sign was turned off, William went to the restroom. He had returned and was just settling back into his seat when a middle-aged flight attendant approached them carrying a tray with an open bottle of champaign and two pieces of plastic stemware.

April was continuing to look out the window and so did not see this. William did and said, "Wow! You people sure do treat business travelers well."

At hearing his voice, April turned to see what William was referring to. She watched as the woman poured the first offering and said, "I'm sorry, but we didn't order any champaign."

"I know, Miss," replied the woman. "Consider it on the house. With the way the two of you have been holding hands and looking at each other, the crew and I figured you were either newlyweds or about to be. So, congratulations from all of us! We hope you enjoy the rest of the flight."

William turned to look at April and was about to say something when he noticed her give him a very short shake of her head. When the crew member had finished pouring the drinks, April responded, "Thank you very much... and please share our appreciation with your crew-mates."

"I will," said the flight attendant and then she moved on down the aisle.

"Why did you allow her to think we're married?" asked William with mild irritation in his voice.

"Because," April replied haltingly, "it would have embarrassed her if we told her we're just friends. Besides, I happen to enjoy champaign, and there's no sense in wasting a bottle that's already open."

"I'll say this, April," William said smiling, "when I'm with you, there's no such thing as a dull day."

"Why, thank you, Mr. Riley," said April as she raised her plastic stemware in salute to William's compliment.

"Think nothing of it, *Mrs.* Riley," replied William as he, likewise, raised his champaign-filled cup and touched it to April's. They shared a laugh; and the humor of that innocent mistake stayed with them all the way back to Detroit.

~ ~ ~ ~ ~

Jeremiah Wheeler considered April's closed office door and looked about for someone he could identify as working with her. Tom Zurakowski was coming toward him.

"I should know that guy," he thought. "Excuse me," Jeremiah said to the unremembered man, "I'm looking for April Smith. I was wondering if you know where she is?"

Unlike the attorney, Tom remembered Jeremiah Wheeler and said, "It's Jerry, right?"

"Right! And you are…"

"Tom," the DIA employee said, his pride wounded.

"Yes, Tom… sorry, names aren't my strong suit. Anyway, do you know where April is?"

"Nope," Tom lied. "Have you tried her at home?"

"Yes, I have," replied the clearly frustrated suitor. "She's not there either and she hasn't returned my phone calls."

"Hey! You're April's boyfriend, aren't you, Jerry," probed Tom knowing it wasn't true.

"Not really," Jeremiah frowned, "just a boyfriend wannabe."

"Well, I'll let April know you were looking for her," Tom lied again. "Or, you're welcome to wait for her if you want. If she's not at home, then I'm sure she's around here somewhere."

"Thanks for the suggestion, but I fly to London this evening. Look — Tom — could you tell her I'll be back in Detroit next Wednesday, and that I'd like to take her out to dinner?"

"Sounds to me like a message you'd be better off writing down, Jerry," said Tom pointing to a nearby desk. "Why don't you write her a note and I'll take it from there?"

"Great idea… Thanks!"

A minute later, the short message had been composed and the folded paper handed off to April's colleague. Tom eyed his competitor as the attorney quickly made his exit from the institute. When Jeremiah Wheeler disappeared around the corner and Tom heard the unmistakable sound of the main doors being opened, he crumpled the note and tossed it into the nearest trashcan.

"There goes your love life, April," said Tom under his breath, "right where it belongs."

~ ~ ~ ~ ~

As April expected, it hadn't made much sense to go back to the institute. It was half-past five when they were finally able to get to April's car.

William suggested getting some dinner and thought it best that they each pay for their own meal. April agreed and soon found a family style restaurant just off Middlebelt Road. By the time she dropped William off at the Renaissance Center, it was just past seven o'clock, and by the time she got back to Birmingham, it was nearly eight — the fading orange on the western horizon the only wisp of daylight remaining.

April parked her car in the designated space matching her apartment number. She pressed the trunk release button on her dashboard and heard the mechanism release. Pulling on the driver's door handle and opening her door, April stood stiffly, locked, and then shut the door.

With bag and briefcase removed and on the pavement, April closed the trunk, took up her bags, and made for her building's locked main entrance. A minute later, she was inside her flat, had already set down her things, and had hung up her coat in the closet.

The tired traveler walked over to her fridge and opened it. A partial bottle of chardonnay from the Leelanau region called to her, as did some camembert. A minute later, her hands were full and April was making for her favorite comfy chair.

She deposited the wine glass and plate on the table next to the chair and went over to the television to grab the remote. After pressing the 'on' button, April sat down and laid aside the remote in order to shed her shoes and roll down her nylons. She put the nylons in the shoes and then set the shoes aside. Picking up the remote again, April scanned through the channels looking for something mindless to serve as background noise.

Finding no programming able to meet (let alone exceed) even that low bar, April turned off the TV in disgust and set down the remote on top of a small stack of trade magazines. She grasped the wine glass and took a sip of the chilled liquid.

In so doing, April noticed her telephone answering machine was blinking red indicating six messages were queued up ready for her to listen to them. She hit the appropriate button and discovered the first message was someone calling around looking to sell replacement windows. April deleted that one before the man got to the end of his tedious speech.

The second message was dead air, but the final four calls were from Jeremiah Wheeler, who came across as the boyfriend he wasn't. She picked up the handset.

"It is time to tell him," she concluded in a whisper.

While the journey back to Detroit was exhausting, being with William had mitigated the drudgery. This conversation with Jeremiah, April knew, would close the day on a sour note.

"It has to be done," she told herself as she dialed the attorney's phone number.

April had waited months before telling Tom to look elsewhere for companionship and was determined not to make the same mistake with this friend of her father. She removed her earrings as the dial tone switched over to rhythmic pulses. On the fourth ring, she heard Jeremiah's voice but knew immediately she had reached *his* answering machine.

Since April knew what she had to say needed to be said in person, or at least voice to voice, when the beep came indicating she was to begin her message, April merely indicated she had received his calls and asked him to call her back at his convenience. She said, "Good-bye," and hung up the handset.

April drew her legs up and tucked them to the side. She took another sip of wine, closed her eyes, and smiled to herself as images of her and William's flight back from New York played their way across her memory.

"Was it my imagination, or did we laugh for an hour straight?"

April recalled William saying that being mistaken for a married couple had been one of the funniest things ever to happen to him. April — her eyes still closed and her smile still wide — nodded her head in silence as she concluded the same was true for her, as well.

April paused in her reminiscing and opened her eyes. She wondered *why* it had been so funny and concluded the initial humor came from their different racial backgrounds. April didn't know why it made William laugh, but suspected he felt the same as she did.

"I know he's not a racist," she thought to herself. "He just respects that particular difference between us."

While April shared this respect, in truth, her own sense of the ridiculous came from thinking she could be married at all. For the last several years, she had been focused on achieving her career goals and was well on her way to fulfilling them. For her, romance could serve only as a brake on those well-crafted plans. Then, another thought flashed into her mind.

"With William being white, it is like I have the best of everything; I have my career plus I get to experience a great relationship with a guy I know won't threaten it with romance." As soon as that happy thought burst forth, it faded to melancholy: "William isn't going to be around much longer. In fact," she mused, "the harder and more skillfully we work to recover the Strang Tapestry, the sooner he will leave. He'll be back on Beaver Island, and I'll be back to rejecting men like Brad Ausmus throwing runners out trying to steal second base."

April finished the wine and then spread some cheese onto a cracker.

"Well," she continued to think as she ate, "at least we'll always be friends…"

~ ~ ~ ~ ~

William closed out Thursday evening exhausted but content. The time he spent in New York City with April had been a productive interlude surrounded by what was otherwise a disappointing task. Ever since the Strang's disappearance, each day had been for William an axe-blow to the tree of his optimism.

While only the reclamation of Beaver Island's iconic tapestry could restore that confidence, William knew spending time with April at least gave pause to the axeman's strokes.

He fell asleep — now no longer troubled by the urban background noises which a week ago plagued his slumber. Instead, he succumbed to his fatigue thinking how fortunate he was to have a friend in April Smith.

As he drifted into his dreams, William clung to that word — friend — like it was the last barrier to a deeper relationship with April. Whether it was out of naïveté, his present exhaustion, or stubborn denial, William could not see the reality the two of them had created: that their *interlude* was fertile ground onto which had been scattered the seeds of a simple idea.

Love blossoming between two human beings requires no complicated formula or hard-to-fathom machinery. All it takes is time, proximity, and shared passion. First sown on Tuesday evening, those time-honored qualities got a large dose of nourishment Thursday afternoon. By the early hours of Friday morning, indications of a love both genuine and growing began to surface within William.

They came in the form of etherial vignettes involving himself and April. The dreams were varied, vivid, and very erotic. The last one woke William; and, in that hazy place between unconsciousness and lucidity, he reached out for April only to embrace empty bedsheets.

William sat up in his hotel bed disoriented. He cleared the dry, encrusted bits from his eyelashes and looked around the room. It took him a few seconds, but he finally remembered where he was. The red digits next to his bed told him it was 6:38 a.m. Since he had set his alarm for seven o'clock, he reached over and disabled it.

Images from his most-recent dream were still fresh in his mind as he threw back the covers and sat up. His feet hit the carpeted floor and he pulled his toes across the dense nap a few times before standing.

William went into the bathroom and relieved himself. After washing up, he emerged and stepped to the window. Drawing back the curtains, he looked out at his reconstituted vista: the Detroit River flowing down from the North and Windsor, Ontario beyond it. As he stood there, he realized that any and all barriers to loving April had been swept aside by the simple act of sleeping.

"I'm such a fool!" William cried out to a landscape as equally unconcerned with his love life as it was with his state-of-mind.

That the two were, in point of fact, one and the same thing, was of even less importance to the busy people far beneath William's window. If anyone down there could have heard him, at least a few might have agreed with his assessment. In fact, they would have likely patted him on the back in congratulations for his feat of deductive reasoning.

William felt self-deceived. He and April had failed to respect the truth that most successful relationships begin as friendships. By acting married — even for a mere ninety minutes — they had subtly deepened the nature of that friendship.

Ethnicity, William now understood as never before, was an illusionary wall which, from a distance, appeared insurmountably high. But the closer he got to April, the more that wall became a small pile of rocks.

"Am I in-love with her?" William asked himself. "Not yet, but it won't take much for me to hop over that wall. We *must* find the Strang!"

William now saw the resolution of the Strang crisis, not friendship, was his only hope of avoiding becoming a complete fool in front of April. He went back into the bathroom to shower and shave.

Looking at his mirror image, he said, "Remember, old bud, there's no fool quite like the one who falls for the girl who doesn't love him back."

~　~　~　~　~

"William," said an enthusiastic April, "I have a special project for you."

He had entered April's office for the first time that Friday morning — hadn't even removed his coat, in fact. He smiled at her energy; and was happy to see that she was in a pleasant mood.

Within himself, William wondered if she was able to detect the subtle change which had come over him since they had last been together.

"What do you want me to do?"

"I found and borrowed a continental map of the United States. I want you to plot the position of every person we have an address for. Then — when that's done — we are going to scour every newspaper which serves those regions for some mention of a Strang-like sampler. Perhaps we'll get lucky and find mention of some odd piece of needlecraft someone picked up at a yard sale or a flea market."

April could see the doubt begin to cross William's brow and cut him off before he could put that doubt into words; saying, "I know it's a long shot, but we're rapidly running out of options."

William removed his overcoat (his gloves and earmuffs were already pocketed) and hung it on April's coat rack.

"Let me see if I understand what you're saying: you are proposing we switch our search away from the thief and onto the Strang itself. Is that correct?"

"Precisely…"

William went to one of April's office chairs in front her desk and sat down.

"I agree the idea is a good one, but why the change in focus?"

April rocked in her own chair as she considered her next words.

"Well, it's been almost two weeks since you discovered the Strang missing. That means it could have been taken from your museum as far back as six weeks ago. If a Beaver Island resident had taken it, that would have been detected almost immediately — according to you. On the other hand, if it had been stolen in order to ransom it, you would have been contacted by now. Finally, if a professional thief took it, he would have fenced it and we would be hearing whispers of something big being bandied about on the black market."

William could see the logic of her reasoning and nodded his head in agreement.

"What you're implying is that we are reduced to looking for an amateur which means we have to look where an amateur might unload it."

"That's right," April agreed. "The Strang isn't going to turn up in an art gallery in New York or Los Angeles. It's out there somewhere in the nation's heartland, and that's simply too big a haystack for us to explore. That's where this map comes into play," tapping on it for emphasis. "Plotting the names will help us focus our efforts."

"I see now why you called it a 'long shot.'"

"It's the only hope we have at this point, because the other possibility is the thief took it with the idea of keeping it for himself. If that's the case, you'll probably never see it again."

William got up from his chair and removed his suit coat. He hung it next to his overcoat and began to roll-up his sleeves.

"It seems I have my work cut out for me. Show me how you want it done and I'll get started."

"Ok!" April replied. "But there's no room for you to do it in here. I found an empty conference room which isn't scheduled for use until next week."

William began to collect the map and all the other materials. He responded to April without looking at her.

"That's a relief... because, you know, I wouldn't want to be accused of cluttering your office..."

As he brought his eyes up to meet hers, April was shaking a fist at him, but on her face was a mischievous smile.

~ ~ ~ ~ ~

William stretched his arms and tried to shake the boredom from his body. He had been at this project for almost eight hours, but (in his estimation) only completed about half of it. He found the work tedious and himself forced to take frequent breaks just to keep focused. April stopped in twice to offer her own support and to bring him lunch when he told her he was inclined to skip it and continue working.

The one good consequence was he was able to keep his mind away from his feelings for April. He had been worried she might decide to assist him, but April made it clear her work that day was to be spent on the written report she needed to submit to Mr. Risner by the end of business. For Friday, at least, he was alone in the search for the Strang.

"It might turn out to be longer than that," William thought as he stretched yet again, "unless I can get these names plotted."

He looked at his watch. It told him it was almost time to pack up for the day. He was doing just that in order to take it back to his hotel when April walked into the room.

"About ready to leave? William, what are you doing? You can leave that stuff there... no one will bother it."

"I still have a ways to go," William responded wearily. "I'm taking all this back to my hotel room and finish it over the weekend."

"But," April pouted, "I thought I might take you on a tour of Detroit. It won't be quite as exciting as our one in New York City, but our zoo is really nice."

"I'd love to spend more time with you — especially away from this place — but I've given myself until Tuesday or perhaps Wednesday to locate the Strang. If we haven't found it by then, I must get back to Beaver Island to let Perry know it's gone for good. I'm sorry."

"No, William," April replied with sadness, "I'm the one who should be sorry. I shouldn't be trying to distract you when time is so essential. If you're ready by Monday morning, will you give me through the end of business on Wednesday to help you look for it?"

William put everything into his briefcase and closed it up. He stood from his seat and stretched his back as he gave answer to April's question.

"Agreed, but if we haven't located it by Wednesday evening, I'll be taking a bus to Charlevoix on Thursday morning."

April nodded her head in agreement as she killed the lights in the conference room. William followed her out and back to her office where their coats were waiting for them.

She said to herself, "Well... at least I'll be able to resume my regular weekend routine..."

~ 10 ~

Monday morning came and revealed William to be as good as his word. By the time April arrived at the institute, he was waiting by her office door ready to show her the results of his weekend efforts.

Once they had shed their respective coats, William laid out the map on top of April's desk and pointed to towns and cities all across America circled in red. On sheet after sheet of lined paper, he had listed the locales along with the names of the people who had visited Beaver Island in the previous month.

Most of these places had only one name associated with it. A few had two, and some of the larger places had as many as four names listed. No place had as many as five potential targets. Instead of tracking down almost one hundred individuals, April and William now had only to sift through some forty newspapers looking for mention of a Strang-like needlepoint sampler.

"William," April began, "I think we should ignore the big city newspapers for now. Let's begin with these medium-sized towns. They should be big enough to have newspapers and small enough that an odd needlework piece might spark some local interest."

"Fine, but what are we to do with all the folk in these really small towns?"

"Well," April speculated, "we could check with the papers in the county seat nearest to them? People in rural areas especially like to read about the local gossip."

"Don't I know it!"

William and April shared a smile as he brought around one of April's office chairs and placed it next to hers. He stood aside so April could take her seat and then did likewise.

"Oh," he added, "I almost forgot... on the last page is the list of people I couldn't find towns for. What should we do about them?"

April turned to that page and silently counted. "There are only twelve names here, so that's a blessing I suppose."

"Actually... fifteen," William corrected her, pointing to one of the names. "This one — Kerschner — represents a group of four men who came onto the island to fish. Kerschner apparently paid cash for all their rooms, so his was the only name which made it into the registry. I actually remember these guys. My friend Perry had them out on his boat every day for a week. They left the morning I found the Strang missing. I saw them walking to the ferry as I was going to work."

"Well," April conceded, "we'll have to leave them for last. I mean, what choice do we really have?"

"None, I guess…"

For the rest of the day — including over their lunch hour — April searched through newspaper websites in the communities they had chosen to tackle. William sat next to her as they both scanned past page after page of text and photos for any possible reference to the Strang Tapestry.

As William sat next to April, an internal conflict was simmering within him unrelated to the search for the Strang: joy and tedium were duking it out. While looking through stories about mundane happenings was without a doubt a form of torture, being shoulder to shoulder with April begged for a life sentence. The result was William found himself in the strange place of silently both cheering and groaning every time they connected to a newspaper's website.

April, because she wasn't used to spending quite so much time on the computer, began to experience neck and back stiffness. William saw her twist in discomfort and — without having to be asked — got up from his chair, stood behind her, and began to massage her shoulders and neck.

"Ummm… that feels great! If you're not careful, I'll make you stop in about a week."

William chuckled and replied, "Just trying to return the favor."

"What favor?"

"The hand massages you gave me on the airplane, remember?"

"Oh, right…" April said. "Well, thanks. Just make sure you keep your eyes on the screen."

William chuckled but said nothing. He did, however, think to himself, "If she only knew!"

What was distracting him wasn't coming so much through his eyes as it was through his nose. April's intoxicating fragrance wafted up to him like the lazy breeze coming off a garden.

"She must bathe in flowers," he continued to speculate internally. That thought triggered in his mind memories of her which had lately been flooding his sleep. William abruptly pulled his hands away from April and retook his seat.

"Thanks, again," said April, not knowing why William stopped.

"You're welcome," said William as he took his eyes from the computer and looked directly at April. She saw this, turned her head, and smiled at him. As she went back to looking at the screen, William squelched an urge to lean over and kiss her.

"Don't be a fool," he said to himself as he refocused his own efforts.

~ ~ ~ ~ ~

It was now a week since her near-fatal collision with misplaced passion and Rachel O'Riley was finding it difficult to put the incident behind her. Since their golf outing last week, she had felt compelled to speak with Margaret twice about her on-going anxiety.

Her friend and co-conspirator tried to reassure Rachel by passing on the news that Brett Burton had made a brief appearance for his paycheck and then disappeared again. While she agreed with Margaret this was a good thing, Rachel knew there was still nothing keeping the jilted paramour from ruining her life.

Rachel sipped her orange juice and looked out her kitchen window. As she did, the events of last Monday burst through like a nosey neighbor scurrying around spreading gossip. As thrilling as it was to think she could be that out-of-control, the downside of trysting with the young golf pro hung over her awareness like a Florida thunderstorm.

"That's the whole sorry story in a nutshell, isn't it," she told herself. "It's why auto races are so popular: thrill mixed with imminent disaster."

With a sad smile and small shake of her head, Rachel realized for the first time in her fifty years of living that the reality of adventure almost never conformed to the fantasy. She had made a calculated gamble and lost as gamblers mostly do.

"Or did I really lose?"

She replayed in her mind the memory of Margaret standing there in the women's lounge. She recalled being embarrassed and then filled with shame as she waited in the pro shop. That shame then morphed into fear of public exposure and eventual divorce. But none of that had happened to her, and so, eight days out, Rachel reverted back to merely feeling guilty.

"If it hadn't been for Margie, I *would* have lost everything," Rachel realized. "She stepped in and took my chips off the table before I lost the entire stack."

Then the truth that one *marker* had been left behind came to Rachel: her sense of self-respect. She hadn't lost her husband or her reputation, but her pride lay in pieces at her feet. Rachel would never again think of herself as someone who always made good decisions.

"If I had to lose something, perhaps part of my confidence wasn't such a terrible price to pay," she thought. "And I could still lose more, if Brett ever decides to take revenge."

Rachel turned her thinking back to her friend and this time the smile on her face was anything but sad.

"If someone had told me when I was little that my best friend in the world was going to be an older black woman, I would not have believed them."

While she did have, as a child, anxiety about African-Americans, her unbelief had a far simpler explanation: Charlevoix had few black residents in the 1950s and 1960s.

The circumstance which brought her and Margaret together was the combination of two extraordinary happenings: her son's disappearance while the family was on a three-day trip to Mackinac Island combined with the Smith's trip to the island to see their elder son, Allen.

Allen was an Eagle Scout and his troop was bivouacked on the island for the week. They had earned the privilege of being part of the Governor's Honor Guard that summer. It was while taking pictures of Allen and his fellow scouts raising one of the island's many flags that the Smith family came across the young, lost, and teary-eyed William O'Riley.

The Smith family took the child to Marquette Park because it was one of the island's most-visited areas. Rachel remembered seeing her son sitting on the ground playing with Margaret's youngest child. The two toddlers acted as if they had been friends forever.

"It's too bad," Rachel whispered. "That was the only time they ever got to be together…"

After thanking Margaret and Richard and exchanging addresses, James went back to the police station to let them know their son had been located. While he did this, Rachel and Margaret talked the entire time. Twenty minutes later, the two Beaver Island families were on board the Whitney's boat making their way first to Harbor Springs, and then, after dinner, home.

Two weeks passed and Rachel had all but forgotten the incident when a letter came in the mail from the Detroit area. Enclosed with the note was a color photograph of her son sitting and smiling with April who was similarly disposed. Rachel wrote Margaret thanking her for the picture, and later that year, sent them a Christmas card. Margaret returned the gesture, and then over many years, the cordiality between them became a bond of friendship. Rachel stood in her kitchen and knew without any doubt it was this bond which had saved her.

"In fact," she realized, "her gift to me is two-fold: Margaret kept her silence and gave me the opportunity to reflect on my actions."

In the last week, Margaret had helped Rachel understand that she was angry with herself and not with James as she first thought. Rachel was able to voice the truth that she resented marrying the first man she fell in love with; and that her decision to meet with Brett was an attempt to turn back time.

"Instead of learning from my past, I was trying to change it," she remembered herself saying to Margaret.

Rachel finished off the last of the orange juice, rinsed out her glass, and put it upside down in the drying rack. She then gathered her things in preparation of meeting Margaret and Vera for some shopping and lunch. Eight days on and the guilt of her actions still weighed heavy. But, Rachel was determined to dig a deep pit, shed this burden, and cover it with the wisdom gleaned from a lesson learned.

"There is no tinkering with history. There's only my next choice."

As this insight took root within her, Rachel O'Riley made a mental note to one day thank her son for getting himself lost one sunny day on Mackinac Island.

~ ~ ~ ~ ~

William lay on his hotel bed worn down from the day's labors. He never before ached just from reading; and the low hum from the computer monitor still echoed in his ears.

He and April managed to get through twenty-six newspapers before calling it a day. Still, that translated into hundreds of articles — mostly local events they did not care to know about. When they stopped to take a break, William was surprised to discover it was after seven o'clock in the evening. They had been at it for over ten hours!

His thoughts drifted back to April and he found himself thinking, "She's such a relentless ball of energy. After today, it's clear April wants the Strang Tapestry recovered more than I do. But, it's gone for good. All we're doing is treading water until I head back to Beaver Island Thursday morning."

William thought about how good a friend April had become to him; how being with her was by far the best thing to happen to him amid the whole, frustrating mess. He closed his eyes and imagined the two of them in an intimate embrace. He scoured this scene for any sign of hesitation.

There was none. The image was as natural as breathing and felt just as necessary to his life.

Overwhelmed by both a sadness and a joy which each threatened to make him weep, William knew he was in-love. It was no longer a foolish possibility or even a pleasant dream. If it hadn't been for the relentless nature of the day's work, the spasms of desperation he endured throughout their time together would have broken to the surface. Time and again, William had to remind himself to accept April's proximity as sufficient.

William felt a jolt of awareness as he remembered the last time he used that word to describe his life.

"What an evil word *sufficient* is," he spat. "I hate it! For five years my job has been *sufficient*; I was sure it was everything I needed in life."

He rolled out of bed in a state of self-loathing as he realized just how easily he had slipped back into accepting crumbs in place of real food. Walking over to his window, William drew back the curtains and viewed the vista before him.

"I was such an idiot for taking over from my father," he said to the bustling world before him. "Why did I do it?"

He felt like the object of a long-running scam; the fraud of the sting compounded by the mark's continued unawareness. The Strang Tapestry — which for years had been the central icon of William's life — now meant nothing to him. His awareness of just how ridiculous his life had become kept this insight as fresh as an undressed wound.

He closed the curtains. The relentless purpose of even nocturnal Detroit was mocking his naked and restless spirit. Making his way back to the bed, he sat down, propped his elbows on his knees, and buried his head in his hands. The irony of his present circumstance pulled a short but sour laugh from his lips.

April Smith — who two weeks ago had been a stranger — now occupied the inner sanctum the Strang once claimed... only she didn't know it.

"That somehow makes sense," he voiced, "the Strange couldn't care less who *worshipped* it, and April can never know how much I care for her."

As he sat rubbing his hands over his face and head, William took solace from the fact he had traded his devotion to the Strang Tapestry for something much better: the intimate connection to another human being.

"Compared to what I had been loving," he said to the room, "there's nothing foolish about loving April."

William knew this connection would always be there... right up to the moment he told April he was in-love with her. The relationship they had and which they both valued would be shattered by his attempt to grasp the improbable.

"No," William confirmed to himself, "I'm not a fool for loving April. I would only be a fool for telling her. Two more days and it will all be over.

Two more days and it is back to Beaver Island and my job as the barely alive court jester."

Moisture began to pool in the corners of William's eyes. He wiped it away with his fingers as he rose to begin preparations for bed. As he did so he wondered: "Is this the same feeling soldiers experience before going into a battle they don't expect to survive?"

~ ~ ~ ~ ~

The telephone was ringing when April got to her apartment door. She unlocked it and ran to the device just as the ringing stopped. Looking on the LED display, she saw that the caller had been her mother. It was almost nine o'clock. April went back to close her apartment door then took off and hung up her coat.

"I'll call her back in a few minutes…"

Ten minutes later April was ready. She sat in her favorite chair in her pajamas and pressed the first number on her phone's auto-dial feature.

"Hello?" her father said.

"Oh, hi, Daddy… how have you been?"

"I'm doing great, sugar. Do you want to speak with your mother?"

"Sure, but while I have you on the line I thought I would catch up with *you*. How is Grandma? Mama said she took a tumble last weekend. Is she feeling better?"

"She's back to her old self, sugar," Richard Smith said with resignation in his voice.

April heard it, laughed, and said, "All right, Daddy, I'll let you go. Hope your golf game is improving."

"It is, April... here's your mother..."

"Honey," said Margaret, "I just tried calling you. Were you indisposed, or just getting back from a dinner date?"

"Wrong on both counts, Mama," April replied. "I was just getting home from work when you called. I tried to get to it, but you had already hung up."

"Work!" her mother said with shock. "Dear, you work too hard. Why don't you put in for some vacation time and come see us?"

"I just might do that. I'll need a vacation after this week. We might want to push back our calls until nine-thirty or so for the next couple of days. Tomorrow and Wednesday, at least, are going to be repeats of today."

"Does this have to do with the mystery project you're working on? When are you going to be done with it?"

"Mama," April sighed, "I really can't discuss it. Now, how are you doing?"

"I'm doing just fine. Oh, Mrs. O'Riley was asking how you were and sends along her 'hello.'"

"Tell her I said, 'hello' as well. Look here, Mama, I'm really beat. If you don't mind, I'm going to cut this short and go to bed. Are you ok with that?"

"Yes, but please take better care of yourself, honey," replied Margaret. After this, the duo shared their 'good nights' and hung up.

April shook her head as she placed the phone on its base unit.

"I guess once a mother... always a mother," she said in a whisper.

April rose and went into her bedroom — turning off the lights in the process. She pulled back the bedsheets and crawled under the covers. Just before drifting off to sleep, April thought, "I wouldn't mind a back massage right about now..."

~ ~ ~ ~ ~

Over the last three days, William and April estimated they had looked through more news articles than either of them had ever previously read. By the time they gave up the search for the Strang Tapestry on Wednesday evening, April openly expressed her doubts to William.

"I think we made a mistake in how we conducted our search..."

"April, your idea was solid. The problem is the tapestry not the strategy. The Strang is gone... that's all there is to it. For more than two weeks we gave it our best efforts. Tomorrow morning, I leave for the island, and when I get back on Friday, I'll let Perry and the rest of the people there know it's gone for good."

"William," said April as she reached out a hand to touch his arm, "I'm truly sorry. I know this must be a huge disappointment for you. Are you going to be all right? They won't fire you for the Strang's loss or otherwise blame you for losing it, will they?"

"They might," William responded after thinking about her question for a few seconds. "And maybe they would be right to do so. Regardless, I'll be fine. After all, there's more to my life than one old rag."

April nodded her head and then turned away from William to switch off her computer.

"At least we both found a friend," she said as she again faced William. This elicited a big smile from April's soon-to-be ex-client.

"It has been the best thing about coming to Detroit. I'm just sorry I wasn't able to take you up on that offer to tour around the city. You know, I haven't been able to explore this building let alone go to the zoo. Of course, it's not like I was on vacation…"

"Do you think you'll ever get back down here?"

William sighed and looked around April's office. He said, "I don't know, April. It would be difficult coming to Detroit and *not* thinking about the Strang."

"I know what you mean," said April as she nodded her head, "I was wondering if you might be reluctant to get together with me for the same reason."

As soon as those words left her mouth, William lunged at and grasped April by both her arms. He appeared to her as a man panicked by a pending tragedy.

"No, you're so wrong, April," said William with an impassioned voice. "If I ever came back here, it would only be because I wanted to see you again. You're my friend, and I always want us to remain friends."

William almost said what was on his heart, but stopped himself. Realizing he was perhaps holding onto her too tightly, he released his grip, dropped his arms to his side, and stepped away from April.

April wasn't sure what she was seeing in Williams's face. Disappointment, certainly, but she wondered if there was something else going on. She began to ask him, but thought that would be too intrusive a question. She instead chose a different tack.

"Would you like to go out to dinner with me tonight? I know a good French restaurant, and the menu is even printed in English!"

William gave a tired chuckle and shook his head, saying, "No. Thank you for the offer, but I think you'd best take me back to the hotel. At this point, I'm just done. John will bring me here tomorrow morning around eight o'clock, but I would like it if you could take me to the bus station. I need to be there by 10:00 a.m."

"Well, at least you'll have a chance to look around the institute tomorrow," said April. She finished putting on her coat, turned off her office light, locked, and closed her door. She took hold of William's arm much as she had done in New York City, saying to him teasingly, "Come on, handsome... let's find a new way to get you back to the Ren Cen..."

Ten minutes after the couple had left the institute, Jeremiah Wheeler appeared at April's office door. While he had been in London, he accessed his home answering machine and heard April's message.

He was stumped by no mention by her about his suggestion they go out to dinner this evening to talk about their relationship. Finding no note on her door for him, the lawyer decided to drive over to April's apartment. When he arrived there twenty minutes later, it was apparent she wasn't there, either.

"Margaret was right. I have to be patient with her," he said under his breath. "I'll give her two more days to call me back. If she doesn't, I'll go back to the institute during the day. Just let her try to avoid me, then!"

~ ~ ~ ~ ~

Thursday morning arrived with William again waking before his alarm sounded.

"This is getting to be a bad habit," he said under his breath. He rolled to his right to check the time. Since 5:17 a.m. was only thirteen minutes ahead of when he wanted to get up, he decided to allow the annoying tone to happen as planned.

That idea survived for all of two minutes before the twitchy energy inside William pulled him to a seated position. He reached behind the side table and pulled the clock's power cord from the wall socket. He snatched up the lifeless device ready to propel it into the next realm in a hundred pieces, thought better of that plan, and settled instead for wrapping the cord around the clock and stowing it in the drawer under the table's surface.

William rubbed the crust from his eyes with the thumb and forefinger of his right hand. Then he craned his neck to stretch out muscles which had become stiff during the night. He took-in a deep breath and let it out slowly — his eyes fixed on his luggage waiting only for his toiletry bag and night clothes to be stowed in an outer pocket of the suitcase.

For a moment, he entertained the thought of having April come get him at the Renaissance Center instead of John. He even went as far as to pick up the telephone — the unit now resting alone on the table top. He put it back as soon as he realized this choice was selfish in at least two ways: Waking April from a sleep she absolutely needed; and second, burdening her with his profession of love.

William pressed his fists onto the mattress and pushed himself to standing. This did nothing to dissipate his annoying agitation. In truth, it amplified it. Worst of all, he had packed and repacked his luggage last night, so there was no legitimate outlet for his nervousness in that direction.

The immediate saving grace for William came in the form of his full bladder. He padded over to the bathroom, shed his sleepwear, turned on the shower, adjusted the temperature, and then sat down to relieve himself.

Thirty minutes later, he was showered, shaved, and dressed for one final morning to be spent in April Smith's orbit. William had resigned himself to the decision of spinning away from her before saying or doing something which would ruin their friendship.

That this was the most fraudulent choice he could make mattered little to William. Soon he would be back where he belonged and April could pick up the threads of a career she had set aside to assist him.

"Besides," he spoke to his mirror image as he adjusted his tie and brushed some stray lint from his suit coat, "how can you really be sure this isn't desperation instead of love?"

His reflected self declined to make a reply.

William turned from the silence, switched off the bathroom light, and walked over to a low dresser upon which sat the TV he used not even once. He pulled out his wallet and removed a crisp twenty dollar bill from the fold and placed it under the note he had composed for the maid the previous night.

He walked to the room door, opened it, took up his luggage, and allowed the door to close of its own accord. The loudness of the latch made William wince in guilt.

By the time he reached the lobby, it was nearing 6:10 a.m. William thanked the staff behind the check-in counter, gave them his two room keycards, and went off in the direction of the breakfast buffet. Another hotel employee ushered him to a small table where William set down his bags before making his way over to the buffet.

"I'm going to miss this restaurant almost as much as I'll miss all the showers I've taken," he mused as he picked up his plate. After filling it and returning to his table, William sat down and ate in complete silence. At twenty minutes to seven, he was finished and awaiting John's arrival seated on one of the many sofas scattered around the lobby.

By eight o'clock, both men were walking into the institute; William with his bags in hand, and John holding nothing save a solemn countenance. For William, the drive to the DIA had seemed more like a trip to a funeral home than anything else.

William found April in her office, asked for, and got her permission to leave his luggage just inside her doorway. Try as she might, April just couldn't cheer her friend. Eventually, she stopped trying, and for that, William was grateful.

William found it almost impossible to be in proximity to April. Twice he had to suppress the urge to confess his love for her.

"Perhaps," he thought to himself, "having her take me to the bus station is a mistake…"

Having John take him instead did cross his mind but then William realized this would only hurt April's feelings, and that was something he vowed never to do.

"April," he said as he hung up his coat and scarf, "I'm going to look around for a while. I'll swing back here in about an hour to see where we stand in terms of needing to leave, ok?"

"Ok, William… Try to have some fun." Even as she spoke those words, April knew William wouldn't.

She sat down and turned on her computer (having arrived at her office only moments before William). April scanned her desk looking at the material which, over the last three days, had defeated them so completely. The way she figured it, there was still about twenty-five percent of the targets remaining to be searched through. Now, however, William was leaving and Mr. Risner would soon be redirecting her energies to other, more important projects.

When they had given up last evening, April was about to examine newspapers from a few of America's larger locales. Both she and William had made the choice to bypass major urban areas like Washington, DC or Los Angeles because of there being too much material to search through.

But, there were publications in many second-tier cities which were prime targets. April read over the list they had compiled: places like Pittsburgh, Atlanta, St. Louis, Dallas, and even Denver. What came to her as she looked it over was the thought to go ahead and do it anyway.

"Why not? Mr. Risner hasn't given me my next assignment, and I have at least an hour before William and I leave for Southfield."

With a nod of her head, April threw aside her hesitation and began working the recently abandoned plan. The list was in alphabetical order. In fifty minutes, she had made her way through Atlanta and was reading articles from the *Dallas Examiner* when her eyes fell upon a name which seemed familiar. April scrolled back a few paragraphs until the name came into view: Mrs. Marla Kerschner of Richardson, Texas.

"Why do I know that name?" April asked herself as she began looking around for William's list of Beaver Island visitors. Not finding it, she went back to the article and continued reading. She hadn't gone more than a few sentences when the hairs on the back of her neck stood up and she got a tingly sensation all over her body.

The article was about Mrs. Kerschner's odd needlepoint sampler with an arcane text no one seemed to know anything about. The authors of the piece made reference to a photograph, but April found the picture was absent from the internet version.

Then April saw William's list peeking from under a pile of stray papers and took it into her hands. She turned page after page until she got to the last one.

"There it is!" she said out loud. "I knew that name sounded familiar..." She spelled it out loud: "K-E-R-S-C-H-N-E-R."

April compared the name on the list to the woman's last name and saw they were spelled exactly the same. And a moment later, when April came across mention of the woman's husband bringing it back from a recent fishing trip, April knew without any doubt she had found the whereabouts of the Strang Tapestry.

With trembling hands, she instructed her computer to make a copy of the article. The printer was just finishing the task when William strode into her office.

"Well, I think we'd better be going."

April turned to William with the article in her hand and excitement in her eyes, and blurted, "You bet we're going, William! It's a good thing your bags are packed, because you and I are flying to Dallas!"

April thrust the newspaper article into William's hand, which he took with questioning eyes. April waited for a certain look on his face to burst forth. A minute later, William's reaction again exceeded her expectations.

With their excitement echoing off the surrounding walls, the two young people managed to sit down to absorb the improbability of their success.

"You did it, April!" William said with a heaving chest. "You're the best!"

"*We* got lucky," she replied shaking her head, "and you know it, mister! I could just as easily have pitched this junk into the trash as look through it one more time. Perhaps we could have come up with a strategy to find it quicker, William, or a hundred other things could have happened which would have made finding it impossible."

"True…"

"If you want to thank someone, thank Mrs. Kerschner… she's the one who took the Strang to the newspaper."

"What do we do next?" William asked like a kid on his first trip to a theme park. "Do we contact Mr. and Mrs. Kerschner directly, or do we call the Dallas police?"

"Whoa, there," April interrupted, "slow down, William. We can't call the police because we don't know the circumstances of how the Kerschner's obtained the Strang. Did Mr. Kerschner steal it, or did someone else take it and give it to him? And the last thing we want to do is to alert them."

"Ok, then what do we do?"

"The first thing we do is to get down to Texas as soon as possible. Do you remember when I agreed to book the airline reservations the next time?"

"Yes…"

"Well, William, this is that *next* time. I'll get started on booking the flight. Why don't you go up to Mr. Risner's office and give him the good news… though he may already have figured it out, if you catch my meaning."

The words, "I'm on it…" had barely graced April's hearing before she lost sight of her tall friend as he bolted from his chair and out her door. Thirty minutes later, William walked back into April's office as she was finishing up a phone call. The look on her face was not a happy one.

"What's the matter?"

"We're not getting down to Dallas today… that's what. The earliest booking I can arrange is for tomorrow afternoon."

"That's fine by me, April. I'm sure I can afford one night's accommodation at some airport motel."

"William," April replied, "I'm not supposed to say anything, but the DIA has an arrangement with the Renaissance Center: we loan them pieces of artwork which would otherwise be in our storage rooms, and they loan us hotel rooms for VIP clients like yourself."

"You mean..."

"Yes, your room has cost us nothing. Sorry, but there's no way we have the funding to pay for your accommodations for two days let alone for two weeks."

"Still, it's nice to be considered important..."

"And you are important... at least to me," April reassured him. "That's why I booked two adjoining seats on our flights to and from Dallas. We are set to arrive there around four o'clock in the afternoon... Central Time."

"When do we fly back?"

"The next day, William, which means I'll need to get us some rooms as well. I'll make sure they are a*djoining* rooms..."

William cringed at the emphasis of that one word since it was an aspect of traveling with April which he had yet to master. He sat down again and watched as April completed their travel plans. April hung up her phone and rose from her desk chair.

"Wait here while I take this information to Mr. Risner's office. He has to approve these travel plans and issue vouchers to the airline and hotel in Dallas."

"Right..."

"While I'm gone, why don't you think about where you'd like to go or what you would like to do today, because we are taking the rest of the day off whether or not Mr. Risner approves."

"So, we're playing a little hooky?"

"Don't you think we've earned it?"

"I do... Ok, I'll ponder... you wander..." he said as he jerked his head in the direction of April's open office door. She returned his impish smile and laid her hand on William's shoulder as she went past.

When April returned, she looked dolefully at William, saying, "Sorry, but we can't play hooky."

"Why not?"

"Because before I was able to broach the subject, Mr. Risner told me to take you out and celebrate."

"Drat! I was looking forward to being naughty... never played hooky before..."

"Oh, well... me, neither," added April. "So, what do you want to do today? Go for a drive around town? The zoo?"

"The zoo sounds like a lot of fun. But before we go anywhere, I want to say how much I appreciate everything you've done for me, April. I know this is going to be a boost to your career here at the Detroit Institute of Arts."

April sat down in the empty office chair next to William and drew it close enough to take his hands in hers.

"William, you are very welcome, but I want to make something clear to you: When I first took on this assignment, I did it for the reason you mentioned. But, all that changed after I got to know you and especially after what you did for me in New York City."

"Thank you," William interjected.

"I'm not done, you big goofus! You became a wonderful friend to me, William, and I'd like to believe I helped you for the same reason."

"Please forgive me," William said nodding his head, "you're right, and my words of appreciation should have reflected that truth about us."

April ignored his attempt at an apology, and instead, continued to drill her gaze into William's own eyes.

"Years from now — whenever this job gets me down — I'm going to remember what we did for each other, and those thoughts will help me get through the tough times. And when you go back to Beaver Island, I'm going to miss you very much, William, so you'd better call me from time to time."

With that, April reached out and hugged William. And as he hugged her back, he began to wonder if April was a friend to a fool or a wise man.

~ 11 ~

April noted William's nervousness, leaned over, and began whispering into his ear, "What's wrong? This flight is going to be just like the last one. Here... take my hand." She reached to him with her right hand and clasped William's left in it. William mumbled something and April had to ask him to repeat it.

"I said, 'I'm not nervous about the flight.'" April began to speak, but William cut her off: "And it's not about the Strang Tapestry, either."

"Fine, William. Then what's going on? You've been on edge since I picked you up from the hotel."

From the moment the two of them left the institute yesterday morning for a trip to the Detroit Zoo, William had promised himself he wasn't going to do something foolish. And up to this moment, he'd been able to keep that promise; covered as it had been under a cloak of superficial activity.

Without it, William's resolve lost all cohesion. Their success in locating the Strang had, in essence, backed him into an emotional corner with only one way out: he had to tell April the truth.

"If not for my sake, then at least for hers," he voiced in his head as he looked into April's orange/brown eyes. "I'm in-love with you," he said evenly.

Like the flipping of a switch, the shaking in William's hand ceased. April looked at him and smiled as if he had just made the silliest joke possible, but the look on William's face never wavered.

"You're kidding, right?" April asked as her smile vaporized into a tight, thin line.

All William could think to do was to shake his head from side to side in the most subtle manner he could muster.

"I mean…" April continued. "Do you know what you're saying?"

"I know," William confirmed, "and I'm as serious as a heart attack."

"What are you going to do?" asked April as her own hand now began to tremble ever so slightly. William felt the tremor and — carefully lifting the back of her hand to his mouth — applied the lightest of kisses to it.

"I've done it already. As hard as I've tried not to, I've fallen hard for you April. You may or may not be happy to hear it, but you deserve to know."

April's face was frozen in shock as he lowered their hands back to the armrest between their seats.

"You're saying it is up to me now," April said with a rising inflection. "Of all the crappy things to do just before…"

"Do you like me?"

April stopped speaking and looked directly into William's eyes. She whispered to him, "Yes."

"And you consider me to be your friend?"

"I think of us as *very* good friends, William. You already know this. But, it isn't fair of you to say this to me…" she pleaded.

"You *are* right, of course," William said as he closed his eyes for a moment and shifted his weight in his seat. "Love is a lot of things," he continued, now looking again at April, "…but it is rarely fair. Look… I am sorry for dropping this on you like I did, but as I said, you deserve to know and to know right now."

"Why now?"

"Well, for one thing, to give you time to think. In a couple of days, this whole tapestry business will be over. For another, I wanted you to know my love for you isn't connected to what's going to happen in Texas. Finally, I was going to explode if I kept it in any longer," he said as he smiled at April. She smiled back at him weakly, but said nothing. "You're still holding my hand."

The ambient noise within the plane swirled around April like confetti. In spite of being seated, she felt an unmistakable sense of falling. That turned out to be the plane's lift on takeoff pressing her back into the seat. She hadn't even remembered them taxiing to the runway.

April turned her head to look out the window at the Michigan landscape speeding by under their feet. She thought to herself, "Why me?" but decided not to pose that particular question to William. It was a good five minutes before she was able to compose her thoughts.

"William," she began, "I've never before been friends with a guy like I am with you, so I know we have some-thing special." William nodded his head in that way which conveyed to April his understanding. "I may even love you," she continued, "but, I've been at the institute for less than two years and I'm just now getting good at my job. I don't know if my life can handle a relationship as complicated as ours would almost certainly be."

"Yes," William agreed, "I was thinking along those same lines myself. But a minute ago you told me how unfair I was being. Think about this: if I never let you know you had the possibility of this wonderful relationship, how fair would that have been to you?"

"True," April nodded in agreement. "Then again, we've known each other for less than a month. How can you be sure you're in-love with me?"

"Oh, that part was easy! The longer we've been together, the less important finding the Strang Tapestry has become to me. Even now — after we've located it — I don't care whether we get it back or not. At first, I couldn't figure out why because my work has always come before anything else in my life. Then yesterday I remembered my mother saying she knew she loved my father because he made her forget about her dreams. That's the effect you have on me, April. That's how I know I'm in-love."

April stared at William slack-jawed and gut-punched; certain he had just plagiarized her soul. Here she was holding hands with a man who felt about love and relationships the same as she did. Apart from that, William Riley occupied little of the other criteria she had about the man she eventually wanted as her life's mate.

April looked down at her hand gently cradled in his. She *was* still holding it and, even midst the shock of his confession, never once considered letting go. She looked away from William and sent her mind aloft amid the clouds like the jet which carried her body.

"Why now?" April thought to herself. "And why this man of all people? I was so looking forward to this trip to Dallas and getting the Strang back. Now, all I want is to get out of this airplane and go back to the security of my normal, boring routine…"

April looked over to reengage William in conversation and was surprised to see he had fallen asleep. She smiled and shook her head.

"I should have seen it coming," she said under her breath. "He got me to New York, was always such a gentleman, and he never made a pass at me." Then a thought entered April's mind and her surprise turned to awe: "He told me he loved me already knowing I would choose my career over him!" The longer she considered this, the more April thought William to be the most courageous man she ever met.

A member of the flight crew appeared next to William and draped a blanket over April's foolish friend.

"Your husband certainly doesn't mind flying, does he?" she whispered to April.

April began to explain that they weren't married, but the attendant had already moved on to other duties. April again looked at William. This was the second time an airline employee had mistaken them for a married couple.

"What do they see when we're together?"

Whatever it was, it wouldn't be fair to think it was all William's doing. At that moment, April came to the realization she was in-love with this naive, slumbering resident of Beaver Island. But instead of filling her with elation, it only magnified her sadness. April was determined to be just as courageous when it came to her career.

~   ~   ~   ~   ~

The tone accompanying the 'Fasten Seatbelt' sign awakened April. She eyed the blanket which covered her from just under her chin to her knees, then glanced to her right at her smiling companion.

"I don't even remember being sleepy," she told herself.

"We're landing," William confirmed.

Sometime during her nap, William had released her hand from his. April took both her hands and peeled the blanket away amid a frenzy of static electricity brought on by the dry cabin air. William took the covering and folded it up.

The flight crew was busy with their pre-landing duties, and the attendant who mistook them for being married accepted the folded blanket and asked them to bring their seats forward. The woman's Texas-sized smile reminded April of the quandary she was in.

As the airplane began its final descent into Dallas/Fort Worth International Airport, April touched William's arm to get his attention.

"William, I thought about what you said earlier. I don't think I'm ready for a relationship as complicated as this one promises to be." William nodded his head in understanding as April continued to justify her thinking, asking him, "Why can't we just remain friends, William? Who knows what might happen in a year or two."

To this suggestion, William shook his head in disagreement.

"Why not?"

"You know, April... I mostly despise modern love songs..."

"What are you babbling on about?"

"Bear with me... I'm coming to my point. Modern love songs... most seem written by people who haven't the first clue about what real love is. On the other hand, there is this old Sinatra number which sums up my thinking perfectly: The song is *All or Nothing at All*. April, having half a love doesn't appeal to me, and if you search your heart, I bet you'll find it doesn't appeal to you either. The love I feel for you is what it is, and I can't and won't dilute it to make your decision easier. I'm sorry..."

April had listened to William's every word, but was intent on making him agree to her way of thinking. William sensed what was coming and interrupted her before she could speak.

"Look, April, we're about to land." William said pointing out the window at the quickly approaching ground. "We need to focus on getting this job done. We'll have plenty of time to talk later."

"How can you say that, William?" a clearly panicked April exclaimed. "We have to talk about this *now*!" April could see how her outburst had drawn the attention of surrounding passengers. She lowered her voice and continued: "You're not leaving much room for compromise."

"None, actually..."

"What?"

"April, if we were of the same background, there *might* be some room for compromise, but still not much for the reasons I've already given.

Since I'm white and you're black, there is *no* room for hesitation and *no* do-overs. For us to be together, neither of us can have the smallest doubt in our minds. Think about it. You know I'm right on this point. Now, let's go get the Strang Tapestry and then we'll be in a place where we can talk some more."

A few seconds passed as April considered William's proposal. Then she nodded her head and said, "Agreed, but let's not drag things out at the Kerschner's home. We go there, explain who we are, find out how they acquired the Strang, and hopefully retrieve it without involving the police."

The wheels chose that moment to make contact with the runway. The *thump* from a harder-than-usual landing and the ensuing swift deceleration of the airplane jolted the couple from their contentious conversation. Each was found to be seeking out the other person's hand to hold; the irony of this action bringing smiles to both their faces.

Twenty minutes later, the two of them had collected their checked luggage and April watched as William contacted their hotel via the courtesy phone near the baggage claim exit. And fifteen minutes after that phone call, they stood near the entrance to their hotel — having left their suitcases at the concierge station — with only their briefcases in hand; waiting for a shuttle to take them to the car rental agency.

April glanced at her wristwatch. It was now just after five o'clock on a hot Friday afternoon. The evening Dallas commute loomed, and the notion that everything in Texas was bigger threatened to empty April of whatever confidence still remained within her.

It took the two tapestry-hunters the better part of ninety minutes to find the Kerschner's house in Richardson. When they did, April pulled the car to the curb, put the vehicle in park, and turned off the engine. She opened her door and got out.

April looked around the up-scale neighborhood. Except for the sparse number of trees, it reminded her of her childhood subdivision. William was waiting for her by the sidewalk leading up to the Kerschner's front door. When she got beside him, they strode together the final feet of their improbable journey.

Reaching the entrance, William found himself closer to the doorbell, so he pushed it. He looked over at April and smiled, thinking, "She seems as nervous as I am."

They both heard someone moving to the front door, and this only heightened their shared tension. The door — a heavy-looking, carved wood variety with a vertical, smoked glass inset — swung open and a beaming Marla Kerschner considered them from behind the screen door which now separated them.

"Yes, may I help you?"

William cleared his throat to respond, but it was April who spoke first.

"Mrs. Kerschner, we are here because we read the write-up about your interesting needlework sampler. Would it be possible for us to have a word with you about it?"

"Yes! Yes!" she effused. "Please come in," she continued as she opened the screen door. "You wouldn't believe all the calls and letters I've received. You know, I even got a call from the governor's wife a few days ago," said Marla as she leaned over to April to add, "She knits…"

April immediately understood this coded message of disapproval and frowned appropriately. The look on William's face indicated he hadn't been able to interpret Mrs. Kerschner's cypher.

Without warning, Marla paused midway down the front hallway. April and William almost bumped into each other before they realized the reason: There — framed and centered for all to see like the photo of a favored son — hung the Strang Tapestry.

For almost three weeks, William Riley's greatest fears were that he might never find the Strang or that he would find it in ruins. Therefore, along with the shock of finding it was the surprise to see that it never looked better.

April's ongoing conversation with their host faded from William's focus as he bent forward to examine the tapestry more closely. He didn't know how she had managed it, but Mrs. Kerschner had removed the old tea stain which had been part of this treasure for over eighty years. William was about to congratulate her on this achievement when he noticed movement to his side; Marla was leading April into her living room. He followed them.

"Please sit anywhere," William heard the proud tapestry owner say. "May I get you something to drink? Coffee? Tea? Something cold?" April was about to politely decline so as to hasten what was sure to be an unpleasant visit, but this time it was William who got in the first word.

"Tea would be wonderful Mrs. Kerschner, if it's not too much trouble."

"It's no trouble at all, Mr…"

"Oh, I'm terribly sorry. We do have you at a disadvantage. I am William Riley and this is April Smith."

"Mrs. Kerschner," April now piped up, "I work for the Detroit Institute of Arts and Mr. Riley here is the foremost expert on your unique piece of needlework."

"Wonderful! I'm so excited and pleased you've come. Perhaps you can answer some questions I have about it. No one else has a clue. Let me put on some water for the tea, and then we can sit and talk all about it."

After April watched the elated woman turn the corner, she turned to William and punched him in the arm.

"Ow! What was that for?" William winced as he rubbed the site of April's surprise assault.

"You know," his companion hissed. "We agreed to get this over as soon as possible! We have a plane to catch… remember?"

"Yeah, tomorrow morning," he whispered back. "What did you expect me to do, grab the dang thing and run out the door like some kind of repo man? This day is going to be a lot worse for her than it is for us, so let her play the proud hostess for a few more minutes. Besides…"

April sat down on a nearby sofa and motioned for William to join her.

"What? Besides what, William?"

William was just about to reply to that question when Marla appeared with a plate of assorted cookies and placed them on the coffee table in front of them.

"These are leftover from a party we had recently celebrating the newspaper article. I had them in our fridge, so they may be a bit cold… Take one… I'll be back in a moment."

"Things just don't add up" said William in a slightly louder voice. "I've been wondering about this since before we left Detroit. If her husband stole the tapestry while he was on Beaver Island, why did he let her be interviewed? No one is so foolish as to wave around stolen artwork for all the world to see."

"What was that about 'stolen artwork'? Are you implying that my sampler was stolen?"

Marla Kerschner stood in the threshold between the kitchen and living room with a silver tea service in her hands and a scowl on her face. Both young people rose from the couch as she edged forward, placed the tea service on the table next to the tray of cookies, and then straightened up with her arms folded across her chest.

"Ah, yes..." said April. "Mrs. Kerschner, my colleague and I have some questions about how you came to be in possession of the Strang Tapestry. There's no question as to its authenticity, but we are at a loss about some other matters."

"What is the Strang Tapestry?" asked the increasingly irate woman. "You know, before I say or do one more thing, I'm going to need to see some identification."

William reached into his rear pants pocket for his wallet, and April reached for and opened her briefcase.

"The Strang Tapestry," April began to say as she handed her DIA employee card to their hostess, "is the name of the needlepoint sampler you have hanging in your hallway."

Marla examined April's identification and also William's business card identifying him as curator of the Beaver Island Historical Museum. She handed them back and sat down in a chair opposite the sofa.

April exchanged her identification for the file folder containing the photograph of a white-gloved William holding up the Strang. She handed it to

Marla who looked at it and then cast her eyes to the man seated across from her.

"My husband," Marla began to say in a flat tone, "went on a fishing trip to Beaver Island last month. Are you suggesting he stole — what did you call it — the Strang Tapestry, while he was there?" Marla handed the photo back to April and sat back in her seat, enveloped in defeat.

"No, Mrs. Kerschner," William answered. "We just don't have a good understanding of how the Strang got from a locked, roll-top desk in Michigan to your wall in Texas."

"We were hoping," added April, "you could enlighten us."

As April finished speaking, the sound of a garage door being opened could be heard coming through the living room wall. Marla answered April as her eyes snapped toward the noise; the anger in her voice as obvious as sin.

"No, *I* haven't the slightest idea, but I know someone who does."

Marla rose from her seat as did William and April. For many seconds, silence filled the room as the trio waited for Phil Kerschner to make his anticipated entrance. When he finally dropped his car keys on the kitchen counter and entered the living room, he found himself staring back at three sets of questioning eyes.

"What going on? Has someone died?"

"Not yet," spat his wife.

"You won it in a poker game?"

Marla and William looked at each other because they had both spoken those words in perfect unison. Marla turned back to her husband and continued by herself.

"Phil Kerschner, you son-of-a-bitch, you said you bought it for me!"

"Now wait one damn minute, here," Phil replied. "I did not tell you how I got it. You just *assumed* I bought it for you, Marla. Besides, in a way, I did!"

"What does that mean, Phil?" asked his wife, taking this moment to sit back down in her chair.

"Your friend," Phil continued, but now addressing William, "what's his name?"

"Perry."

"Yeah, your buddy Perry asked me what I thought was worth fifty bucks. He took us around that museum of yours, but it all looked like junk to me... no offense, son."

"None taken," replied William, himself sitting down; done-in by Phil's revelation.

"Anyway," continued Phil, "he tried opening this old desk drawer because he said there was this gold-something inside it. He was so drunk Larry had to turn the key for him. Well, as soon as I saw it, I said, 'Yeah, that'll do.' So, he took it out and we went back to the game."

"Let me see if I understand you correctly, Mr. Kerschner," interjected April, herself sitting, "you got the Strang Tapestry from William's friend in lieu of fifty dollars?"

"Sure... That's the nut of it," Phil answered. "I thought it might be worth that much." April tilted her head in William's direction and rolled her eyes. Phil looked at his three gut-punched judges and attempted to further acquit himself: "Look here... it didn't matter. That turned out to be the last hand, anyway. Your friend passed out, and the rest of us decided to call it a night. We had to get a few hours of shut-eye because the ferry to Charlevoix was leaving at nine the next morning."

"William," April asked quietly, "did your friend have the authority to remove the Strang Tapestry from that drawer?"

"I don't... yeah," William shrugged, "I guess so. I operate the museum, but the tapestry is part of the Whitney Family Collection and Perry — as king — is the technical head of the Whitney family. Honestly, it's his to do with as he pleases."

"See, Marla," Phil gloated, "it was a legit deal! And I did get it with you in mind. So, what do you have to say about them apples?"

Phil's sheepish wife got up from her seat and gave her husband a tentative hug.

"But, these people came looking for it Phil. Maybe they want it back?" Turning to face William and April, she asked them, "Is that why you came here... to take it back?"

April began saying something about the historic nature of the Strang Tapestry, but William tugged on her elbow, asked the Kerschner's for a moment to speak with her in private, and took April out toward the front door. There, they carried on a quiet conversation the Kerschner's could not hear. A minute later, it was over and the two young people returned to the living room.

"Mrs. Kerschner," said April, "as far as we can determine, your husband is correct: this was a legitimate transaction, albeit an odd one. We do not have the authority to compel you to return it."

William noted the look on Marla's face now matched the elation with which she first greeted them. This time, the hug she gave her husband was anything but tentative.

He and April began to collect their things — the tea unpoured and the cookies uneaten. The duo made their farewells to the happy tapestry owners and were escorted to the front entrance. Marla had one final question for them after Phil opened the door.

"Oh, Ms. Smith, for how much should we insure the tapestry?"

April looked over to William who nodded. She said, "Mrs. Kerschner, I'm not authorized to give you advice in a matter like this. All I can say is that if the Detroit Institute of Arts owned that piece, we would not insure it for anything less than five hundred thousand dollars. Please enjoy the rest of the evening."

As April and William reached the rental car, the Kerschner's remained in the doorway to their home staring at the departing couple with their mouths open. April saw them and smiled.

"I believe we saved their marriage... or perhaps prevented a homicide."

"Possibly," replied William as he opened his door and got into the rental, "I doubt she would have killed him if we left with the Strang, but — yeah — given how angry she was at the prospect of having to return it..."

"Well," April sighed as she, too, got in, "lose an expensive tapestry but save a marriage... not bad for one day's work."

The drive back to the car rental agency was difficult for April. Silence again filled the space between them as William's attention seemed taken up by Dallas's version of suburbia. April's thoughts, on the other hand, gave way to her brain's more pressing need to keep them out of a traffic accident.

Before she was able to adequately process the anti-climatic event this day had become, April realized they were standing in front of the door leading into William's hotel suite.

"I didn't expect you to leave the Strang with the Kerschner's," she said.

"I know what you mean," William replied nodding his head. "It wasn't my original plan, I'll admit. But once it became clear to me Perry could have told me where it was from the start, I realized that even if he didn't let it go on purpose, he sure didn't want it back. I can't blame him... he never wanted to be the king."

"But, William," April gushed, "it's worth so much money! And what about Mr. Risner? He wants the Strang for the institute's State of Michigan Collection."

"You know... the people of Beaver Island — and my family in particular — have thought so much about that cloth that we kept it hidden in a drawer for over a century and took it out once a year like it was some kind of prophetic rodent. As far as I'm concerned, the Strang is right where it belongs: with people who will truly love and appreciate it. And as for John Risner, well... he can negotiate with the Kerschner's now."

William inserted his keycard and turned the handle when the light showed green. April stopped him from entering with a hand to his arm. "But, what about you? How can you go home empty-handed?"

"Oh, no," William replied with smiling eyes, "I found what I *needed* to find. Have a good evening."

With that, William kissed April on the cheek, entered his hotel room, and gently closed the door to his suite.

~   ~   ~   ~   ~

April had been sitting on one of her hotel room's two beds for the last thirty-three minutes; her head in her hands and weeping in utter frustration. In her whole life, she had never before felt so lost. She reached over and picked up the room's telephone in order to call her mother, wiped her eyes, and then remembered her mother owned no cellphone, and — even worse — April had no idea where her mother was this time of the day. April slammed the handset back down onto the base unit.

"What *is* the matter with me?" she asked the space around her. "This should be a no-brainer! He's white… I'm black… case closed!"

April's heart, however, knew the situation was far more complicated than her simple equation implied. The truth was, she ached for William to kiss her again. April touched and traced her fingers across the cheek which had received his most-recent one; her skin giving the false signal that his lips were still there. She again tried to justify her logic.

"I've known him for less than a month…"

From some deep, unimpeachable place within April's psyche came the rebuke to all these pathetic rationalizations and it burst forth into her consciousness like a sunrise.

"He loves *all* of you, girlfriend!"

Now that April understood the shape of their relationship, all the pieces which had been puzzling her for at least a week began falling into place: Her body, she now recognized, oozed desire whenever William was near. Her brain, however, warned her not to jeopardize her career.

"Am I really in-love with him?"

April possessed scant experience by which to make that determination. She did, though, have one means of measuring her feelings, but feared to use it. Passion and reason were in mortal combat over her destiny. Then passion chose that moment to gain the upper hand...

William heard a quick succession of raps on the door connecting April's suite to his. He was naked and peeking around the corner toward the source of the sound. The shower was running and he was just about to step into the tub.

"William," April called out to him, "open this door. I need to speak with you. It's important."

"Um, April, I know I said we would talk later, but I was just about to take a shower. All I have on is a towel," he yelled as he grabbed one and wrapped the plush fabric around the lower half of his body in order to make true his statement.

"It doesn't matter. We need to talk right now!"

"Can you give me a minute to put on some clothes?"

"No, just open the door, please."

William — who had made his way over to the connecting door by this point — reached out to unlock and open it, but hesitated. He said under his breath, "This isn't a good idea."

Then again, April sounded like she was about to break down the connecting door if he didn't do as she asked, so he did. What he saw when the barrier swung open almost made him drop his towel...

William never imagined any woman could be so top to bottom beautiful, but April — standing before him in nothing save a matching set of purple-flowered undergarments — erased every prior fantasy he ever had concerning females of the species. Her breathing was labored, as if she had been running, and the effect made her breasts rise and fall. William noted how they were keeping perfect time with his own beating heart.

He floated to her through the threshold, and the two of them embraced as if the moment had been rehearsed a hundred times. April released her lips from his and placed them near her love's left ear

"I want you *so* much, William! Please make love with me..."

William felt the heat radiating from April's body and marveled at the smoothness of her flesh upon his own. He looked down. In spite of their differences in hue, he was having difficulty determining where his skin ended and hers began. April's fragrance was a tonic he forever wanted to imbibe. But, from some taste and odor-free corner of his mind, a single, sane thought crashed his euphoria.

"Yes!" it said to William. "But not like this! Not like this!"

Without speaking, William took April's hand and led her over to the bed where she had removed and folded her outer garments. The two of them again pressed their lips together amid a frenzy of stroking and hugging.

April reached around behind her back to release the clasp to her bra. William shook his head and brought her hands back around and placed them within his between their bodies. April looked at her beau with questioning eyes. William answered her thoughts by reaching past April to grab her blouse. He held it up so that she might put her arms through the sleeves.

"April, I love you more than I can ever say with words," William began, "and I so much want to make love with you right now and for the rest of my days. But we just *can't* do this... not when we're about to go our separate ways. If we have sex now, we could never be sure if it's out of love or merely desperation."

April felt the soft material caress her fingers as each arm gained entrance to her recently shed top. She actually surprised herself by how easily she was permitting William to dress her — first her blouse, and then other things. He was slow and gentle in his actions, and it was no small irony to April that William was doing this loving and grace-filled act dressed only in a towel.

William bade April to sit on the bed. He bathed her feet and legs in kisses before rolling each nylon up and securing it to the garter belt he had put back on her moments earlier.

From William's perspective, dressing the woman he loved was not at all a fight against his passions. Because he had made peace with his emotions, this was more so an assurance of not taking advantage of April. And, from his stance, she was vulnerable — and not just because she was half-naked. William knew in spite of how April had greeted him, she had yet to resolve her inner conflict between love and career.

William bent down to pick up April's skirt which had fallen to the floor. She placed her hand on his shoulder to stop him and said, "You don't have to do any more, William. Please sit across from me."

"Don't feel embarrassed April," William said, taking a spot on the other bed, "and I hope you understand I'm not rejecting you. It's just that…"

April held up her hand which had the desired effect. She spoke softly, "It's ok, William, I do understand. And you're right… I am desperate for you. I didn't realize how desperate until a few minutes ago. Thank you for being a gentleman and giving me the space to sort all this out. I know now I'm in-love with you. But, you've been trying to tell me all day that love isn't enough, is it?"

William was silent for a moment, then he voiced what both of them were thinking: "We would be fools to ignore our racial differences. Sure, there are pressures from society to consider, but it really comes down to our families. What would your parents say if they knew I was white? Hey! I'm sorry, April. I don't even know if your folks are alive."

"Don't worry," she smirked, "they are, but *I* might not be if I told them about us. I had the thought earlier to phone my mother, and I would have, but other things got in the way. What about your parents?"

"Well, they *are* good friends with an African-American couple, so I know they aren't racists. But, I don't know how they might react if I told them the woman I want to marry is black."

April rose from her bed and sat down next to William. She took one of his hands in one of her own; slipping her fingers in between his; asking, "You really want to marry me and not just date me? Now who's being desperate?"

William blushed and looked down at their joined appendages. He replied, "I'm not desperate, April. I've just figured out my feelings faster than you have. The way I see it, your feelings will either catch up to mine or they won't."

"All or nothing at all, right?"

William brought his head up, looked deeply into April's eyes, and nodded his head. This time, it was he who got a peck on the cheek. April stood and pulled William up after her. She said in a louder voice, "Go on... go take your shower... only it better be a cold one! I think you'll need it. I know I will."

~ ~ ~ ~ ~

William rapped lightly on April's hotel room door. A few moments later, she opened it.

"Good morning, April... I'm all packed. I thought we might want to take advantage of the restaurant here in the hotel before taking the shuttle to the airport."

The manner in which April considered the man standing in front of her made William think he might be a selection on her menu.

"I dreamed of you last night..." she said as she reached out for his hand. William gave it to her.

"Same here..." he responded, "just like every night for the last ten days. But, it's going to take more than dreams to solve our problem." Even as he said this, William found himself leaning through the opening to meet April mouth to mouth. The kiss was as wet as it was magnetic — dragging their bodies into a collision as close as can be accomplished while clothed.

"Good morning, William," April managed saying after they disengaged. "Breakfast sounds great. Why don't you go grab us a table while I finish packing? I'll only be a minute."

"My thoughts, exactly... see you in a few." With reluctance, William exchanged April's torso for his luggage and moved off toward the elevator.

It couldn't have been much more than a minute after William got seated that April showed up at the entrance to the restaurant. William stood and waved to her. She came over with her own bags in hand.

"We have about two hours..." April said as she set down her luggage and took her seat, "... before our flight is scheduled to depart. I called the airline and they told me it's still listed as being on time."

April adjusted her clothes and placed the napkin on her lap. When she looked up to engage William's face, he was looking around the room with a strange expression reflecting back to her.

"William, did you hear what I said?" she asked.

"I heard... two hours... on time..." he replied absently. "April, why are all these people staring at us?"

The question pulled April from the bucolic contentment her mind had been in and back to a reality she hadn't experienced in a long time. She scanned the restaurant and confirmed what William saw: most of the other patrons were indeed staring at them.

"This is Texas, William," she deadpanned.

"What does Texas have to do with anything?"

April smiled, shook her head, reached out her right hand to grasp the crystal tumbler before her, and took a sip of ice water.

"You don't have a prejudiced bone in your body, do you," she stated setting the tumbler back down. "It's a big reason why I love you, William. I hope you know that. But, you must also know you and I are in the minority. There remain plenty of people in this country who don't want to see blacks and whites together. Besides, people stared at us in New York City, too."

"Yeah… but not like this! If looks could kill, then we'd be dead. Does this sort of thing happen to you all the time?"

"Not all the time," April replied. "In fact, it happens far less now than it used to. Mostly, I just ignore it… and so should you, William."

A young waiter approached their table and spoke softly to them: "You folks ain't from 'round these parts, are ya?" William shook his head in response. "Well, let me tell ya, mister, ya picked juss 'bout the worst place in the Dallas area to bring your girlfriend. As for me, I don't personally care a hoot… I'm from Austin. If ya want my advice, get something that eats quick. Either that, or grab some chow at the airport," he said, eying their luggage.

William looked to April and then back to the waiter. William replied with a tinge of irritation in his voice, "To hell with them! Will you serve us?"

The twenty-something restaurant employee indicated with a slight nod of his head that he would, but said no more.

"Fine," William continued. "I'll have a cheese Danish and some hot tea. April?"

"I'll have the same. Thank you."

The waiter turned to leave — himself looking around the room at the other customers as he did. When he got out of ear-shot, April cleared her throat.

"It's not easy being in love with me, is it?"

At hearing that, William pulled his energy back to April and bore his concentration into her eyes.

"April, you couldn't be more wrong. Loving you is the easiest thing I've ever done in my life… and the best! Let them stare; who knows, maybe they're jealous because you're so beautiful?"

April's smile broadened at his comment and she took in another sip of water as William continued to speak.

"What's not easy is knowing I have to leave so you can think about what you want. For me, at least, that part is going to feel like dying."

Two and one half hours later, William watched Texas recede from his window seat as the airplane rose higher and higher into the hot, morning air. The region recently experienced its first taste of rain in months, but the moisture had made only the briefest of appearances. Now, drought was again at the state's doorstep.

William sat there with his right arm around April as she snuggled up to him with her head in the crook of his shoulder — the center armrest raised and tucked in between their seat-backs.

At that moment, an odd analogy popped into his head: "I'm going through the same process as that land below. For years, the thought of being in-love has been as insubstantial as a Texas rain cloud; the result being a life so dry it might have been blown away by the weakest of breezes."

William was lightly stroking April's arm. He turned his head and was met by her closed eyes and peaceful features. April, he realized, had burst onto him like an autumn thunderstorm and had brought with her something he hadn't even realized he was without: completeness as a human being. But this quality would evaporate the moment he stepped foot onto the bus back to Beaver Island; and William knew he would go back there as surely as April would go back to her career.

William kissed the top of April's head. She stirred and looked up at him. They both shifted in their seats, placed their arms around one another, and kissed. Some of the other passengers around them stared, but this time neither April or William noticed, nor would they have given a hoot if they had.

When April pulled her lips away from his, William asked her a question, "That felt like a 'good-bye kiss'... was it?"

The joy which shone from April's face faded and then collapsed entirely under the weight of that sad query. William could see the beginnings of tears welling up in April's eyes. He gently placed his left hand on her cheek and — with his thumb — wiped away her escaping emotions.

"Don't cry, April," William spoke in a whisper. "We have to do this. As much as I want to be with you, if I don't go back to Beaver Island, you will *never* have the space you need to figure all this out."

"I know, William," April replied as she straightened up in her seat. Taking hold of his moistened hand, she continued: "We've both been living in a kind of unreality, and while we are in it our love makes perfect sense." William smiled and nodded his head while April finished her thought: "But, will that sense stand up to the demands and pressures of our real lives? That's the test, isn't it?"

"Yes…"

"I'm sad," she finished, "because I'm sure it's a test I can't pass."

"I know what you mean, April," William concurred. "We're asking a lot from one another… more than most couples can generally expect or deliver. But look, we are still in our *unreality* as you call it for a few hours. Let's enjoy it while it lasts. One way or another, the rest will take care of itself."

"I'll agree to that, William, but would you please call me when you get home?"

"April, you know we can't do that or anything which smacks of normal boyfriend/girlfriend stuff. We are *way* past any dating phase in a relationship. We already know how we feel... we just need to determine how committed we are to those feelings."

"So... right up to when I drop you off at the bus station this evening, we have it all. Is that what you're saying?"

"And when I get on that bus," William continued, "the nothing at all takes over... yes, that's exactly what I'm saying. We have to be together on this, sugar, or we don't stand a chance."

"You called me *sugar*, William! That's what my father calls me," April said as joy rushed back to fill her face. "So what if I decide I want it all?"

"Come look for me," said William with a shrug of his shoulders. "Heaven knows I'll be easier to find than that old rag."

They broke out in gentle laughter which ended as April followed along with the next obvious question: "But, what if I *don't* come looking for you?"

It was William's turn for his smile to fade into oblivion. The look on his face not only passed through April, but pierced the veil of time to glimpse some as-of-yet brutal moment. He continued stroking her hair, and it appeared to

April he was unable to respond. William eventually cleared his throat.

"We'll still love each other, April. We'll just not get to see how beautiful our children would be."

With those words, April realized the entire day was one, long, gut-wrenching good-bye kiss.

~ ~ ~ ~ ~

The door to April's apartment closed, and the young woman glided past her small kitchen and into her living room. Seemingly without direction from her brain, the scarf and coat she had been wearing were shed and draped over the back of a nearby chair.

April looked around at her surroundings and thought to herself how unfamiliar and how much lonelier they seemed to be. It wasn't fair, she knew, to blame her current emotional state on her living space.

"I'm the lonely one," she confessed as she placed both hands on top of her overcoat and dropped her head in exhaustion. "William, you were right!" she called out in a voice which chanced waking her neighbors. Then she lowered her tone to continue, "Your absence does feel like nothing at all."

April glanced at the clock which hung over her kitchen sink. It confirmed what she was feeling within her body: the day was almost completely spent.

The bus from Detroit had been over an hour late in getting to Southfield. And the only good thing about that was the extra time it gave her and William to cry with and console one another. In the process, though, the condensation within April's car had become so thick, they were forced into the chilled air just to make sure they saw the bus when it arrived.

April pushed her body away from the chair and went over to her telephone answering machine. She scrolled through the names and numbers. As she expected, her mother had tried to contact her repeatedly earlier in the evening. So had Jeremiah Wheeler.

April wanted to call her mother in spite of the lateness of the hour: she yearned for someone to pour out her heart to, and her mother certainly fit the bill.

"But if I tell her what's been going on," April mused, "I'll have to tell her William is white." She sighed and knew she was not ready for *that* conversation. Neither was she ready for any confrontation with Jeremiah. She collapsed onto her easy chair and rubbed her puffy eyes.

April had to keep reminding herself William was white even though it was one of the reasons she felt certain their relationship wouldn't survive.

"A white boy!" she effused. "Toss this relationship into the 'experience file,' girlfriend," April quietly told herself as she pretended to shoot hoops with a nearby trashcan. "At least you now know what *actual* love feels like."

"Yeah," her inner voice replied, "it feels like the world's greatest massage followed by the world's worst car crash."

As April rose to begin making preparations for bed, she tried to assure herself that soon everything would be ok. She would give Mr. Risner the Kerschner's telephone number, along with her opinion on how open they might be to selling the Strang Tapestry. The look on their faces had told April everything she needed to know: this was going to be a fantastic gift for her boss.

"I wonder if it will be enough of one for me?"

~ 12 ~

April ran past Marshall Fredericks' grave. Every time she entered Greenwood Cemetery, she made it a point to pass by the sculpted gazelle which crowned his marker. April guessed if her friends and family knew this was how she often spent her weekend mornings, they might think her a bit off the beam. For her, though, the place was a runner's paradise: quiet, open spaces; scant vehicular traffic; and plenty of nature for her to take pleasure in running past.

Because April lived near the by-passed section of downtown Birmingham (a block west of Woodward Avenue), her choice to run through the cemetery made sense. By the time she walked over to it, her legs were stretched enough to safely transition to running. And after her six-mile course was completed, the distance was again perfect to cool down over.

As April ran, she thought about William. For her, this was new ground: it was the first time she permitted herself to think about *any* guy during one of her running sessions. Today was also just the second time since meeting William that April had made the choice to do any running at all.

April grasped this moment as a chance to fully jump back into her previous, William-less life. But, this particular session wasn't being as helpful as she had hoped it would be; her leg muscles and lungs groaned in that particular way which belied a lapse in athletic routine.

"Tomorrow will be easier, girlfriend," she said to herself as a kind of motivational mantra. "You just watch… on Sunday, you are gonna *kill* this course!"

An hour later, April was a sweat-soaked mess as she walked the final hundred feet back to her apartment and felt for her pulse on her left wrist. She arrived, but continued to pace around waiting for her number of heartbeats per minute to drop below seventy. That was always her cue: the session didn't end until that level was achieved. April prided herself on maintaining a resting pulse which hovered near fifty-five… most of the time.

Lately, she was sure that had not been the norm. Whether it was due to sitting behind her desk or from being in-love, she blamed William for her elevated numbers: "Not that he even knows anything about this side of me," she silently realized. "But, regardless, I *am* out of shape."

When April closed the door to her apartment, she noted the light on her answering machine blinking — telling her a message was in the process of being recorded. She ignored the device.

April hated the decision to brush aside her mother's attempts at calling her, but by the time she had crawled into bed Friday night, she knew this *test* William was asking her to go through was something she needed to do without assistance.

"Can I live my life and be happy without him in it?" she remembered asking herself while laying there under her flannel sheets. April spent hours in bed in an elusive search for sleep. Time and again she came back to that question above all other questions. At four o'clock Saturday morning, sleep found her. At half past eight, sleep decided it was needed in a different time zone.

This fact lay behind April's decision to return to her usual activities. Reengaging with her routine of running was the first element in April's plan. Going out to lunch with an old high school girlfriend was the second element.

At 12:30 p.m., Saturday afternoon, April strode into a cafe in Birmingham frequented by the women and men of her generation. Her friend Sarah was already seated in a two-person booth off to the left and was facing the door. They waved to each other and April began unravelling her scarf. She tossed it onto the bench against the wall, but left her coat on.

"What's new, April?" her friend asked. "It's been, what… like three weeks since we last got together. Have you really been *that* busy?"

"I've been more than busy, Sarah," April said. "Let's see... I've been to New York City... to Dallas... you?"

"Go on... rub it in. You know I'm stuck in Warren for at least another year."

"Still," April pointed out, "...working for GM at their Tech Center — that must be heaven for an automotive engineer."

"It's young, good-looking, well-paid, single guy heaven, April," her friend replied with a glint in her eyes. "Do you know the ratio of single female engineers to single male engineers?"

"No, but math was always one of your best strengths, Sarah. So, am I to assume by your comments you are dating someone?"

"Not *someone*, April! I've been on dates with twelve different men just since the beginning of the month."

"Wow!" April said with a tinge of disgust mixed with her surprise. "Seems to me either you are playing the field or the field is playing you, girlfriend. Say, have you placed your order yet?"

Sarah looked at April with unrestrained anger in her eyes. April knew her mouth had just gotten her into trouble... again, but after what she had recently been through, April was in no mood to hear about Sarah's score-keeping.

"What's gotten into you, April? I haven't seen this side of you in seven years. Go on... spill it!"

"What? To you? No possible way will I share with you anything about my love life, Sarah! You are one of the biggest gossips in Oakland County."

The cafe's teenage waitress interrupted them to take their drink orders and then moved off.

Sarah looked around and lowered her voice, saying, "I know you all too well, April. You can't share what doesn't exist."

"You are more right than you can ever know, Sarah," April spat, "so let's just move on to the weather, sports, or one of the other banalities we usually yammer on about when we're together."

Instead of taking April's advice, Sarah got up from the table, grabbed her overcoat and hat, and exited the cafe without further comment.

April put her head in her hands and rebuked herself for her rude behavior: "Well, that certainly wasn't part of any plan," she said under her breath.

The waitress came back over, asking sweetly, "Is your friend coming back?"

"I don't believe so. Don't bother bringing her drink."

"Do you still want something to eat?"

"Yes," said April looking over the menu. "I'll have a cheese Danish... and please change my drink to hot tea."

"Yes, Miss..."

~ ~ ~ ~ ~

A bracing wind blew through William's hair as he stood on the foredeck of the ferry. The boat rocked noticeably from side to side; movement caused by the four-foot swells all around them.

William gripped the railing and reflected on the journey he had made in the last twenty days. It had been much more than a geographic voyage: he had experienced a sea-change in attitudes and priorities. Yet, nothing could top the delicious discovery of love coupled with the agony of letting it go.

The longer William stood there, the more he realized what he'd let go of was only the hope of love. What he felt for April — and he was sure she felt for him — may have been real, but it wasn't the entire reality between them. That reality included their racial differences, but even that wasn't the most difficult factor weighing-in against them.

April, William knew, was a woman in possession of a job she valued greatly. He understood their love was a threat to that career — and that there was literally nothing he could do about it.

William had great respect for reality when it came to relationships. He knew from previous experience love between two people was never enough to overcome any differences they might have. He knew, as well, that differences came in two types: differences of substance and differences of style.

William discovered that differences of substance were things like fundamental values, religion, and attitudes about children. These would wreck any relationship no matter how deep the love. He had learned the hard way that while there weren't as many of these differences, they were always the deal-breakers.

Differences of style were another matter. William learned that every couple shared hundred of these. What mattered was how these differences were perceived. Were they celebrated by the couple, merely tolerated, or just plain ignored? One bit of irony was this: how a person perceived differences of style was itself a difference of substance.

So, too, was the weight a person gave to his or her career. William felt no anger toward April for her choice of job over him. Had April entered his world a few months ago, he would have made the same choice. Now, no job William might do would ever again be that important to him.

Beaver Island grew larger on the northwestern horizon. A light rain began to fall, or perhaps it was just the spray thrown into the air by the ship's bow. Whatever the source, it persuaded William to return to the enclosed cabin. The ferry was nearly empty. He chose a seat next to one of the many windows.

William looked at his hands. He was surprised to see they weren't shaking like they normally would be on this trip. At first, he thought it was because he had become emptied of all feeling. Then, the real reason came to him: He wasn't numb as he first surmised. The events of these last weeks had simply placed this ferry ride into its proper context. William lifted his hands and turned them over and back again. Their steadiness established the truth: he now knew what real turbulence felt like, and this wasn't it.

And yet, William *was* empty — just not in the way he first imagined himself to be. In spite of finding the Strang Tapestry, he was returning home without it. He had found something even more precious, but a relationship with April increasingly looked to be a hollow pursuit as well.

The only object of value he was returning to Beaver Island with (besides his suit) was a new-found sense of self. While he cherished it, this rebirthed identity meant *new* William would never go back to *old* William's job. So, he would be without that, as well.

William shook off this shroud of gloom and mentally reviewed the plan he would set into motion as soon as he disembarked: "I'll see Perry as soon as possible… if for no other reason than to inform him about the Strang. But, I also need to tender my resignation. Perry will have to take it to the village council for their approval. But, first things first: I need to sleep."

The captain's voice sounded from the ship's intercom informing the passengers and crew the ship was five minutes from docking. William stood and made his way to the lower deck where he'd left his luggage and from where all persons exited the vessel. He exchanged greetings with a crewman who had taken up his position nearby.

This ferry was the same one piloted by William's grandfather up until the man's death. As a child, William had known every member of the crew by name. These ferrymen, though, were strangers to him. William wondered if the residents of Beaver Island would appear to him just as strange. "I suspect I'll look different to them," he thought. "Heck, I hardly recognize myself anymore!" In William's way of thinking, this alone was proof positive his new resolve was not a fleeting thing but a substantial change.

The ship made her final approach to dockside and was promptly secured. William heard the whine of the motorized winch used to lower the ramp. Its job was completed when the clang of metal on metal pealed throughout the open compartment. William looked to his watch. It told him it was 5:35 in the evening; only five minutes past the scheduled arrival time.

Six passengers disembarked, including William who was the first one off. With his luggage in hand, William walked past empty slips and small watercraft hoisted onto metal-framed dry-docks.

He paused to say hello to neighbors he passed in the street. William smiled and made small-talk as he made his way back to his apartment like he'd been gone only a few hours. The sheer unreality of these conversations first surprised, but ultimately horrified William.

"I can't believe how two-dimensional everyone now seems," he said to himself as he opened the main door to his apartment building.

Upon entering his flat, William dropped his luggage in the spare bedroom, took off his coat and earmuffs, laid those on top of the luggage, and walked directly to his refrigerator. He opened it and grasped a bottle of water. This he opened and drank in one, long series of swallows. There were no phone messages for William to sort through because he did not own an answering machine.

William completed all the chores which needed doing before he could permit himself the luxury of taking a nap. He had been hungry as well as thirsty, but fatigue was the more insistent tempter.

Within ten minutes of returning home, William was asleep on his bed fully clothed down to his shoes. Except for a drowsy trip to the toilet sometime on Sunday, he would not fully awaken until Monday morning.

~ ~ ~ ~ ~

Monday morning unfolded just as April thought it might. Now she was returning to her office after conferring with Mr. Risner and giving him the written report concerning the Strang

Tapestry which she had assembled Sunday afternoon and evening.

Her boss was even more delighted by the information than she first anticipated and agreed with her assessment that the Strang was now far more obtainable than it ever previously had been.

Between her work on the Strang Project and what she had been able to accomplish in New York City, John Risner informed April that a promotion and raise in salary would be coming her way.

April said she was happy about this turn of events, but her lack of any real enthusiasm so surprised her boss that he asked her what was wrong. She just smiled, shook his hand in thanks, and declined to say any more about it.

Her latest mission accomplished, the successful career woman sat behind her desk with her office door closed. April tried to look through the stack of inner-office memos which had accumulated in her absence, but her heart just wasn't into that kind of drudgery. She turned on her computer, but the moment her screen came alive, she switched it off again. Someone knocked on her door and April immediately sat up in her chair; saying, "Please come in."

The door swung aside and the taut frame of Anthony Munoz stood considering his colleague with worry written across his brow.

"Is everything all right, April? Risner just filled a bunch of us in on what you've been up to, and I came by to say, 'Way to go, girl!', but he also said you didn't seem too pleased. Is there something I can do for you?"

"I don't know, Tony," said the melancholy girl, "but come on in. You might be the only person I can speak with right now. Close the door and sit down." Anthony did. As he was making his way to one of her chairs, April drew in a deep breath and asked, "Tony, what if Angelina had been a white girl? Would you still have married her?"

Anthony had not been expecting *this* question, but he sensed April was looking for honesty, so he gave it to her

"April, Angelina is half Caucasian. Her mother is from Minnesota. But, to me, it wouldn't have mattered if her daddy had been from there as well. Hey! Did I ever mention I was born in Mexico? My folks brought us into the United States illegally in 1976, — they told us — so we could watch the Bicentennial celebrations up close. I found out later my dad was just being funny, but he was dead serious about raising us in America."

"You're not still considered an illegal alien, are you, Tony?" April asked him.

"No, we got all that straightened out under President Reagan. But, listen up, April… we struggled for years trying to make it here. And every day, my parents told us we needed to hold onto the good things — and especially all the good people — this country had to offer us. My two sisters married anglos and my folks love them. Love, April… that's what it's all about. I love Angelina. I would have married her if she had been purple." April laughed at Anthony's last comment, and continued rocking back and forth in her chair; thinking on what he had told her. "This has to do with that Riley guy you've been hanging with for the last three weeks, doesn't it?"

"Why do you say that?" asked April as she ceased rocking.

"Come on, April! Do you think we're all blind here? There's not a person at the DIA who doesn't have an eye for detail. Those of us who know you best all knew by the time the two of you left for Dallas."

"Knew what, Tony?"

"What else? That you were in-love with one another. Jeez! You know, they made me go around wiping up the floor where the two of you had been drooling…"

April threw a pencil at Anthony, but was nevertheless laughing at his animated descriptions. "Oh, stop it, already! Ok, I'll admit it: we were in-love! You happy, now?"

"Happier, apparently, than you are." Anthony replied. "So, where is he? Did you guys break up?"

"No," April responded curtly, "you can't end a relationship until you begin one. Ours never really began… he wanted it to, but I was…" April looked at her friend and shrugged her shoulders.

"What, April… you were what?"

"I was… afraid," she finished casting her eyes up to the ceiling.

"Ok, you love each other, but you're afraid. So, I get that you asked me about Angelina because Riley is white, but April, it still doesn't answer my question, 'Where is he?'" The hesitation with which April resisted Anthony's question made him rise from his seat. "Look, you asked to speak with me, April. I want to help you, but I'm too busy to deal with your bull…"

"I'm supposed to go find him once I decide if I want to have it *all*," April blurted out. "It is like this test: is William more important to me than my career."

At hearing this, Anthony didn't leave, but neither did he sit back down. He just stood before his friend looking exasperated. He prodded her.

"Ok, so what did you decide?"

"I don't know, Tony. I'm supposed to give it some time…"

"Sweet Jesus!" Anthony yelled. "You rich kids are all the same: simplifying the complicated and complicating the simple. April, if it takes you longer than ten minutes to finish your little test, well then *hermanita*, you had better go back to school." Anthony now came around April's desk and turned her chair to face him. "Come on, April, was he just a white-boy plaything you had fun keeping on a leash, or are you desperate for him?"

April pushed Anthony away as memory of her abortive lunch with Sarah and her criticism of her friend's dating strategy flashed before her. April rose from her chair with all her latent frustrations now coming to full froth.

"What do you want to hear, Tony, that I couldn't sleep last night? Well, I couldn't! I can't eat, and I can't get him out of my head. And it doesn't matter to me that William is a white guy. I think it would be easier for me if race was the problem, but I'd be lying if I said that."

"So," Anthony stated with his arms folded across his chest, "you were being serious when you told me it's a choice between him or your career."

"Yeah, I am. I want him, Tony. But what happens to my career if I go after him?"

April collapsed back into her chair, and Anthony knelt down in front of her. He reached out to embrace April. She responded by hugging Anthony and weeping inconsolably into his shoulder.

April's colleague patted her on the back and then separated from her so he could continue their conversation.

"April, you are over-thinking this *test* of yours. In my opinion, the entire thing is a trick question… a false equation. There is no *choice* between him or your career. There's only the question, 'Do you want your work here to have *real* meaning?'"

"What do you mean? My work here has…"

"Stop, April!" Anthony interrupted. "It's me you're talking to, not Tom. You can be a robot… come in here day after day and do your job. That's the April I've known up to two weeks ago. A lot of people here at the DIA do it and nothing gets in their way. But, if you want your work here to have *real* meaning, that comes when you are being completely loved by someone and loving them back the same way — like we've seen with you and Riley. Wouldn't you agree, Mr. Risner?"

Unbeknownst to April, John Risner had entered her office and witnessed the latter half of her conversation with Anthony. He approached April's desk and sat down.

"He's right, April. You would be a fool to let William get away. In fact, he was a fool for not asking you to marry him, if he loves you half as much as I've seen your love for him."

April wiped her eyes, grabbed a tissue, and blew her nose. She responded saying, "He did ask me, sir. I just couldn't give him an answer."

"Well, young lady," John replied calmly, "it seems to Anthony and myself that you have your answer, don't you." John stood up and indicated to Anthony that he should do the same. He continued, "April, as of this moment, you are officially on vacation. You have two weeks. If I heard you correctly and you're supposed to go find William, well then, go find him. And when you do, tell him you came looking for him because you want your work around here to mean something special."

~ ~ ~ ~ ~

Joyce Whitney opened the backdoor of her home and motioned William into the mudroom just off her kitchen. William waved to her, entered, and then wiped his feet on the area rug just inside the door. She was still on the telephone — the long, coiled cord stretching impossibly across the length of the kitchen.

"No wonder I couldn't get hold of Perry," William deduced in silence.

Joyce brought the conversation to a quick conclusion with the words, "...he's standing right in front of me," hung up the handset, and turned to face William. "I heard yesterday morning that you got back," Joyce said cryptically. "Perry and I thought you might stop by Sunday evening."

"I don't remember much about Sunday... except it felt a lot like my pillow..."

Joyce nodded, then said, "Perry's down in his office."

"Right... Thanks, Joyce I'll..." William began to say, but Joyce cut him off.

"Before you go down there, I have something I want to show you. Come with me, Bill."

William closed the backdoor and did as instructed. She motioned him over to her husband's small desk in the corner of the dining room and lifted up Perry's odd calendar.

"What are you and Perry cooking up? The day you left," she continued, "he took this calendar — and one for next year — and created this odd countdown. Look…"

William took hold of the calendar for the current year as Joyce pointed to the space for October 23, 2000, (which was that present day). Under that number, Perry had written another: '160.'

William gave it back to Joyce and looked to her with indifference.

"So? What does it mean?"

"You tell me. Perry's numbering system runs backwards all the way to next April. And on April 1, 2001, there is a big red circle around that date. There's something going on here, and a lot of us on the Rock think that *something* is connected to the Strang Tapestry. Are we right? Do Perry's strange numbers have anything to do with the Strang?"

William smiled, shook his head, and let out a small chuckle — marveling at Perry's not-so-subtle way of telegraphing his true feelings.

"Joyce, I'd better let Perry explain this." She was about to protest William's statement, but he cut her off: "Look… I will say this: it does have something to do with the tapestry. I'm here to speak with Perry about it. When I'm done, I'll tell him to come up here and fill you in. That's the way this is going to work, Joyce. Now, if you'll excuse me..."

A dumbfounded Joyce watched as her usually mild-mannered and easy-to-manipulate neighbor strode out her backdoor and down the gently sloping hill to her husband's work shed.

William reached the structure's side entrance and found the door already open. Perry had his back to it, and so did not see his friend enter. The first indication Perry had that he was no longer alone was William's question to him.

"Hello, Perry. How about a game of poker?"

Perry spun around on his heels and looked into William's eyes trying to gauge his friend's mood, but an honest-to-goodness poker face stared back at him. He picked up a nearby rag and wiped the grime from his hands.

"Crap..." he huffed, "you found it already... Damn! I would have bet good money you wouldn't have been able to catch up to it so fast. Well, so much for that..."

"Haven't you just about scratched away any gambling itch you might have had?"

"Yeah..."

"What I don't get, Perry," William continued to say as he found a place to sit, "is you giving it up for just fifty bucks? If it had been me... I think I would have asked for at least a hundred."

"Be glad I didn't, Bill," Perry said as he found a spot to sit near his friend, "otherwise, it would have cost you more to get it back."

"You mean, it would have cost *you* more, Perry."

Perry closed his eyes, grimaced, and then reached into the rear left pocket of his pants for his wallet.

"What do I owe you, anyway?"

"Nothing."

"What do you mean, *nothing*? The guy didn't just hand that old rag over to you for free, did he?"

"I mean it didn't cost me anything to get it back because I didn't get it back. The Kerschners own the Strang Tapestry now. Phil Kerschner essentially bought it from you for fifty dollars."

Perry rose from his seat — a confused look plastered across his face — and struggled to find the right words to say.

"Bill," he finally spoke, "what kind of game is this? You could have gotten it back from them. Why didn't you?"

"Because after I heard about that poker game, I realized you didn't want it back. And, it turned out, I didn't want it back, either."

"Oh…" Perry let out in response as he retook his seat.

"What do you think folks will say when they find out what happened?" William asked his friend. "I spoke with Joyce before coming down here. Apparently everyone on the Rock knows something fishy is going on with the Strang Tapestry."

"What did you tell her, Bill? Oh God, you didn't tell her about that poker game, did you?"

"No, Perry, I haven't told *anyone* about that poker game, and neither will you! But, we're going to have to tell them something, so we better put our heads together and come up with a good reason why you sold the Strang."

"You got any bright ideas, old bud?"

"Not really, *old bud*… but, in my opinion, simplest is best — whatever you say, keep it simple… and vague. Don't start with grand details or you'll end up tripping over the lies and falling into a puddle of truth. Oh… I also came over here to give you this." William reached into his coat's inner pocket, then pulled out and handed to Perry his letter of resignation.

Perry opened the folded paper, read it, and then looked again at his friend; saying, "What's going on here, Bill? Nobody's going to blame you for the loss of the Strang. Why resign? Are you pissed at me for making you go on some wild goose chase?"

"Whoa! Slow down, Perry. My resignation has nothing to do with the Strang Tapestry or you sending me anywhere. It's just personal, that's all."

"What the hell does that mean?" asked Perry, standing once again.

"It means," William replied, standing up himself, "I found out my job isn't as important to me as it used to be. And, it also means I need time to think about my future."

"Whatever you say, Billy boy," said Perry after a moment or two of looking into his friend's face. Then Perry took a different tack if for no other reason than to change the subject. "So, Bill, how did you find it?"

"I didn't. April found it."

"Who is April?"

"April is Ms. April Anne Smith... one of John Risner's assistants. She is young, very pretty, and married to her work." William paced around Perry's organized chaos and passed his hands over his head trying to keep from saying too much about April.

"Your poker buddy, Phil," he continued, "gave the Strang to his wife. She got a write-up about it in their local newspaper. Eventually, April found the article. The woman's last name seemed similar to one of the names I put together on a list of people who had been to Beaver Island in the month of September. April matched the names and then read where the wife mentioned about some fishing trip her husband went on in Michigan. Bingo! We go to Texas, find the Strang, leave said Strang behind, end of story."

Perry's face took on a bemused look as he tried to keep up with his friend's synopsis of his last three weeks. He cleared his throat when it seemed like William had finished.

"So, what are you going to do now?"

"Don't know...you need anyone to help crew your boat next year?"

"What... you?" Perry laughed. "You hate the water. And even if you didn't, you're all thumbs when it comes to fishing. I'd lose business with you on board."

William stared at his friend with a mock expression of hurt. He replied, "Thanks for the vote of confidence..."

"Don't mention it," replied Perry, slapping his friend on the back. "But, hey... I'll see what I can do about helping you find another job. I owe you at least that much for *not* bringing the Strang Tapestry back here."

The two men stood in silence for a few moments until Perry intruded with a question which had been on his mind since William first left.

"I have to ask you one thing... The Strang... was it really worth half a million bucks?" William slowly nodded his head, a smile and dancing eyes slowly merging onto his face. "And it was mine to unload?" Perry continued asking.

Again, William silently confirmed that fact, but then felt compelled to do more.

"Yeah, but what's money compared to your freedom?"

"For that kind of money," replied the now dejected King Perry the First of Beaver Island, "I could have been a little less free for a little while longer…"

~   ~   ~   ~   ~

April had been awake for almost thirty-six hours straight. So, in spite of being given time to go find William, she felt the first best thing she could do for herself was to get some sleep.

She had arrived back at her Birmingham apartment shaking like someone possessed with seizures. It was the perfect external manifestation of how she felt on the inside; but not much of an asset when it came to resting.

"Sleep… yes! But not yet… First I have to call William… need to call him and let him know I'm on my way."

April ran over to her telephone, picked it up, and then dropped it on the floor because her hands had lost their ability to grip. That gave her inner voice the time it needed to slow down her thinking.

"NO!" it screamed to her in opposition. "Do *not* call that man. He told you there are no half-measures. Calling him makes it seem like you want him to come back down here to you. You must go to William and tell him in person."

April stood still and deliberately slowed down her breathing as she knew how to do. She carefully placed the telephone handset back on the base unit and sat down on the easy chair.

"I'm not going to take the easy way," she said out loud. "William found me. Now it's my turn to find him. But not yet, girlfriend... First you need some sleep. Then pack a bag and drive up to Charlevoix later this afternoon."

The mention of the town which connected Beaver Island to the mainland prompted April to get up. She needed to find a map of Michigan.

"Charlevoix... Charlevoix..." she repeated to herself, "where is that dang map?"

April searched through every drawer in her apartment until she found an old Michigan roadmap stuffed in the back of one of her kitchen drawers and unfurled it.

"Charlevoix has to be on the western side of the state... up by Traverse City somewhere... here it is!"

April put her left index finger on Charlevoix's location and her right index finger where Birmingham was. She consulted the map's distance guide between cities and found them to be almost three hundred miles apart. It was going to take her four hours or more just to drive there.

Even with her depleted mental faculties, April knew going to Charlevoix later on that day was not a good idea; she wouldn't get there until well after dark.

"Ok, then," she decided, folding up the map but leaving it on the countertop, "I'll leave for Charlevoix early Tuesday morning and get to Beaver Island by mid-day."

April went back over to her telephone and disconnected the power cord from the base unit. "Sorry, Mother…Jerry…" April spoke to the inert device, "but the next voice I want to hear is William's."

~　~　~　~　~

After his talk with Perry, William joined him as the two of them walked back up the hill to the Whitney's house. Instead of going inside with him to watch Perry tell Joyce the sanitized version of the Strang transaction they had concocted, he told Perry that he needed to go back home and call his folks.

William thought his father, especially, deserved to hear this story from his son before some other islander got to him. "Besides," he mused, "I haven't heard their voices in over three weeks. They must think I've dropped off the face of the planet!"

In every way which mattered, William realized this was precisely what had happened. When he finally dialed their number, his mother answered.

"Hello... O'Riley residence."

"Hi, Mom," William said sheepishly, "how are you?"

"Oh, Billy," Rachel answered, "I'm fine. What about you? Your father and I tried calling you last week, but you must have been out. You sound tired."

"I am, Mom, just not in the way you mean it. Hey, is Dad there, too? I need to speak with both of you."

"He's in his den. Just one moment, honey..." William could hear his mother call out for his father. "Jim! It's Billy on the line. He wants to talk to you." She then resumed speaking with her son, "What's happened? Are you in trouble?"

James O'Riley picked up the telephone in his study and added his voice to the conversation, "Hello, Bill. What's the news from home?"

William smiled to himself. His father always began their phone conversations the same way. It had gotten to be a kind of joke because usually there wasn't anything news-worthy from Beaver Island.

William took a deep breath and sat down on his sofa. This conversation was going to be the rare exception to the rule: "Well, that's why I'm calling you. There is, in fact, a lot of news to tell you both."

"Has someone died, Billy?" asked his mother.

"No, Mom, it's nothing like that. The news I have is that Perry Whitney sold the Strang Tapestry to a couple from Texas."

There was a long, silent void in the connection between Michigan and Florida which William's mother finally filled.

"Well, thank goodness for small miracles! I knew that boy had brains."

Taken aback by her outburst, William felt compelled to get some clarification. He asked, "What did you say, Mom? Dad, did you hear what she said?"

"I did, Bill," James O'Riley replied, "and if she hadn't said it, I would have. That damn piece of cloth has been a monkey on the back of every Whitney and O'Riley for the last hundred years. Good riddance to it!"

William was totally flummoxed. He simply hadn't expected this kind of response from his folks. Anger? Probably... Mild irritation? Maybe... But, outright glee? Never!

"Dad," William continued, "I don't understand. If you felt that way, then why did you allow me to take over from you at the museum?"

"It was what you wanted to do with your life, Bill. Who was I to get in the way of that?"

"In that case, Dad, you'll probably be glad to hear I've resigned as the museum's curator and as the head of the Chamber of Commerce... both effective immediately."

"I'll say this for you, Billy," Rachel gushed, "you've never been one to do something halfway! So, tell us... how did all this come about?"

"Actually, Mom, I'd rather tell you that in person. I've booked a flight for tomorrow from Traverse City to Chicago. I connect there with another flight to Tampa. I thought I would come down to Florida for a visit... if that's ok with you, that is."

"Son," replied his startled father, "are you kidding? That's great! We'll pick you up at the airport. What time does your flight arrive?"

"Dad, I'm not really sure. I made the reservations over the phone this morning. I wrote down the information, but I seem to have misplaced the paper it's on. The airline will have the tickets waiting for me in Traverse City. I tell you what... I'll call you from Chicago before the second flight departs."

"That sounds good to us, Bill," his father said.

At this point, William's mother couldn't help but be herself and offer a bit of motherly advice.

"Billy, are you sure you want to fly? You've never flown before. Maybe you could take the train instead."

"Actually, Mom, in the last three weeks, I've been to Detroit, New York City and Dallas... and I've flown four times."

"My God, Bill," his father exclaimed, "now *that's* what I call news! That must be some story you have. But, story or not, your mother and I will be glad to see you tomorrow. Have a safe journey. I'm going to hang up now and go pry the phone out of your mother's hand. Otherwise, you'll never get any sleep tonight. Bye, Bill!"

"Don't listen to him, Billy. He's the one who won't be able to sleep tonight. Good-bye, honey... I love you!"

"Love you, too, Mom," said a relieved William.

~ 13 ~

By Tuesday morning, news of the Strang Tapestry's sale was universal to the residents of Beaver Island. Except for a brief tirade laid upon Perry by his father, the news brought surprisingly little protest from the islanders. Those who did voice an opinion complained more about the secrecy of the transaction than about the transaction itself.

Perry told Joyce the tapestry was sold to cover a debt... leaving out the details about the value of the sale or the nature of the debt. From there, Joyce served as the perfect broadcaster of Perry's tale. By Monday evening, most folk on the island knew what had happened. Perry also took pains to absolve William of any involvement in the transaction.

William finished his breakfast and took care of his dishes. Ten minutes later, he hauled his cleaned and folded laundry from the basement laundry room and was repacking his suitcase. By eight o'clock, he was out the door and on his way to catch the morning ferry.

As he watched Beaver Island recede into the horizon, this time William felt he was going back to his life instead of away from it. He shook his head and marveled at the difference the last three weeks had made. And he thought of April. He hadn't told Perry — or even his parents — the whole story lest in speaking about his hope for love it might burst like a soap bubble. But, his feelings toward her were still as strong and as passionate as they ever had been.

By the time the ship docked in Charlevoix, William decided on a course of action designed to give his hope more substance.

"Certainly," he thought as he disembarked, "I should be able to find a suitable one in Florida which would fit April's tastes."

He would do it tomorrow morning. Perhaps it would turn out to be all for nothing, but William had to prepare himself for the possibility of it being all for everything.

He walked to Bridge Street — Charlevoix's main thoroughfare — and looked for the taxi he had hired to drive him the fifty-five miles to the Cherry Capital Airport in Traverse City. While in that vehicle going south, William unknowingly passed April as she drove north to find him. They had missed each other by less than one hour.

~ ~ ~ ~ ~

April held onto the guide rope as she made her way down the ramp from the ferry to the pier. Her only piece of luggage was a handbag draped over her shoulder which held two changes of clothes, her purse, some toiletries, and a few other things she thought she might need for her stay on the island. A larger suitcase containing the remainder of her vacation needs was back in Charlevoix in the trunk of her car.

The ferrymen helping to secure the pitching ship looked upon her with utter astonishment. It wasn't difficult for April to figure out why: she imagined few black women ever stepped foot onto Beaver Island by themselves.

"To these men," April realized, "I'm as rare as a hot day in winter." At this point, she really didn't care how uncomfortable her presence was making others feel. Someone had to know where William was. "On an island the size of this one," April continued thinking, "there couldn't be all that many places for him to be."

"Miss," a man asked her, "do you have any other bags?"

April shook her head as she pulled the collar of her clearly inadequate coat tighter around her neck. "I'm actually looking for someone. Can you help me?"

"I'm sorry, Miss, I don't live on the Rock — that's what the locals call this island. If you go to the King Strang Hotel over there," he said, pointing to it, "the woman behind the desk probably can help you… she knows everyone — and everything — on Beaver Island."

April nodded, shook his hand, and then began the slow, wind-swept trek to the large building in the direction the man had been indicating. Although it was mid-afternoon, the sky and season made it seem more like dusk.

The streets of St. James were mostly empty of people, but everywhere April looked, the lighted homes and businesses gave off the warm glow of community. Old cars dotted the streets, alleyways, and side lots of the village. And with every step she took, April felt as if she was walking further backward in time.

Ruth Doherty heard the hotel's front door open and looked up from her book. She wasn't expecting guests today, so she blinked twice over the top of her bifocals as a wind-blown, young black woman approached her desk. At Ruth's age, not much shocked her anymore. But...

"Between this girl, the mess in the museum, and the sale of the Strang," Ruth quipped under her breath, "October sure is turning out to be an exceptional month for surprises."

"Good afternoon," April spoke.

"May I help you, Miss? Were you looking to book a room?"

April ran her fingers through her hair in a vain attempt to undo nature's effects. She also readjusted the collar on her coat. She said, "No, ma'am, I don't think I need a room. But, I was told by one of the dockworkers you might be able to help me find someone. I'm looking for William Riley. Does he live anywhere near here?"

Ruth Doherty opened her mouth to speak, but then found she didn't know what to say. After a few seconds, she finally found her voice.

"Sweetie, I'm going to call our local township supervisor. I think you need to talk with him."

Now April became alarmed. She said, "Is that really necessary? I'm not here to cause any trouble."

"No," Ruth smiled and replied, "you don't understand. Billy O'Riley and Supervisor Perry Whitney are best friends. I'm pretty sure Billy left on the morning ferry and Perry may know where he went. It's too bad… you must have passed each other in Charlevoix."

"Are you certain we're talking about the same person? I believe William's last name is Riley, not O'Riley."

As Ruth dialed the Whitney's phone number, she looked upon April as a teacher might consider an error-prone student.

"Yes, sweetie, he's the same person. Billy dropped the O part of his name about ten years ago, but he's the only one who did. That's about as rebellious as kids around these parts get — still made his folk as angry as a disturbed nest of hornets."

A male voice answered and Ruth spoke to it: "Supervisor Whitney, there is a young woman here who needs to speak with you." There was a pause as Ruth listed to a question. "I don't know her name, but she says she's looking for Billy O'Riley." Ruth endured a second pause, then snapped: "Yeah... I thought you'd want to know... that's why I called!"

As she hung up the phone, Ruth spoke under her breath, "That apple sure fell close to the tree..." Returning her attention to the young woman before her, she asked, "What's your name, sweetie, and how do you know Billy? Tell me *all* about it while our esteemed supervisor gets his boots on."

April returned the woman's smile but began to wonder just how far back in time she had traveled.

~ ~ ~ ~ ~

Perry opened the outer door to William's apartment building for April. She stepped into the hallway and he followed right behind her continuing their conversation.

"No, I'm sure Bill won't mind you staying at his place for the night... seeing you're a friend of his and all. Besides, it will be a damn sight cleaner than the hotel. Not that the hotel is dirty, mind you, just that Bill is a bit of a clean freak... if you know what I mean."

"Yes," replied April, "I do. I seem to be surrounded by them, in fact."

The two of them climbed the stairs to the second floor and Perry pointed to his friend's place. April was astonished to see Perry open William's apartment without the need of a key. Perry saw her surprise, and so felt compelled to say something.

"Um, nobody locks their doors on the Rock. We don't have much in the way of crime."

April nodded and stepped into William's apartment like she was entering a shrine. This was a special place to the man she loved and was looking for. He had been in these rooms not more than seven hours ago. She took silent steps as if hoping the space would speak the secret of its resident's whereabouts.

Perry edged around her and looked into William's bedroom. It was as clean as ever. He continued to address her.

"In here is where you'll sleep tonight. My wife — her name is Joyce — my wife will bring you some dinner in about an hour. We would have loved for you to stay with us, but the boys... well, you probably know how young boys are."

April nodded and removed her coat. Perry took it from her and hung it in the bedroom closet. When he returned to her side, she said, "I take it you are the King of Beaver Island, Mr. Whitney."

"Please call me Perry, and yes, I guess I am… for another one hundred and fifty-nine days, that is. What do I call you?"

"Call me April, Perry," she said with a smile. "Don't you have any idea where William went?"

Perry motioned for April to take a seat on William's old Victorian couch. She did and was surprised by how springy it was. "April, you have to understand… Bill was here for barely forty hours. Then he repacked his bags and lit out again. We had only that one conversation I told you about on our way over here. I thought for sure he was going to kill me when he found out the truth, but he came back here a changed man. He quit his jobs, but he was acting real strange in a happy-go-lucky kind of way."

April blew out a breath and suddenly felt very small. She confessed, "I'm afraid I am the cause of that, Perry. Your friend *is* a changed man, and I'm the one who changed him."

"I thought Bill said you were the one who found the Strang?"

"I was," April confirmed. "But that's not what I'm talking about." Perry was confused, and it showed in every aspect of his body. Before he could say anything, April continued speaking: "Perry, William… ah, Bill talked about me, didn't he? What did he tell you?"

Perry rose from the chair next to the dining table he'd been sitting by and paced around scratching his balding pate.

"Oh boy! Well, he told me your name, of course, and that you were pretty. But..."

"But, Bill didn't tell you I was black, did he." April finished for him. "And I also bet he didn't mention that he's in-love with me."

Perry sank back onto the chair which creaked in protest. "You're right, April, you'd win both those bets. Bill didn't mention either of those details." Perry let loose with a short burst of laughter, his right hand coming to a rest over his mouth.

"Is it really so funny," April asked, "to think your friend could fall in love with a black girl?"

"Forgive me, April, but it's not that, though, you have to admit, it *is* a surprise. I was laughing because the idea of Bill being in-love again with *anyone* is really out there for most of his friends. Did he tell you about getting burned by his long-time childhood sweetheart when he was a high school senior?"

"No, I didn't know about that," April replied. "Thanks for telling me, Perry. It actually explains a lot of the things William... I mean, Bill was saying and doing."

"And what you said," Perry added, "explains his odd mood when he came back. So, you followed Bill here to... what... to tell him you were in-love with him, too?"

"No, Perry, Bill already knows I love him. But, I was concerned about the race thing, and even more than that, I was afraid of what being with him might do to my career."

"Bill did say you were *married* to your work."

"He was right about that... until yesterday, that is. I came to Beaver Island to tell him I was ready to face all those fears as long as we could face them together. Now, I don't know what to do."

"Well, April, don't do anything until you've had a hot meal and a good night's sleep. Would you believe me if I told you my mother still tells me stuff like that? Anyway, that's her advice, not mine," Perry said as he rose to leave.

April smiled, stood up herself, and gave the startled monarch a hug.

"Your mother sounds a lot like my mother," April said to him as she pulled away. "Thank you, Perry. I see now why Bill considers you to be his best friend."

Perry Whitney, stunned Supervisor of St. James Township, left April's presence to walk back to a wife who — he was certain — wouldn't believe a word of what he was about to tell her.

"Bill," Perry whispered as he looked back at his friend's apartment, "what the heck have you gotten yourself into?"

~ ~ ~ ~ ~

Only thirty minutes had passed since Perry's departure, but April thought she could detect the odor of food. Then a sound very much like someone tapping the toe of a shoe against a door came from the direction of William's entrance. She got up from the sofa where she'd been reclining, stepped lively down the hallway, and opened the door.

"Hello, please come in Mrs. Whitney. Your husband said to expect you in an hour."

"Call me Joyce, please. Well, it was an easy meal to make tonight, and I wanted you to have your's first. So, I guess I am a bit early. That's ok, isn't it?"

"Certainly… And thank you so much for your hospitality," April added.

"Should I call you 'April'?"

"Yes, please do. Here, let me help you with that…"

Joyce looked at April with a mixture of astonishment and curiosity as the two of them marched the meal to William's kitchen countertop. Joyce then checked to see that the aluminum foil was still secure over the two platters.

"Joyce, do you have time to sit and talk awhile, or must you get back home to your family?"

"Oh, I have some time. Perry and the boys know how to eat on their own, and besides, I brought enough food for the both of us."

"That's what I thought," April replied with a smile. "Joyce, I'm not really hungry and I can see by the look on your face Perry told you about the conversation the two of us had."

"And I can see why Bill is attracted to you... Not much gets past those eyes of yours, I imagine. He also has an appreciation for detail... as I'm sure you've gathered from his apartment."

"Yes," April agreed, "and I'm looking forward to sleeping in that beautiful antique bed I saw a while ago." Both women exited the kitchen and sat on the couch. April continued to speak. "Joyce, I'm going to be up-front with you: I'm concerned about how Bill's folks — and the people of Beaver Island for that matter — are going to react when they find out Bill's girlfriend is black. Can you tell me if I have anything to be worried about?"

"Wow! You weren't kidding, were you? Well, the two of you will get nothing but support from Perry and me. That much I can guarantee. But, April, I'll be just as up-front with you and say there will be a few folk on the Rock who won't like it very much. They may or may not hold their tongues in front of you, but they *will* have an opinion about your relationship. As for Bill's folks... I can't say. But, hey! That could be where he has gone. They live in Florida, you know."

"Yes, he did mention that," April replied, "but he didn't say *where* in Florida."

"I believe they moved to Clearwater..."

"Really?" blurted a surprised April. "Do you know his parents' address?"

"Not off hand, but Bill must have it around here somewhere."

"Well, Clearwater was going to be my next destination anyway, Joyce. That's where *my* folks live, too."

"Talk about a small world…" Joyce voiced. April looked down at her hands and gave out a sigh. Joyce immediately understood why. She said, "You haven't told them either, I take it."

"It is worse even than that, Joyce — if you can imagine. They have this black attorney all picked out for me to marry, and they don't even know I'm in love with someone else."

Joyce stood up and placed a hand on her new friend's shoulder. She asked in sympathy, "April, are the two of you ready for the crap about to be thrown at you? My parents had a conniption when I told them I was marrying Perry, and that was just because he was a fisherman."

April seemed about ready to burst into tears, so Joyce sat back down and gave April a hug — which the younger woman gladly returned. "Don't worry, April, if Bill is worth finding, he's also worth keeping. It's just going to be harder than you thought. Look, I'm going to warm up our dinner. You just sit back and relax."

"I can at least *try* to do that," agreed April.

"Look here," Joyce pointed out, "under the coffee table is one of Bill's old family albums. Why don't you grab it and get yourself acquainted with his folks?"

"Thanks, Joyce, that's a great idea. And thank you, again… for the food and… everything."

While Joyce went into the kitchen, April pulled out from under the coffee table a thick, three-ring photo binder. She sat back on the sofa and placed the heavy folio on her lap. She swung back the cover and began leafing through the pages, but hadn't gone far when she was drawn to an image which was both familiar to her and, at the same time, out of place.

Joyce was startled from her efforts by April's voice: "No! It can't be! This is incredible… just totally incredible!"

Hurrying back into William's living room, Joyce found April staring at a page in the album and shaking like a leaf.

"What's wrong, April? What's incredible?"

"This is, Joyce," said April pointing to a photo of Bill sitting with a small black girl in Marquette Park on Mackinac Island. "My parents have this same photograph framed and sitting on top of their piano."

"But, how is that possible?" Joyce exclaimed.

"*I'm* the little girl in this picture, Joyce. Do you know what that means? It means I know where Bill is! I know his folks and have been to their home. They live not more than a five minute walk from my parents."

Skeptical, Joyce formulated a way to test April's claim: "April, did Bill ever tell you the names of his parents?"

"No…"

"Ok, there is a more recent photograph of them in his bedroom. I'm guessing you haven't seen it."

"I haven't been into his bedroom, Joyce."

"Perfect… I'm going to go get it."

Moments later, Joyce returned with a picture frame pressed against her chest, the back facing April. She said, "If what you are saying is correct, you should still be able to tell me the names of the two people in this picture." With that, Joyce turned the frame around.

"That's Jim and Rachel O'Riley…" Joyce nodded her head in amazement and handed the photograph to April, who continued, "My mom said the O'Rileys were from northern Michigan, but if she ever said anything about them being from here… well, I must have forgotten."

April's companion finally found her voice: "Perry told me I wasn't going to believe his story. Just wait until he hears mine."

Forty minutes later — as Joyce was walking into her home — she continued to roll recent events over in her head. While happy for April and Bill, she wasn't convinced the couple would find either set of parents eager to bless their union just because they were already friends. She saw Perry sitting by himself in the living room.

"Well, Joyce, what do you think? Isn't April just as I described her?" Joyce took a seat opposite her husband but did not immediately respond. "What's the matter?"

"Perry, do you remember the first time you met April?"

"Sure… Today at the hotel…"

"Nope… you met her once before… a long time ago…"

"What are you talking about, Joyce? The only other time in my life I ever met a black girl was on that trip Bill's family and mine took to Mackinac. It was that little kid we found Bill playing with in the park."

"That's exactly right," Joyce confirmed.

Perry wasn't expecting the response Joyce gave him, so it took a few seconds for the implications of what she had said to bore into his brain.

"You mean…" Perry began slowly.

"Go on, hon, you're almost there…"

"You mean to tell me that April — the woman Bill is in-love with — is the same little girl in that old photo?"

"Bingo!"

"Does Bill know?"

"Not yet…"

"Holy, crap!"

From an upstairs bedroom came two young voices… "Daddy said, 'crap'! Daddy said, 'crap'!"

Perry and Joyce snickered as their sons segued their father's explicative into a new bedtime song. Normally, Perry would have disciplined them for such an outburst, but not this time. Instead, he said, "Wow! Would I love to be a proverbial fly on the wall when he does find out."

"You and me both, Perry," replied Joyce shaking her head in amazement. "You and me both!"

While the Whitney family was having their bit of fun at William's unknowing expense, April was on William's telephone speaking with an airline representative trying to book a flight for tomorrow afternoon to Tampa from Detroit Metro Airport. She wasn't making much progress…

"Hello, Ms. Smith?"

"Yes, I'm still here."

"Look, I'm sorry. Every seat on every flight leaving Detroit after ten in the morning is booked. There is some availability on both the 8:00 a.m. and 10:00 p.m. flights."

"I can't make that first one. I don't think the ferry even gets back to Charlevoix until around ten to ten-fifteen in the morning."

"Then my best advice is to get to Detroit as soon as you can and wait near our ticket counter to see if someone will sell you their ticket."

"Thank you for your time, ma'am. You were especially kind to check with the other carriers for me."

"Well, I sure hope you find him, honey."

"How did you know?" said April, stunned at how apparently transparent she was.

"Listen, honey… as desperate as you sound, it could only be one thing. I mean… nobody's in *that* much of a hurry for sunshine, are they? Bye, now…"

"Good-bye," April replied after a moment's hesitation, but the woman had already hung up.

~ 14 ~

April pulled her rental car into her parents' driveway, turned off the engine, leapt out, and ran to the door. It was locked, so she opened it with the house key they had given her.

"Mama, Daddy, it's me… April," she called out. "Hello? Is anyone here?"

She looked at her watch. It told her it was five-thirty Wednesday evening on October 25, 2000. April furrowed her brow in confusion.

"The folks are still part of the cocktail generation," she said under her breath. "Where are they?"

For Richard and Margaret Smith, imbibing an evening cocktail was as traditional as tea-time was for the British. April had been so sure of where she would find her parents that she hadn't thought about what to do if they happened *not* to be at home.

As April pondered her options, she also thought about how fortunate she was to even be standing in their home in the first place. She managed to get to the airport by one o'clock. And after only ten minutes of asking around, a college student agreed to sell her his ticket for $700. In spite of what he thought, April knew she got the better end of that deal.

Then the obvious reason for her parents' absence hit her and April was back out the front door in a flash. She locked up, but even that easy action took time as she dealt with her excitement.

She turned and began walking to the O'Riley's home. April drew in some deep breaths as she felt her head pound from her heart's rapid beating.

"What do I say to him if he *is* there?" she asked herself. "And what about his parents? Has Bill said anything to them about us?"

Suddenly, an old and annoying habit reared up as April found herself about to bite her nails. She pushed both hands down to either side of her frame and flared her fingers. Her mother's suggestion of what to do immediately came to her: "April, dear, when you feel like biting your fingernails, go for a run instead." It had been how April came to be part of her school's track and field team… by substituting a good habit for a bad one.

So, April ran. She ran in one of her favorite, most comfortable designer outfits that she liked to wear when traveling. April ran and didn't care how silly it might look to anyone in the neighborhood. The only problem with running was that it got her to the O'Riley house much faster than she wanted. Acting reflexively, the index finger of April's right hand pressed the O'Riley's doorbell. The door opened and April looked into her mother's face.

"April!" Margaret effused. "What on earth are you doing here? When did you get into town? How did you know your father and I were over here?"

Before April could answer any of these questions, her mother embraced her and gave her a kiss on the cheek. Then Margaret pulled her daughter into the house, closed the door, and began leading April deeper into the residence.

"April, this is such a coincidence, but you'll never guess who's here... little Billy O'Riley! Only, he's not so little anymore. You probably don't remember him. You'll have to wait a moment — he just went to the restroom — but, he's the boy in that picture your father took while we were on Mackinac Island when you were four. Well, he surprised his parents yesterday by coming down to Florida for a visit, and they invited us over to meet him. Isn't this wonderful?"

"Margie," Rachel called out to her friend, "who was that at the door?"

"Rachel, Jim," Margaret began to say as William emerged from his parents' powder room and turned off the light, "you'll never guess who just walked in! Billy, I bet you don't remember..."

"April!" William shouted. "How in heaven's name did you find me here?" And before any parent in the room could react, William ran over to and swept April up into his arms. The two young people kissed like it was to be their last one.

Margaret stumbled backward in shock, and the rest of them, likewise, assumed looks ranging from incomprehension to confused horror. When the pair finally came up for air, April was at last able to say something to someone.

"I was desperate to find you, Bill, so I could tell you I'm ready to face whatever may come, and to say, yes, I will marry you." They kissed again — their parents looking at each other trying to figure out what in God's precious name was going on.

After disengaging from his intended, William cleared his throat and stepped over to his stunned parents... passing by Richard Smith in the process who was trying to flag his attention without much success.

"Mom, Dad, this is the woman I've fallen in love with. Her name is April Smith. She lives in Detroit. April, these are my folks, James and Rachel O'Riley."

April stuck out her hand and giggled. Rachel took it in hers. "Hello, again, April," she said, looking at April and William with furrowed brows.

Before William's father could explain that they already knew her, William had turned both April and himself around to complete his introductions. "I almost forgot, April, I'd like you to meet..."

"My parents, Bill. Richard and Margaret Smith are *my* parents."

"What?" William asked no one in particular as he swallowed... hard. "I can, uh... I mean... we can explain this."

"You goddam well better, young man!" Richard Smith boomed. This time, Margaret made no attempt to curb her husband's foul mouth.

~   ~   ~   ~   ~

April opened the door to the O'Riley's guest bedroom. William was lying on the bed... on his back... with his fingers locked together behind his head and his eyes staring at the ceiling.

"Well," April began as she stretched out next to him, "I think they took that pretty well."

"Which part?" sighed a worn-out William. "The part about wanting to get married, or the part about us not having sex yet?"

April slapped him on the head. "My mother didn't even ask me that in private, so don't go making stuff like that up, you dirty-minded white boy!"

William smiled and blew her a kiss. "I really do love you, you know. Thanks for finding me."

"My pleasure, mister."

William sighed a second time, and April turned to her side and propped her head up with her hand. "I had it all figured out," William lamented, "how I was going to ease my parents into the idea of them having a black daughter-in-law... assuming, of course, you came looking for me. But the more I think about it, the more convinced I am the way it happened was the best we could have hoped for."

"What do you mean?"

"I mean... look what happened: our parents got the news at the same time; they were able to pretty much blow up together; and, most importantly, they got to see how genuine and deep our love is for one another. In spite of their obvious shock, our folks know it wasn't an act on our part designed to impress them."

"Yes," April concurred, "that was something my mother pointed to about ten minutes ago when she pulled me aside to ask if this was what I really wanted."

"So," William said, switching subjects, "what do we do now that the hard part is over?"

"Oh, you are *so* wrong, stud," April replied, now sitting up in the bed. "That stuff we just went through," she said pointing in the direction of the O'Riley's living room, "that was the *easy* part! The hard part is only the rest of our lives together. But if you want something to do in the short-term, you can do me the honor of going out and buying me an engagement ring. And let me tell you, Billy boy, it better be big! I got me a lot of suitors to fight off back in Detroit!"

William smiled, unclasped his fingers, and reached into his left pants pocket. When he pulled his hand out, in it was a small, square jewelry case. He opened it and April gasped. It was the largest diamond she had ever seen on a ring.

"When did you get this?"

"This morning… at a store here in town…"

"But, you didn't know I was coming…"

"No, but I hoped you might someday. I just wanted to be prepared in case you did. Here, let me put in on you."

April stretched out her left hand and William placed the ring on the appropriate digit. It was about a size too big for April's finger. She wiggled it around to demonstrate. "We can go tomorrow and get it re-sized, Bill. Don't worry. I absolutely love it."

"So, April Anne Smith, does this mean you will marry me and love me forever?"

"Yes, William O'Riley," she responded with emphasis on William's missing O, "I will be your wife. As for the rest, it occurs to me I may have been in-love with you pretty much my whole life."

April leaned over and kissed her man as he reached for and pulled April on top of himself. A moment later, Richard Smith cleared his throat as he lightly rapped on the bedroom door.

"Um, kids…" began the much calmer father, "sorry to interrupt, but could I have a word with the two of you?"

April rolled off William, and the two of them sat up on the bed. She responded, "Sure, Daddy. Is everything ok?"

"Everything is fine, sugar. You know, April, Bill's folks were planning to take him out to dinner tonight. Jim and I were just talking and we wondered if you would mind the four of us taking you both out... you know... an engagement dinner."

"That's generous, sir," William responded. "Thank you. I think we would like that. April?"

April brushed a stray hair from her face and added her thoughts: "Yes, that's a fine idea, Daddy. You know, I haven't eaten since breakfast."

"That was going to be my next question," Richard said, offering a weak smile. He paused and then continued, "April, your mother insisted that she go and bring your grandmother over here. She and Mrs. O'Riley left a few minutes ago. And Bill, your dad is on the phone to the restaurant seeing if it's possible to change the reservations. I thought while things were quiet, I'd come here and ask you something the four of us were wondering about. Sugar, are you..."

"Pregnant?" his daughter finished for him.

"Yeah," confirmed the retired engineer.

April and William looked at one another and broke out laughing.

"What is so funny about that?" Richard responded as if he had just been insulted.

"I'm sorry, Daddy. Bill and I were just talking about how none of you had asked that question yet."

"The thing is, sir," William added, "we haven't had sex yet."

"You haven't?" Richard said in amazement. "Oh, well… forget I asked, then. Ok, yeah…" he said as he edged back out of the bedroom.

April felt honor-bound to make a complete confession: "I tried, Daddy, but Bill…"

"No! That's ok, sugar. I don't need to know… I mean, I don't *want* to know… I mean, I'm going to go check on those reservations. I'll leave you two alone, now. I don't mean so… Uh, that's a real pretty ring, sugar," said the visibly shaken parent as he tried to right himself but kept scuttling his efforts. "You have fine taste, son… in jewelry, I mean… and women, too!" he said, looking at his daughter.

April watched her flustered father make his way back down the hall. She then turned and stared dumfounded at William.

"I don't believe I have *ever* seen my father so undone. He's usually such a rock when it comes to his emotions."

"Well," William offered, "he'll get over it soon enough. At least he won't have anymore surprises to deal with this evening."

April agreed and put her arms around her fiancé. This time, when they kissed, it was with the joyous knowledge it would definitely *not* be their last one.

~ ~ ~ ~ ~

Vera Smith heard tapping on her door and ambled over to see who was calling on her at this hour of the day. Pulling aside the laced curtain which covered the small window, she was surprised to see her daughter-in-law and Rachel O'Riley standing there. She unlocked and then opened the door.

"Margaret, Rachel… what's going on? Why are you here? Is Dick all right?"

The younger women stepped into her apartment and Vera closed the door behind them. "Richard's fine!" said Margaret curtly. "Well, I wouldn't exactly say he's *fine* right now, but he's… Something has come up, Vera. Grab as much of the Smith Family genealogy as you can and come with us. Have you eaten dinner? No… Forget that I asked. You are joining us regardless."

"But, we agreed," Vera pleaded, "that now wasn't the right time to tell them! And yes, I've already eaten my supper. What's come up?"

"Vera," Rachel said, "forget about our agreement. This is more important. Please, go get those folders you showed us last week while I get you a sweater."

"Fine!" said the elderly woman as she went over to her desk and opened the bottom drawer. "But, where are we going?"

"First to Rachel's house and then to dinner," Margaret said tersely.

"But I told you I already ate."

"So," her daughter-in-law replied as she and Rachel escorted Vera out of the apartment, "order a whiskey... Believe me, you'll need it."

~ ~ ~ ~ ~

In spite of repeated questions from Vera, Rachel and Margaret were able to deliver her to the O'Riley house without divulging their secret. On the way over to Vera's place, the two mothers had agreed April and William should be the ones to tell Vera about their plans to wed. After a ten minute drive, the three of them had exited Margaret's car and were walking into Rachel's home.

April heard her grandmother's voice and said as much to William, "Come on, husband-to-be, let me introduce you to my Grandmother Smith. And whatever you do, please call her Grandma."

"You got it, sugar."

"Good answer, Bill... Besides, soon she'll be your grandma by marriage."

The two young people got off the bed and — holding hands — walked down the hallway and into the living room. Vera Smith's face lit up when she saw her youngest granddaughter.

"Oh, pumpkin! When did you get into town?" Vera hugged and then kissed April on the head and cheek. Then she spied William. "Who is this young man?"

"Grandma, this is our son William," Rachel spoke before April could respond. "I, however, call him Billy."

"Grandma Smith," William addressed the Smith family matron while extending his right hand, "it is a pleasure to meet you."

"It's nice to meet you, too," Vera replied, shaking the young man's appendage with her own. "Now, will someone please tell me what is so dang important that you felt the need to kidnap me from my evening rest?"

An awkward pause filled the room, and then Margaret took hold of Vera's arm and led her over to the couch.

"Perhaps you should sit down, Vera."

Vera did while clutching the dog-eared file folder. She eventually replied, "Ok, you got me so I can't spill anyone's drink. Now, what's all the fuss about... besides the news that April is in town, because it's got to be more than that!"

James O'Riley smiled at Vera's spunk and took a seat near her. The other parents did the same which left April and William as the only two still standing.

April reached out for William's hand and he gave it to her. She said, "Grandma, Bill and I met a few weeks ago. We fell in love and now we are going to be married."

Vera sat there with her mouth agape. She stared at her granddaughter and then turned her attention to the girl's mother, saying: "And, Margaret, you've known about this for how long?"

"Mother," Richard responded, "we only just found out about this ourselves. We didn't even realize until today the kids knew each other. Furthermore, *they* didn't know who the other person's parents were."

"What?" asked Vera. "Forget it," she said, preempting her son's attempt at clarification. "I got the gist of it. So pumpkin," she said, now speaking to April, "you want to marry young Mr. O'Riley, here, do you?"

William started to correct her, but Vera raised her hand. Strangled sound ceased emanating from William's mouth and it closed like a trapdoor. "I know all about you dropping the O part from your name, so don't bother." Turning back to her son, Vera continued, "He seems like a nice enough boy. So, what's the problem? Is he too tall for her?"

That question drew laughs and smiles from everyone — except Vera, for whom it seems like the most serious of inquiries. Richard scratched his head and looked at his wife as if to say he wasn't quite sure how to verbalize the thoughts which were on his mind.

"There's no problem, Mother. I just thought you might be concerned because Bill is... white," Richard said, delicately.

"He's not white. He's family." Vera deadpanned.

"Grandma," April exclaimed, "that is *very* generous of you to say! Thank you."

"Generosity has nothing to do with it, pumpkin," Vera replied, "William is your cousin."

While April and William didn't quite know what to do, their respective fathers were not so unsure: Richard and James both laughed uproariously. Margaret and Rachel just looked at each other and winked. Rachel finally broke the spell.

"She's not kidding, Jim. You and Richard are cousins, too."

Richard looked over to his wife who nodded her head in confirmation. Not convinced of this, he turned to his mother.

"Mother, is this true?"

James suddenly jumped to his feet in realization. "Of course! Peter Edward Smith!" he said, looking to Vera whose smile confirmed his guess.

"Who the blazes is Peter Edward Smith?" Richard yelled as he, too, rose from his own seat.

Vera pulled out the ancient lithograph from her binder and handed it to the men.

"That's him," said James to Richard, pointing. "Oh, good Lord! See how much the kids look like the couple in this picture. The resemblances are uncanny…"

The three older women gathered around the men and all stared at the racial pioneers in the print and then at their flesh and bone counterparts before them. Not long after this, everyone in the house had an eerie sense that — by either a natural or a divine influence — this particular branch of a truly American family had come full circle.

~ ~ ~ ~ ~

Jeremiah Wheeler pulled up to the curb in front of the Smith's home, parked, and turned off the engine. Even from out by the street, he could tell some kind of party was underway.

"Dick and Margaret sure do enjoy their retirement years," the attorney said under his breath. But Jeremiah also knew this to be a good sign. He looked at his watch which told him it was almost midnight. "Perhaps this means April is here in Florida. She sure as heck disappeared from Michigan…"

For over a week, he had tried to contact April at the DIA or at her apartment. He had left any number of messages but had never heard back from her. And then, yesterday, he stopped into her workplace only to be informed that April was on vacation and that no one there knew where she had gone.

On a hunch, Jeremiah had taken a late flight to Tampa to see if, by chance, April had decided to visit her parents. He hadn't wanted to call and give her the opportunity to spin some lame excuse as to why she couldn't go out with him.

"I'm tired of being patient," he spat as he walked to the Smith's front door. "Being patient was not a good strategy…"

He got to the door and rang the doorbell. An indistinct voice called out from inside and moments later, the door opened and Jeremiah found himself standing toe to toe with a broadly smiling William Riley.

"May I help you?"

"Yes," responded Jeremiah; momentarily taken aback by this unexpected person, "I'm looking for April. Is she here?"

"Come in, come in, fine sir," said William as he dramatically swept his arm through the opening like a matador challenging his opponent. "April, it's for you."

Jeremiah cautiously stepped past William into the Smith's foyer. From this vantage, he could see his old mentor. William closed the door and strode toward April who was making her way toward Jeremiah who cleared his throat.

"I apologize for interrupting your party, Dick, but I was wondering if I could have a word with April?"

"Well, Jerry... there she stands. Ask her yourself... she's a big girl. She can even walk and talk all on her own."

"Yes, sir... right!" Jeremiah replied, laughing nervously at his mentor's not-too-subtle dig. "Thank you." Now he looked April in the eyes. "Hello, April."

"Hi, Jerry... How have you been?"

"I'm good. Nice party you're having, though I didn't realize your family stayed up this late."

"Yes, we've been celebrating ever since we got home from dinner. Is there something you wish to speak with me about, Jerry?"

"As a matter of fact, there is. Could we go somewhere and talk in private?"

To this request, April shook her head, saying, "No, Jerry, if you have something to ask me, just ask it. My father doesn't own a gun."

"Yes, I do," came the cryptic correction from the father in question.

Again, Jeremiah gave out a nervous laugh and then cleared his throat for a second time. He said to April, "Right, then... April, I came here to ask you to go out with me on a series of dates. I'm thinking of maybe five or six to begin with. Frankly, I'm hoping that if we can just spend some time together, we could get to know one another better than we already do. Then, after a few weeks, who knows what might happen between us."

April continued to smile at Jeremiah, but said nothing for many seconds. Finally, she turned to William and addressed him.

"Bill, would you give me permission to date Jerry?"

"Why are you asking him, April?" Jeremiah asked with indignation.

"Well," she replied, "I just found out this evening that Bill, here, is my cousin."

"Your cousin!" laughed Jeremiah to the point of grabbing his stomach and bending himself almost in half. But, he soon discovered himself to be the only one doing so, so he stopped. "Well, even if that's true, what does that have to do with you dating me?"

April thought about this for a few seconds and nodded her head. "You're right, Jerry, it has nothing to do with it. Ok, how about this, then: Bill, here, is my fiancé."

Now Jeremiah really cut loose with a gut-busting, nose-snorting chortle of a laugh. But, when he straightened up and looked around the room, he was still the only person laughing.

William tapped April on the shoulder to get her attention and said to her, "Sugar, as your future husband, I do *not* give you permission to date this fine specimen of humanity." Turning to Jeremiah, he continued, "Sorry, Jerry, but I'm a bit selfish when it comes to family. You understand, don't you?"

"No!" Jeremiah Wheeler screamed at the entire gathering. "I don't understand any of you people! April, I like you, but I'm tired of being jerked around. Dick, we've had our fun, but I am done with you and... and... your whole, damned incestuous family!"

Before Margaret could speak one word of rebuke for such a foul display, Jeremiah pivoted and rolled out of her home — slamming the front door behind him. A few seconds later, the young attorney could hear the sound of laughter billowing from inside the Smith's home as he stormed toward his set of wheels.

~ ~ ~ ~ ~

Monday, November 6, 2000, was a clear, mild day in Detroit. It was also April's first day back at work after having been ordered to take a vacation by John Risner. For April, it had been the best fourteen days of her life — except that each subsequent day kept topping the previous one.

Upon entering the institute, both she and William felt it best to check-in with Mr. Risner before going back to her office. Along the way, the couple caught the eye of a number of colleagues — all of whom congratulated her. After the third such occurrence, April finally said something to William.

"Did you tell anyone?"

"No, sugar, did you?"

"Not a peep… And you know I have yet to go through all those voice mail messages back at the apartment."

"Maybe it's the ring. After all, it's not *that* subtle," he pointed out.

"No, it's not. Then again, neither are you."

"'It takes one to know one,' as they say."

On the executives' floor, April spotted her boss coming out of someone else's suite. She caught his attention and the department director practically ran over to them.

"I was hoping to find you, April, before anyone else did," he said slightly out of breath. "Has anyone told you the news? Hello, William. I wasn't expecting to see you again so soon. How are you?"

"John, we are both doing great."

"What news, Mr. Risner?" April asked.

"The Strang Tapestry, obviously! We have it! The Kerschner's sold it to us for $410,000.00. It's already on display in our State of Michigan Collection."

"That's a wonderful development, John," William said reaching out for and shaking the man's hand. "It's now where you said it belonged three years ago… well, done!"

"That *is* wonderful news, sir," April concurred, taking her turn at shaking her boss's hand. "And it explains a few comments we got as we entered the building. But, Mr. Risner, I wanted to speak with you about what my next assignment is going to be."

"Well, April, I have space in my schedule around ten o'clock. How about then?"

"That will work for me, but sir, Bill is here to inquire after any openings he might qualify for."

"You moved to Detroit, William?"

"Permanently," he emphasized as he and April held up their left hands.

"You got married already?"

"Nine days ago, to be exact," said April.

"In Clearwater… with our family around us," William added.

"Then it was off to the Virgin Islands until two days ago," April continued to explain.

"We're living in April's apartment until we can find something larger in our price range."

"So, William" John said, "you want to come work for me."

"Only if you agree to call me Bill from now on."

"Well, Bill," replied John, smiling, "the DIA is in need of an assistant curator for our State of Michigan Collection. You'll have to go through all the regular hoops, but if you apply, I guarantee you'll automatically be at the top of the list of candidates."

"Thank you, Mr. Risner," replied William.

"Ahh, right! I understand," said John with a glint in his eye. "Well, now, — business aside — allow me to be the first person here at the Detroit

Institute of Arts to say congratulations to the newlyweds: Well done, Mr. and Mrs. Riley!"

"Not quite, Mr. Risner," April corrected her boss. "We go by Bill and April Smith."

So astonished was John Risner that he actually stumbled a step backward.

"You took April's last name in marriage, Bill? There must be a story somewhere inside that decision and I'd love to hear it."

"Maybe someday, Mr. Risner," said William. "For now, let's just say I would have been a fool not to."

Disclaimers and Acknowledgments

April's Fool is a work of historical fiction. As such, the story should not be construed as factual history. As for the fictional characters and organizations depicted within the work, any resemblance to real entities or persons is a coincidence.

The Beaver Island Chamber of Commerce has been an invaluable source of inspiration and support in the bringing of this work to publication. I would like to especially thank Mr. Stephen West of the Chamber for his providing of the cover photograph taken from a NASA satellite. For information about Beaver Island and King James Jesse Strang, please visit the website: chamber@beaverisland.org. The Chamber's address is: P. O. Box 5 Beaver Island, MI 49782, or call the Chamber for information at: (231) 448-2505.

I also wish to thank Elaine West who has served as an editor for this work. Jill Jollief and my wife Darlene also have provided editing and proofreading services. I thank them all profusely for their time and talents! Finally, I would encourage folk to check out Elaine's Beaver Island newspaper, *The Northern Islander*.

— Harry J. Truman
   March 16, 2017